"I don't say things I don't mean, Renee."

If Daniel Barnard hadn't said she was prettier than her sister Meg, Renee would have believed him. He didn't seem the kind to use flattery to disarm an opponent. But she *had* heard him say it, a mistruth so blatant she was instantly suspicious. *You're not so bad looking,* she might have bought. Prettier than Meg—never.

Except…there might be a man somewhere who thought she was. Both men and women had incomprehensible tastes sometimes. Fortunately, nature had the common sense to shield people's vision with blinders.

More likely, Daniel had simply forgotten what Meg looked like, and the compliment had been an idle remark. Not a lie exactly, but not words to hold close to your heart.

Still, it wouldn't hurt to stay for dinner and see, would it?

"Thank you, then. A man who can cook is a wonder I've got to behold."

A slow smile warmed his face, making her see it in a different light. That first time, she'd thought him plain except for those extraordinary eyes. But now she knew she'd been wrong.

Or else, nature was in the process of manufacturing a pair of blinders for her—custom fit.

Dear Reader,

This is my first real trilogy—three books written back-to-back and planned together. I set about writing what is essentially a really long novel that happens to be broken into three separate parts, each with its own love story. What an undertaking! My editor occasionally had to remind me who was born when, and that oh, yeah, the antique mall used to be the old police station, but hey, I'll freely admit to anyone how absentminded I am!

What was exciting about this project was the fact that I could really write about family. Life has driven wedges between three sisters who had once depended on each other, trusted each other. PATTON'S DAUGHTERS is about coming to terms with the past, and about reconciliation and learning to trust again. Of course, the love and support of some fabulous men doesn't hurt!

So here's hoping my great big novel works: that you find each book totally satisfying on its own, but you're also compelled to read on. And here's hoping, too, that you close the book and reach for the phone to call your sister or brother, just as I did.

Sincerely,

Janice Kay Johnson

THE WOMAN IN BLUE

Janice Kay Johnson

TORONTO • NEW YORK • LONDON
AMSTERDAM • PARIS • SYDNEY • HAMBURG
STOCKHOLM • ATHENS • TOKYO • MILAN • MADRID
PRAGUE • WARSAW • BUDAPEST • AUCKLAND

ISBN 0-373-70854-8

THE WOMAN IN BLUE

This edition published by arrangement with Harlequin Books S.A.

® and TM are trademarks of the publisher. Trademarks indicated with ® are registered in the United States Patent and Trademark Office, the Canadian Trade Marks Office and in other countries.

Visit us at www.romance.net

Printed in U.S.A.

Since this book is about family, it seems right to dedicate it to Karl. Whatever distance there may be between us, you'll always be my beloved big brother.

CHAPTER ONE

HAVING YOUR DOG present you with a human skull was a hell of a way to start a day.

Daniel Barnard had thought it was going to be a good morning. He'd awakened with the rooster, whose crow rang just the right note as far as he was concerned. And the weather was perfect, he saw as soon as he stepped out onto the front porch with a steaming mug of coffee in one hand. He sat down, as he always did, on the rustic Adirondack chair that faced due east.

The back porch was for evenings, when the sun set like liquid gold over the Sisters, a trio of mountains as sharp and cantankerous as the elderly Robb sisters in town. But the front porch was for morning, when the sun poured glorious colors over Oregon's high desert country as if trying to make it the most beautiful place on God's earth. And maybe succeeding.

The coffee warmed him from inside until the sun's rays touched his face like a gentle hand. He set down the mug and thought about the morning's chores. These days, Daniel had enough help on the ranch. He no longer felt as if twelve hours weren't half long enough. He didn't shovel much you-know-what in the barn anymore; that was the job of hired hands. He concentrated on tenderly caring for the mamas waiting to foal and training the stock that had made the Triple B famous for world-class cutting horses. Back right after Granddad disappeared his father died, and times had been tougher. A hell of a lot tougher.

But no reason to remember that right now. The day was too full of promise for dark memories.

Daniel stood and saw Lotto trotting across the scrap of lawn he watered and mowed just to please his mother, who said a house wasn't a home without grass. The big yellow Lab had something in his mouth half the time; he liked tennis balls or branches so big he couldn't get through doorways. At the creek, he'd dip his head all the way under to pick up rocks that would probably wear his teeth down. Lately, he'd even taken to fetching home some weathered bones. A long-dead deer or elk, Daniel figured.

But today...what in tarnation did he have? If it was a rock, it was a damned big one. And grayish-brown, not red like the dirt around here. Something about the perfect curve of the top made Daniel uneasy.

He whistled. "Lotto, here, boy."

The dog came obligingly. He didn't mind showing off his treasure. Daniel's uneasiness grew as the Lab neared, that oval, dirty...something clutched awkwardly in his broad jaws.

By the time Lotto galumphed up the porch steps, Daniel knew. Even with soil clinging to it, he knew. He crouched and held out his hands.

"Let go, boy."

The dog whimpered, his brown eyes anxious, and held on tight.

"Lotto," Daniel said sharply.

The yellow Lab reluctantly released his prize, and with a sigh sank onto his belly on the painted porch floor. Daniel was left with the skull in his hands.

He turned it to face him—truer words had never been spoken, he thought with sick humor. Empty eye sockets stared at him. The lower jaw was missing, but the upper teeth were pretty much intact, and when he tilted the skull he saw something that made his stomach turn. Metal in one of those teeth. This was no ancient Indian burial. And that hole in the top suggested things he didn't like to contemplate. Especially since he guessed he knew who this was.

"Granddad," he whispered. "It's you, isn't it?"

RENEE PATTON strolled into the office that still felt like her father's but now belonged to the acting po lice chief, Jack Murray. She'd known Jack most of her life, though he was two years older, her sister's contemporary rather than hers. He and Meg had been high school sweethearts, but he'd never come calling after Meg had run away from home. To this day, Renee had no idea whether Jack had known Meg was going, or whether they'd broken up before she'd left. He'd never mentioned Meg to Renee, never asked if she heard from her sister, and Renee sure as heck hadn't brought up Meg's name.

What she did know was that he'd also dated Abby, Renee's younger sister, a few times about a year ago. Apparently Jack had a thing for Patton women. Just not for Renee, the plain sister.

Oh, yeah. It stung.

He glanced up now, one dark brow lifted. "Catch the punks?"

She snorted. "You kidding? Long gone."

They got calls like this twice a week on average. Vandalizing mailboxes was a favorite recreation for local teenagers. The county deputies faced the same thing. Not much could be done; even within the Elk Springs city limits, country roads abounded. Houses stood far apart, traffic was sparse. But lately one particular neighborhood had been victimized every few days. Some folks had given up and had canceled mail delivery. A few put out portable mailboxes and took them back in come late afternoon. Others had fortified theirs with concrete and metal pipes, which functioned as a red flag waving does for a bull. The vandals had done some creative work on those boxes. Post office security had asked for help, and she was darned if she was going to admit failure.

"I'm thinking about setting up a video camera," she said, perching on the edge of Jack's desk.

He grinned, softening a face rough-hewn enough to be called homely. Not that any woman in her right mind would think such a thing.

"Go for it," he said.

Her heart rate accelerated, but she ignored what had become an automatic response. Aside from the fact that Jack wasn't interested in her—never had been, never would be—he was too much like her father. He'd become more so since he'd moved into this office. She knew he was campaigning to keep it, which was fine with her. Becoming police chief was something of a dream of hers, but she wasn't ready yet. She knew the city council wasn't ready to hire a woman, either. But Jack would move on; he liked the power that went with the job, and soon he'd be chafing at the limitations of the Elk Springs Police Department compared to the bigger county sheriff's force that patrolled the area outside the various city limits. Heck, for all she knew, he lay awake nights lusting after an FBI badge.

Elk Springs was all she wanted. Maybe this town hadn't been good enough for Meg, but it was for Renee.

"Hey, Jack," called the dispatcher, whose desk sat just outside his office. "Here's a good one. Daniel Barnard says he has a human skull."

"The rancher?"

Renee swiveled to better hear the answer.

"Yup. Says his dog brought it home."

Jack grunted. "If it's human, it's bound to be from some old Indian burial. Still, somebody better go see." His gaze fell on Renee. "It's all yours."

She rose with alacrity. A human skull. Now, that sounded more interesting than a mailbox bashed in with a baseball bat. "Do I know Daniel Barnard?"

"His dad was Matthew Barnard. The Triple B?"

"Oh, yeah." She frowned. Seemed as if she remembered a Barnard boy about Meg's age, too, but she couldn't seem to picture him. "I can find the place. It's in the city limits?"

"Yeah, Matt kicked and screamed because when they redrew the line his taxes climbed, but the city wanted Butte Road because they were talking about taking cinders from that little lava cone past his place. Then they opened the quarry at Ponderosa

Butte instead, but they couldn't be bothered to take back what they'd done, even for Matt.''

Renee recalled hearing about that, too. ''On my way,'' she said cheerfully, sauntering out the office door.

The whole city police department—all fifteen officers—drove Bronco 4x4s. Winters here in eastern Oregon were long and cold. Heavy snowfalls at this elevation only came two or three times a season, but the ice stayed.

Of course, that long cold winter was also bringing prosperity to Elk Springs, in the form of a new ski area on Juanita Butte. The influx of outsiders brought more crime, which made life interesting for a cop, but also changed the personality of a town where you used to be able to leave your doors unlocked. Renee curled her lip as she passed an espresso stand. Seemed as if one stood on every corner. A steaming cup of coffee wasn't good enough for folks anymore. At least, not the urbanites who came from Seattle and Portland to ski.

She was glad to leave the central district, cross the Deschutes River, low from summer and fall, and find herself almost immediately on ranch land. Except, even here big fancy houses were cropping up on every bare ridge. More than 5,000 square feet, some of them, and they were vacation places! Renee couldn't imagine that much space echoing around her. She liked to feel enclosed, snug. As it was, by herself in the house Daddy had left jointly to her and her younger sister, Abby, Renee was rattling around like a lone pea in a pod.

The Barnard spread was the last on Butte Road;

if you went on past their gate, you'd come to the foot of the area's smallest cinder cone, red with scrubby ponderosa pine clinging here and there. Target shooters came out now and again, maybe a few teenagers who liked sliding around on the steep slope of loose cinders near the bottom, but otherwise the road was a dead end, in more ways than one.

At the turnoff, letters burned into a slab of wood supported by two peeled poles announced the Triple B Ranch. Renee didn't mind seeing that the road to the house was packed firm with red cinders. Yesterday's rain had left most unpaved roads shin-deep in rust-colored mud.

The ranch was picture-perfect: split-rail fences, gray-blue barns and an old ranch house nestled among the grove of cottonwood near the creek. A second house had been added some distance away, on a spine of ancient crumbling lava exposed to winds and driving snow. The small patch of green lawn in front was incongruous, surrounded as it was by the bare knuckles of lava and the gray-green sage. Beyond the barns, broad green pastures were the product of huge rolling irrigation sprinklers.

A shiny blue pickup sat outside the newer place; a modest sedan down by the old one. At the Y, Renee turned toward the modern house with its big porches and shingled, natural cedar siding. A yellow Lab raced alongside the Bronco, barking the whole while.

As she parked and turned off the engine, a sharp whistle silenced the dog, who reluctantly went to the man who came down the porch steps. Squirming, the Lab stayed behind his master.

Renee never liked being dwarfed by a man. No mystery why she felt that way, but insight didn't always help. She tended to be her stiffest when she came up against somebody like this rancher, a solid 6'4" if he was an inch. Big shoulders, big chest, lean hips, strong legs. Short dark hair. His face was saved from being uninteresting by his eyes, an electric blue. It wasn't just the color, either; they were intelligent, perceptive, intense. She darn near squirmed just like the dog.

The man nodded. "Officer." His gaze touched on the name plate pinned to her chest. She'd never been so glad not to be buxom.

She didn't bother to introduce herself. "Daniel Barnard?"

"The same." His voice, slow and deep, went with his looks.

"I hear you found a skull."

He nodded toward the house. "Come on in."

She followed, appreciating the simplicity of the porch railing and the front door, topped by a window shaped like a fan. Inside, she knew right away no woman had had anything to do with the decorating. The entry was half mudroom; a rain slicker and a parka and an olive-green duster buried a coat tree, and several pairs of boots lined the wall. She caught a quick glimpse of the living room to the right. Wood floors, plain white walls and leather furniture weren't softened by pretty cushions or knick-knacks. Big windows, wood-framed, let in floods of light that touched on the one spectacular painting above the couch and some smaller, quieter ones—pencil sketches, she thought.

But Daniel Barnard led her the other way, into a kitchen so neat she had to shake her head. Maybe there was a woman around, after all.

"Coffee?" he asked.

Attention riveted on the dirty, discolored skull that sat smack in the middle of the maple table, Renee shook her head.

"Your dog brought you this."

"Yup." He leaned against the island countertop and watched her. "Some other bones, too. I just didn't pay any attention to them. I rounded up what I could find. They're in that box there."

She glanced. One long heavy bone that might be a femur, which she seemed to remember was a good thing as it could be used to determine height and maybe gender. A cluster of others as dingy as the skull. A couple of ribs—she could see the arc.

Renee circled the table to see the gaping eye sockets. No lower jaw, which wasn't surprising if this skull had kicked around out there for Lord knew how many years. And definitely human, unless Sasquatch really existed.

"Any idea where the dog got these?"

He shook his head. "Not a clue. I'll try following him, if I can do it without him noticing."

"Chances are, it's an old Indian burial." Those cropped up from time to time, exciting everybody until the coroner took a look at the bones.

"Not unless this fellow's shaman moonlighted in dentistry," the rancher said.

She gave him a sharp look. For the first time she noticed how tense he was. Shook up. For all his casualness he was too still. The hand that gripped the edge of the tile counter showed white knuckles. A muscle danced in his jaw.

Interesting. And gratifying. She hadn't liked feeling as wriggly and timid and obedient as his dog.

Back to the skull. Renee guessed she ought to pick it up to see what he was talking about. Irked to discover she was capable of squeamishness over something so long dead, she lifted the damn thing. It was lighter than you'd think, dry and grainy.

And, yup, an upper molar had a filling, the kind most people ended up with.

"You're right," she agreed. "It looks modern to me." Gingerly, she turned the skull in her hands. A pale groove and several gouges made plain where the dog's teeth had gripped.

"About ten years ago, my grandfather disappeared." Daniel Barnard met her eyes when she looked up. His tight jaw betrayed emotions he'd otherwise clamped down. "Senile, but my mother wanted to keep him at home. He just wandered out one night, in December. We never found him."

Bet that had made for a jolly Christmas.

"I'm sorry," Renee said simply, and he inclined his head in silent acknowledgment. She tilted the skull back and studied those teeth again. "I doubt this is your grandfather's...uh, remains, though."

Without even looking, she felt him go on alert, like a Labrador retriever spotting a quail. "Why?" he asked.

"Come here." Renee held the skull higher, waiting until he covered the few steps to her side. "Except for those two fillings, these teeth aren't bad."

A thought came to her. "He still had his own? Your grandpa?"

A frown drew Daniel Barnard's dark brows together. "Yeah," he said doubtfully. "I'll have to ask, but I don't think he wore dentures."

"Still, most old people I know have had lots more dental work than this. Bits have broken off, and they have bridges, caps…" Renee shrugged. "These are in better shape than my teeth."

"Or mine." He exhaled. "I should've seen that."

"It's natural, when you know a man disappeared on your place, to figure this is him. Question is—" she carefully set the skull back on the table "—who else has disappeared?"

A small silence followed as they both stared at the empty eye sockets and crumbling bone. After a moment she gave herself a shake. "Well. I'll just take these with me."

"You know anything about bones?"

"Not much," Renee admitted. "Some basics are covered at the police academy. I've done a little reading. The coroner is good, though. He can tell an amazing amount from a femur. I'm hoping that big one there is a human femur."

"Could be deer and cow bones mixed in. Lotto isn't very discriminating."

The dog had stayed on the porch. "But he's brought these home recently?"

"Yeah, I've noticed him carrying bones around just this last…oh, week, ten days. I just figured it was an antelope or cow." He grimaced. "Until this morning."

She nodded. "We'll have more questions, once we know something about this fellow."

The rancher's gaze followed hers. "Or gal."

Now there was a thought. The uncomfortable reminder of her own mortality shuddered right through her. Someday, that's all she'd be. Right then, she hoped as she'd never hoped before that her minister knew what he was talking about.

"Would you like a bag?" Daniel asked. "To put that in?"

She'd felt his eyes on her; he must have read her morbid thoughts. The offer showed some sensitivity. No reason the skull couldn't just sit on her front seat, but she didn't much like the idea of it looking at her, or gazing ahead as if hoping it could see out the windshield, and turning it to face the upholstery seemed sort of…cruel.

Another shudder touched her. "Thank you. I would."

He produced a brown paper grocery bag and even set the skull in it for her. She thanked him again and reached for it. His voice stopped her.

"You're Meg Patton's little sister, aren't you?"

Was she? She didn't even know if her older sister was alive.

"I'm the middle sister."

His eyes stayed trained on her face. "What ever happened to Meg?"

"I have no idea," Renee said shortly.

He apparently didn't notice she didn't want to chat about her family. He made a sound. "I can see a resemblance."

Distant, she guessed from his tone. Her throat

closed, and she had to grit her teeth. Hurt, after all these years? she marveled. Or was what she felt grief?

"Meg was the pretty one," Renee said carelessly.

"Was she?"

Saints above, he actually sounded surprised! As if he had never noticed. Renee suppressed a snort. Maybe those vivid blue eyes didn't see as much as she'd thought.

"In a dress," he mused, "I think you'd be plenty pretty."

She was standing there surrounded by bits and pieces of a dead man, and Daniel Barnard was... Well, she wasn't sure what he was doing. Flirting with her? She had trouble believing that. Insulting her? Probably.

"You don't think women belong in a uniform?"

His eyes opened wide, ostensibly in surprise, although this time she sensed some pretense. "Did I say that? I just thought, in some floaty dress, or maybe one of those crinkly skirts..." He shrugged, nodding toward her dark navy uniform. "That outfit just looks too much like a man's."

Definitely insulting her.

"No, it looks like a police officer's," Renee said through her teeth. "Man *or* woman. Now, if you'll excuse me, I'll be on my way to the coroner."

A groove deepened in one lean cheek. "I didn't mean..."

"I'm sure you didn't." She set the bag with the skull atop the bones in the cardboard carton.

"I'll take it," he said, voice tight. Before she could argue, he hefted the box without a glance at its contents and strode toward the door. Not much she could do but trail him, like the little woman.

Everything deposited in the Bronco, she climbed in and slammed the door, rolling down her window just a bit.

He bent down. "You'll let me know?"

Renee eyed him narrowly. Was he really so naive? Hadn't it occurred to him yet that skeletons weren't strewn in everybody's backyards? Sure, a few people went missing for reasons that didn't involve a crime, like his grandpa. Most dead folks not tucked in a grave, however, were dumped somewhere because they'd been murdered. Which meant she'd have a few thousand questions to ask.

Assuming, she reminded herself, with an involuntary flicker of a glance toward the brown paper bag set atop the box on the passenger side of her front seat, assuming those bones told the coroner enough to give any grounds to ask those questions.

"We'll be in touch," she agreed, and drove away.

BOBBY SANCHEZ laid the bones out on a table, more or less in order. "Mostly less," he said with a chuckle. "Lot of gaps here."

As she watched, he discarded a number of bones. "Deer," he'd remark, tossing one aside, or, "Cow."

Balding and potbellied, the coroner had kept his position for the past ten years without much opposition when elections rolled around. Partly, that was because of police support. With training in forensic anthropology, he knew his stuff and was genuinely useful to police investigations. Today was a good example.

Renee waited, outwardly patient, while a half hour dragged into an hour, then more, as he examined the small collection, measuring the bones and turning them in his hands and humming to himself.

Inside, she was anything but. One thing bothered her most. Hadn't anybody missed whoever these remains belonged to?

She'd spent the past few hours shying away from that speculation. She of all people knew how easy it was, if someone walked out of your life, to assume that person had gone of her own volition. If someone you trusted told you she'd left because she didn't want to be bothered with three kids, you shrank inside. You didn't say, *Wait a minute! Mom wouldn't have gone this way, without even saying goodbye!*

Those were the kinds of thoughts Renee had had on her way back to town, with that box of bones on the seat beside her. She couldn't forget that those teeth looked as if they belonged to a fairly young man or woman. Renee had been just a little girl when her mother, Jolene, had deserted her family. And Jolene had been only thirty-three years old then. Renee had nothing but her dead father's word that her mother had chosen to leave.

The hamburger and fries she'd had for lunch weren't sitting too well by the time she passed under the Triple B arch and turned onto the highway. Renee swallowed the acid in her mouth and stole a glance at the rough knob where the femur would have connected to the pelvis. It was poking over the edge of the carton as if taunting her.

What if these bones turned out to be a woman's?

Her brooding was interrupted when the coroner spoke for the first time in more than a mutter to himself. "I'll fax you a report, but I can tell you the basics if you'd like."

"I'd like." Why else did he think she'd been sitting here on her hands for two hours?

He was succinct. Male, the coroner was certain.

"You're sure about that?" she asked, telling herself she'd known her mother wasn't dead. What she felt was curiosity, not relief.

"No question," Bobby Sanchez said. He continued. The victim had been 5'9" to 5'11" tall. Rangy, not real muscular. Teeth in good shape; he'd seen a dentist regularly—two small fillings meant the cavities had been caught early. Late teens to thirty years old, tops. Hard to tell how long he'd been dead; ten years at least, most likely not over twenty.

"And chances are he was murdered," Bobby Sanchez concluded. "See?" He showed her the vee-shaped cut in the rib.

"But animals must have been gnawing at all these," Renee protested. "What's different about this spot?"

"The teeth marks formed tiny U-shaped gouges," he informed her, making sure she saw the difference. "And by the time animals got to the bones, they would have crumbled, like this hole in the cranium. They wouldn't have had the elasticity to shave clean the way this did. Nope. Had to have happened right about the time of death. Or not long before, because there is no sign of regeneration."

Renee left in a hurry, hoping to catch Jack Murray

before he went home for the day. She pulled into the parking lot behind the station just as he reached his car. When he saw her, he leaned against the fender and waited. She had to give him credit; he never looked impatient. He must really love his job.

Jack listened as she reported the coroner's conclusions.

"Bobby's sure?" he said at last.

"Sure as he can be. That's a quote. He'd like more bones."

"I'll bet he would," the acting police chief agreed dryly. "He's welcome to go hunting."

"Shouldn't we?" Renee tried not to sound too eager. The only murder cases she'd ever investigated were the garden variety kind: a shot fired during a bar brawl, a domestic dispute gone uglier than either husband or wife had intended, a cashier in an all-night gas station/grocery executed during a holdup. Not a lot of mystery, just lives lost or ruined because of hot tempers and panic. But this one, the victim dead ten years or more, identity unknown—this one made her want to find out who the bones had belonged to and why someone had killed him.

Jack frowned. "How long has this guy been dead?" he asked. "Bobby have any idea?"

"He thinks ten to fifteen years. Twenty years at most. Somebody has gotten away with it for a long time."

Jack grunted. "Have you checked to see who might have gone missing within that time frame?"

"I'll do that next. The only one I know of is Daniel Barnard's grandpa," Renee reminded him. "But the coroner says this victim is too young to be him. Not more than thirty years old, he thinks.''

''I'd forgotten about that.'' Jack seemed not to be seeing her anymore. ''I hadn't been back in Elk Springs long. Dan's mother called. Hysterical, of course. She'd turned her back for a minute, and the old man was gone. He was getting pretty confused, and some new medication was making him worse. It started snowing just about the time he slipped away. Covered any tracks and confused the dogs.'' He shook his head. ''After the first hour or so, we knew in our hearts that we were looking for a body, not a lost old man. It was so damned cold, we had to give up, though we hated to with her carrying on the way she was, sure the whole thing was her fault. Nobody could convince her that turning on the news and watching for a few minutes wasn't a sin. We looked again the next day, and the day after, and then when the snow melted. Never found him.''

Renee shivered. With October around the corner and dusk fast approaching, the air had a wintry bite to it for the first time. She pictured a dazed, elderly man, maybe in his shirtsleeves and slippers, just walking away from the lighted house, powdery flakes of snow clinging to his lashes and hair, clouding his vision. Where had he thought he was going? Had he seen someplace else, a mirage that lured him on and on?

She'd read about old people doing that. Nursing homes lost residents pretty regularly. You could understand that; who'd want to stay in one of those places, especially once you'd regressed far enough to forget that you hadn't wanted to be a burden to your children?

But to walk away from your own home, into a snowstorm… Maybe it was instinct, like an animal going off to die. But it was cruel, too, leaving the people who'd loved you to wonder and to imagine you slipping and staggering and finally going down.

Renee shivered again. Those bones were not his, she reminded herself. Any more than they were her mother's.

"Yeah, okay," Jack finally said, straightening and reaching for the car door handle. "Find out who went missing during those years, see if you can come up with any more bones without using much manpower. Ask at the Triple B. Maybe Daniel's mother remembers a ranch hand taking off one night and leaving his stuff behind. At the very least, I'd like to see us put a name to those bones."

"I'll do my best," Renee agreed.

Hurrying into the station, she started thinking about the questions she'd ask. Something told her Daniel Barnard wouldn't like them.

And he'd like even less that she was the one doing the asking.

CHAPTER TWO

DANIEL REINED THE MARE into a whirling pivot to
the left, her hindquarters bunched and her front
hooves flying as she propelled herself in a circle.
Responding to a slight touch of the rein on her neck,
the mare reversed direction, spinning to the right.
Daniel sat loose in the saddle, feeling the power
gathered beneath him, the sweet willingness to do
as he asked.

When he let the rein go slack, she went still, waiting for the tightened legs that would send her surg-
ing ahead. This mare could stop on a dime. Better
yet, she used her head. She could read a steer better
than Daniel could. Not quite four years old, Marian
B Good was going to be one of the best.

Daniel slapped her neck and murmured a few
words. Her mobile ears swiveled to listen.

When he lifted his head, he realized he had an
audience. The lady cop watched from the other side
of the corral fence, her arms crossed on the top rail,
one black-shod foot resting on the bottom rail.

Daniel wondered if he could scare her. Without
pausing to examine the childish impulse, he urged
his horse into a dead run, straight at Officer Renee
Patton.

She never flinched, even when 1,500 pounds of

horseflesh slid to a stop with whiskers tickling Renee's hand. All she did was nod, cool as the snow that stayed atop Juanita Butte year-round. "Mr. Barnard."

"Officer," he drawled, inclining his head.

"I promised to be in touch."

He'd expected a phone call. Those bones had been out there a long time. This wasn't like finding a body with blood still sticky. How interested were the police really going to be in a scattering of weathered bones?

Daniel had kind of hoped for a visit, though; Renee Patton interested him. He'd known enough about her old man that he hadn't been surprised when her sister had run away before graduating from high school.

Funny, though, that nobody except, presumably, her sisters had ever heard from Meg Patton again. After talking with Renee the other day, now he wondered. Runaways were a dime a dozen; when a rebellious teenager vanished, people just assumed she'd gone under her own steam. But he remembered the time Meg spent with her sisters, walking them to school, taking them out for ice cream, bringing them along to the swimming hole on the Deschutes. What would have made her go out the door and never come back, even to see them?

Renee stroked the mare's velvety muzzle, not seeming to mind the steamy breath Marian puffed out with a nicker. The lady cop was as pretty as he remembered, all delicate bones and eyes as big and greeny-gold as a cat's. Her pale blond hair was long, but pulled back so tightly it must hurt.

Her mouth thinned, as if she didn't like his scrutiny. "I need to ask you and your mother some questions."

She'd been wrong about the teeth, Daniel thought instantly, stomach clenching. Those bones had been Granddad's, after all.

"What did you find out?"

"The bones belonged to a young man, between five foot nine inches and five foot eleven. No weightlifter. Probably lean, the coroner thinks."

"Then...definitely not my grandfather," Daniel said slowly.

"Not your grandfather," she agreed.

His stomach should have unclenched, but it didn't. Meg was still on his mind—Daniel remembered her as being tall. "The coroner is sure the bones are a man's?"

Something flickered in Renee's eyes. "He's sure," she said shortly. Was she trying to squelch him, or her own uneasiness?

"I do have questions to ask," she repeated. "I'm told that your mother lives here on the ranch?"

"Over there." A frown coming on, he nodded toward the modest white house where he'd grown up. "My sister's here for a visit right now with her son, too."

"Oh? Well, she might remember something worthwhile. If you can make time for me later, I'll start with them."

Daniel shifted in the saddle, and Marian B Good quivered under him. "Remember what?" he demanded.

Her gaze didn't waver. "Those bones mean a

young man died around here, maybe even on your place. Nobody but the killer ever knew what happened to him. It's like your grandfather. Somewhere there's family who's been wondering all these years. I want to know—"

Her words took a minute to sink in. When they did, he interrupted, "*Killer?* What makes you think something like that? The dead guy might've been some drunken drifter who fell asleep in a snowbank. Or a Vietnam vet living up in the foothills."

"He had a knife cut in one rib. Made around about the time of death, the coroner says."

Daniel swore under his breath. *Murder.* In his backyard.

The mare moved restlessly and he realized his legs had tightened. He soothed her with one hand while he said aloud, "It can't have happened here. Unless it was…jeez, thirty, forty years ago? I mean, I've been here most of my life. My parents have owned this spread since 1959. We'd have noticed if someone upped and disappeared."

"Ranch hands must come and go."

"Yeah, but…" He stopped. She was right. They did. Logical assumption: one of them had killed another after a Saturday night trip to town to hit the bars. Fight over a girl, maybe. "You never did say how long ago the…" He hesitated.

"Victim," Renee supplied.

"Yeah. The victim. You never said how long ago he died."

"Ten to twenty years is the coroner's best guess."

Daniel had recently turned thirty. This murder had happened so long ago, he'd been a kid.

He must have expressed his thought aloud, because the lady cop said crisply, "A twenty-year-old isn't a child."

Daniel grunted, not much liking the speculation in Renee Patton's eyes. What was she thinking? That at twenty he'd have been plenty old enough to commit murder? He went rigid in the saddle and the mare fidgeted under him, edging sideways, tossing her head. He hardly noticed.

God Almighty. The cops would be out here asking questions. People in town would soon be talking. Next time his mother went shopping, folks would hush up when she neared, but she wouldn't have to hear the whispers to know what was being said. Locals would be remembering her husband's sudden death, and the way she'd let her father-in-law just up and wander out into the cold night, never to be seen again. Now a body had been found out on the Triple B, but not Joshua Barnard's. A lot of dying out there, people would say; maybe those others weren't accidents after all.

"Your horse is getting antsy," Renee Patton said, stepping back from the corral fence. "I'll head on down to the house and talk to your mother."

His mother's twin losses, not that many years apart, had weakened her fiber. Maybe she never had been strong, although when he was a child she'd seemed that way. He knew she still cried sometimes, for no reason anyone else could see.

"You're not talking to her without me there," Daniel said flatly, urging Marian B Good toward the gate. As obliging as ever, the mare went through, then turned sideways without him asking so he could close it behind them. He swung off the horse's back and led her to the barn, the cop trailing him.

When he called, a young cowboy came out and took Marian's reins. "Walk her," Daniel said, and Warren nodded, looking curiously toward Renee. Daniel didn't explain her presence.

Renee fell into step with him as he strode between paddocks. "I wasn't planning to grill your mother," she said mildly.

He'd like to believe her.

Daniel said abruptly, "I never told her about the bones."

"Never told her...?" Renee lifted her eyebrows. "Why?"

"Until I was sure it wasn't Granddad..." He stopped. "I figured I would when we knew more."

"She's going to be sorry this isn't your grandfather."

"Sorry?" he began incredulously.

"Never finding a trace is worse than having some bones to lay to rest." Her tone was flat; her face averted now.

The sense of what she'd said penetrated, and Daniel hunched his shoulders. The uniform Renee Patton wore was mannish, but she had a woman's instincts and way of driving to the emotional heart of a matter. She was right—a real funeral would assuage his mother's grief, if not her terrible sense of guilt.

Down at the house, he knocked once, then opened the door. "Mom?" he called.

"Why, Daniel!" His mother appeared from the kitchen. The welcoming smile on her plain, gentle face wavered when she clapped eyes on the woman beside him, then settled into place again. "I'm sorry, Officer, I didn't realize..."

"No reason you should," the lady cop said. "I'm parked over by the barns."

"Is there trouble?" His mother's gaze turned anxiously to him.

Only old trouble that should have been buried ten, twenty years ago.

"No," he said. "Not exactly."

"I need to speak to you," Renee interjected. "If you have a few minutes to spare."

"Of course." His mother's ingrained courtesy kicked in. "Why don't you come into the living room. Can I get you coffee? Tea?"

"I'm fine."

His mother looked at him again; Daniel shook his head.

The front room was more like an old-fashioned parlor: rarely used, a formal configuration of wing chairs and high-backed sofa, dark wood end tables dotted with china figurines Daniel's father had bought for his wife. The only incongruous note was the bright painted wooden blocks scattered in front of the couch. As kids, he and his sister hadn't been allowed to play in here. His mother must be more permissive with her grandson.

Renee chose a chair; Daniel sat beside his mother on the sofa and took her hand. Fine and fragile, it trembled in his. He didn't give the cop a chance to break the news.

"Mom," he said gently, "lately Lotto has been bringing home bones. I, uh, I realized they were human and called the police. I didn't tell you because I wanted to know more first. Officer Patton brought me an update today, and it turns out this doesn't have anything to do with us. The bones are a young man's, and they've been out there a long time.''

Somewhere in this speech, her pupils dilated until her eyes were huge and dark and unfamiliar. At the end, she sagged a little.

Her voice was faint with relief. ''You mean, like an Indian burial? Or some settler?''

''No, Mrs. Barnard.'' Renee was watching his mother with an intensity that scared Daniel, but her voice was kind enough. ''The coroner thinks this man was murdered. Knifed. Probably ten, fifteen, maybe as much as twenty years ago. His body might have been dumped here, but we can't rule out the possibility that he was one of your ranch hands, say. You must have had ones up and leave unexpectedly. Maybe even without taking their stuff.''

A moan rose from his mother's throat. ''Fifteen years ago?'' she whispered.

Renee edged forward in her seat, her expression like Lotto's at the sight of tall grass shivering from the movement of some small creature. ''What happened fifteen years ago?''

Mrs. Barnard stared blindly. Whatever she saw, it wasn't in this living room here and now. She kept making that sound, a soft keening that raised the hair on Daniel's arms.

''Mom!'' he said sharply, his fingers biting into her hand. ''What's wrong?''

She swung toward him, the keening becoming

small gasps. "Wrong?" she echoed, as if not understanding the word.

"What is it?" His throat hurt. Dear God, did he *want* her to say, with a cop sitting here hanging on every word? A wild glance told him that Renee wasn't feeling compassion; she looked predatory. And it was his mother she was hunting.

Not that Daniel knew what he feared; his mother couldn't have hurt anybody, she even trapped spiders and buzzing flies and carried them out of the house to tenderly release them. But it sure as hell sounded as if Mom knew something. About his father?

She looked back at the cop, then him. A shudder worked its way up her thin frame, and she closed her eyes for a long moment. When she opened them again, the pupils were almost back to normal.

"I…" She wet her lips. "You're certain this man was young? He can't possibly have been my father-in-law?"

After an infinitesimal pause, Renee leaned back in her chair, apparently willing—for now—to accept that Mrs. Barnard's distress had been for her father-in-law. "The coroner is quite certain. From the bones he has to work with, he thinks the man might have been anywhere from teenage to thirty at the most. He says that he was under six feet tall, maybe as short as five nine. Probably wiry."

Mrs. Barnard didn't blink. "How can you possibly identify him from that vague a description?"

"Dental records will help."

He'd have sworn his mother's cheeks blanched.

He also had the unpleasant feeling he wasn't the only one to notice.

"Mrs. Barnard, Mr. Barnard." Renee sat unmoving, her clear eyes missing nothing. "I'm going to need you to find your employment records from back then. We might be able to follow up, see if we can trace the men who worked here. Of course we'll be checking neighboring spreads, too. I don't know if your dog wanders that far..."

Daniel would have liked to lie. But the Rosler ranch, the nearest, was a mile and a half away. Lotto liked to keep Daniel in sight. He was never gone long enough to have left Barnard land. Reluctantly, Daniel shook his head.

"Mrs. Barnard, do you remember anything at all that might shed some light on this crime? Any talk, back then, about someone disappearing, or a fight, or ugly feelings? Did your husband complain about a hand who didn't show up to work one morning? You must have a pretty good idea what goes on around here."

Body rigid, his mother said expressionlessly, "Ms....excuse me, *Officer* Patton, hands come and go and my husband was always complaining. After fifteen years, no one story sticks in my mind. We've had as many as half a dozen men working for us at any one time. Sometimes, after a Saturday night in town, one of them will have a black eye or be walking real careful. But, to be truthful, I can hardly even remember names and faces from that long ago. Maybe—" she rose to her feet "—once I find the records they'll nudge my memory. But I can't promise."

It didn't take much perception to realize that Officer Patton was being gently dismissed. Whether she'd have gone if she hadn't been ready to leave anyway was another question. As it was, she, too, rose to her feet.

"Thank you, Mrs. Barnard. I'll be stopping by again. Perhaps I can speak to your daughter then, too."

The air seemed to quiver, and his mother stiffened. "My daughter?"

"She'd have been a child, but children hear things."

Mrs. Barnard's mouth pinched, but she gave a single formal nod. "Yes. Very well. If you'll call ahead, I'll ask her to be here."

Daniel walked Renee to the door. "I assume you remember the way," he said.

Her eyes met his; plainly, she knew why he didn't want to accompany her back. "Of course," she agreed. "I'm sorry that I upset your mother."

"Murder isn't a pleasant subject."

She didn't look away. "No. It isn't. Is it?"

"For God's sake..." he growled.

"Good day, Mr. Barnard." She went down the stairs and walked away without a glance back.

He disliked her a great deal just then, but he also watched her go longer than he should have, because of the way her hips swayed inside uniform trousers that fit her rump snugly. They'd probably been designed for a man.

Daniel swore under his breath. So the lady cop was pretty. She also had a gaze that measured guilt and sized it for prison bars. She didn't give a damn what she did to his mother's fragile sense of peace.

When he went back in, he closed the front door and, for a moment, stood just inside, listening. Had his mother gone back to the kitchen?

But when he went to the archway and looked into the living room, he saw that she'd sunk back onto the couch and sat, spine ruler straight, staring ahead with wide unblinking eyes. Fear laid cold fingers on his nape.

"Mom?"

Her head slowly turned toward him; more sluggishly yet, her eyes focused. "Daniel?"

She sounded as if she couldn't remember why he was here. The fear walked a few icy steps down his neck.

He went into the living room and sat next to her again, taking her hand. It was as cold as he felt inside.

"Mom." He waited until her head swung toward him, until her wide distressed gaze acknowledged his existence. "What happened here fifteen years ago?"

RENEE FOUND, as she'd expected, that it was tedious work following up on the dozens of missing person cases that fell within the ten year span that Bobby Sanchez had suggested.

Some could be eliminated because of gender or age, among them Daniel Barnard's grandfather. She took a few minutes to read the stark police report on the night Joshua Barnard had disappeared into a snowstorm. It added nothing to Jack Murray's recollection. Searchers had indeed combed the ranch land for days; not even a footprint was found. Where had the old man gone? Why?

Just thinking about it gave her the willies. Sure, he'd been senile. But still, he'd chosen to go out that door, walking away from what he knew toward something imagined or real that seemed better. Not so different than what Renee's mother had done. What her sister had done.

Why did anybody shed a life as if it were old skin, unneeded and uninteresting? How could you just let it fall to the ground? Kick it aside as if it were nothing, as if the scars on the discarded skin didn't represent pain, the birthmarks your heritage? As if you hadn't touched other people in that old life?

From long habit Renee was able to wall that familiar emptiness and hurt behind everyday busyness. She searched records, made phone calls, eliminated as possibilities another fourteen men who somebody had thought was missing, back all those years ago. Two had died; one had been discovered dead behind the wheel of his car, which had gone off an icy, little-used road into a canyon. One case resulted from a misunderstanding; the guy had never really been missing. Most had come home again.

One of those, interestingly, was the son of the rancher whose spread bordered the Barnard's. He'd had a police record. Petty stuff, but Gabe Rosler sounded as if he'd been a troubled teenager and young man. When he dropped from sight thirteen years ago, the family panicked, but only a few weeks later he surfaced in San Francisco. Too bad. He'd have been a likely prospect.

But just as interesting was one of Gabe Rosler's buddies who'd vanished about the same time. In fact, people had assumed they'd gone together, only Gabe showed up again, and Les Greene didn't. Greene was into drugs, although he liked hallucinogens, not today's more popular crack. According to his description, he was a little on the tall side—six foot, according to his mother and the high school, where he'd played football before he got tossed from the team for drinking. On the other hand, in Renee's experience, males tended to exaggerate height as much as women tended, when asked, to admit to substantially fewer pounds than they really weighed. Mothers were given to exaggerating, too, as were high school athletic departments.

Besides, given how few bones the coroner had to work with, couldn't he be wrong an inch or two one way or the other?

Greene's mother, she discovered, had died two years ago. Cirrhosis of the liver. Her son had come by his vices naturally, it appeared.

Renee put Les Greene's file on her stack of possibles, then called it a day.

Home was her father's house—she still thought of it that way—within spitting distance of the Deschutes River. The view from the back stoop, Renee told herself, was why she was still in the house despite too many empty rooms and the unsettling sight of her father's recliner sometimes giving an agitated rock on its own.

Chief Patton had kept the place in pristine condition. He painted the house every two years, powerwashed the roof every fall, mowed the lawn twice a week. So far, she'd done the same. How could she not, with him looking over her shoulder? His ghost would never let her sleep nights if the windows were smudged or the grass untrimmed along the fence.

Tonight the darn place felt even lonelier than usual. She almost wished she'd hear a clank of handcuffs as her father's ghost strode down the hall.

She stood in the living room—with the same furniture that had been there all her life—and said aloud, "I should sell the house."

Of course she should. She didn't even know why she hadn't. Her younger sister Abby wanted her to. Dad had been dead…six months. Not long, for the loss of a dearly beloved parent. But Renee hadn't loved him.

She didn't stop in the living room tonight, any more than she ever did. She hadn't sat in there in six months. How could she curl up in the armchair and read, when she could *feel* him in that damned recliner, rustling his newspaper, making edgy comments, working up a head of steam about something.

Even the brief image of him was enough to prickle the tiny hairs on her arms. Renee shivered and hurried into the kitchen, which had always been the domain of the girls. Nowadays, she practically lived in here. She'd even moved the TV to the dining room table.

She stuck a frozen, prepared dinner into the microwave and set the timer, then leaned against the counter waiting. She hadn't cooked dinner in six months, either. Not a real, oven kind of meal. Microwave was good enough for her. Some nights she brought home Chinese takeout or a pizza or even just a burger and fries. Not nutritious, but she'd become sick of cooking. And the only recipes she knew were those her father had liked. Meat loaf. A few casseroles. She could mash potatoes, grill a steak. Her beef stews were probably very good; Dad had always grunted when he dug in, which she'd taken for approval.

What fond memories he'd left her, Renee thought bitterly. He hadn't given hugs or quiet words of praise. No, her best memories were of silence or a grunt.

She reached for the telephone without thought, dialing a number she knew by heart. Her younger sister answered on the first ring.

"I was just thinking about you," Abby said. "What's up?"

"What were you thinking?" Renee countered.

"Just that I haven't seen you in two weeks. Shall we have dinner one of these nights? Tomorrow? No, shoot, I can't do that. How about Thursday?"

Renee consulted her mental calendar. "Sounds good."

They discussed where, made plans to meet. Then Abby asked, "How are you?"

The microwave beeped. Phone held between her ear and her shoulder, Renee took the dinner out, peeled off the plastic top and dumped it onto a plate. She felt like being civilized tonight.

"Oh, I'm okay."

Her sister waited.

"I've just had a weird couple of days. It's this case. Do you know the Barnards? I think Daniel was Meg's age."

They rarely talked about their sister. Abby said only, "No, that doesn't sound familiar. But I don't remember very many of her friends. Don't forget, I was only eleven when she left."

And had seemed younger. In one of those quick flashes, Renee saw Abby curled in a small ball in bed, face wet with tears. Feeling terribly young herself, Renee had still known that, at fourteen, she was now the mother. She'd slipped under the covers and held her little sister, spending the night in that narrow twin bed. Perhaps she'd needed the comfort as much as Abby had.

"Well, Daniel Barnard is a rancher. Quarter horses. The place is called the Triple B." She told Abby about the dog bringing home the skull, and about Joshua Barnard going out into the snowstorm one night and not coming back, and how interesting Shirley Barnard's reaction to the news of the murder had been. Finally she told her sister about the sheaf of missing persons reports she'd been reading.

"It's all made you think about Mom," Abby diagnosed.

"And Meg." Still leaning against the counter, Renee looked down without interest at the cooling lasagna. "Both of them, just disappearing like that... Don't you ever wonder?"

Abby was quiet for a moment. "Whether they're alive?"

"Yeah."

"Of course I wonder!" Unexpectedly, Abby

sounded mad. "When I was little, I convinced myself that Mom was dead, so I could believe she'd really loved us! Because if she's *not* dead..."

"It means she didn't care very much about us."

"Which is probably the truth."

"But we know Meg loved us."

"Oh, sure," her sister said, the anger gone but her voice wry. "I remember the stuff she did with us, and the way she used to shield us from Dad. But, you know, when she left she was only sixteen. Even if she did love us, she was probably still glad to be gone. Away from him. And you were a pain about then, always talking back and making Dad mad, and then you'd yell at her when she tried to head you off."

"Blame *me*, why don't you?" Renee said hotly. As if she hadn't blamed herself often enough.

"I'm not!" Abby denied. "I'm just saying, Meg wasn't an adult like Mom. She hadn't *chosen* to have three kids, then leave them. I mean, how can we blame her?"

Easily, Renee thought. *You weren't the one who had to take her place because she couldn't be bothered with it anymore. You weren't the one who had to become an instant grown-up. Have dinner on the table when Dad walked in the door at 5:45 every day. Take the brunt of his anger.*

But all Renee said was, "She could have written us. Or called."

Again, her sister was silent, speaking at last in a small voice. "Yeah. She could have."

Renee sighed. "I didn't mean to get you down, too. I just...when I saw that skull, I thought it might be Mom. Or Meg, I guess, except at least I saw Meg packing. Mom was just…gone.''

"Maybe someone else should handle this case. If it bothers you so much.''

"No," Renee said swiftly, surprised at her instant resistance. "No, I want to see it through. If I can't accomplish anything else, I'm determined to give this guy his name back.''

"In case…" Abby stopped.

She didn't have to finish. They both knew what she'd been going to say. *In case Mom had been buried somewhere in an anonymous grave. In case they'd never heard from her because she'd died and no one had known who she was, so they couldn't notify the family.*

"Anyway, it's my job," Renee said more pragmatically.

She hung up a moment later, thinking fate had sent her out to the Triple B. No one else in the department would care anywhere near as fiercely as she did.

Acknowledging, even to herself, how strongly she felt, how much she cared about having a name to put on a gravestone, embarrassed her.

It was probably just her mood, she decided. Tomorrow the whole thing would become a puzzle she had to put together. No more.

"Hey," she said aloud to the silent kitchen. "Investigating a murder beats staking out a mailbox.''

She only wished Daniel Barnard wasn't involved. The way he charged her on his horse today had been a challenge, whether he knew it or not. When she didn't flinch, his eyes had held respect. That had meant more to her than she wanted to admit.

But the respect had been gone later. While she questioned his mother, he'd looked at her as if she were some kind of monster. He wasn't going to be any help on this. In fact, he'd be fighting her all the way.

Oh, well, she told herself. It wasn't as if he'd noticed her as a woman. Men didn't. Not the way they noticed Abby. Which was okay by her.

That's how she wanted it.

Renee dumped the now cold lasagna in the garbage, rinsed off the plate and turned on the television.

LISTENING TO THE SOUNDS of her son's departure, Shirley Barnard glanced down at the dish towel in her hands. She had picked it up only to look busy, as if she were herself again, ready to bustle around the kitchen. When the front door closed behind him, she let the towel drop as if it were a piece of trash and went to the round oak table in front of the bay window, where she sank into one of the chairs. The fraying cane seat gave comfortably, shaping to fit her. As it should. Why, she'd sat in this very same seat, three meals a day, for thirty years now! She didn't even have to count back; she'd been pregnant with Daniel when Matt had his grandmother's oak chairs freshly caned for his wife of two years.

In her memory it was only yesterday. She looked at the empty chairs, seeing in her mind's eye countless dinners, Daniel and Mary in high chairs, then as chattering school-age children, and finally teenagers. Joshua, after his wife had died and he'd moved in with Matt and Shirley. And Matthew, always Matthew, presiding over the table, his enormous shoulders filling the worn denim shirts he favored, his blue eyes sparkling with humor and that hint of something private she had to call lust, always just for her. She'd never been afraid of him straying, not Matthew. He'd sworn to love her for keeps, and he had. Even during that awful year when she hadn't wanted him on top of her, when the very idea made her stomach heave, still he had loved her and looked at her with desire and affection along with sorrow.

Shirley had never ever been glad Matt had died. How could she? she thought, shocked even though right this minute she *was* glad. She had loved him with all her being. When Daniel came to the house to tell her Matt had gone over a horse's neck—Matthew! Of all people!—straight into the wall of the arena and was unconscious, she'd rushed out without a coat even though it was winter and ridden in the ambulance with him to the hospital, holding his hand the entire way, terrified by his white still face. He'd stayed unconscious for two days, then died without ever waking up. He was brain dead, they'd tried to tell her, but she hadn't believed them. She'd talked to him, and squeezed his hand, and waited for his eyes to open and that slow sweet smile to curve his mouth when he saw her. His heart was beating—wasn't it—and he was breathing. So how could he be dead, the way the doctors said? It was like the night when Joshua wandered out, leaving the front door open and snow blowing into the front hall. They wanted to give up, and she wouldn't let them. How far could he have gone? He had to still be alive, just cold and lonely and confused. To this day she thought of him that way, huddled out there somewhere.

Daniel had tried to gently pull her away from her husband's side at the hospital. She had screamed at him to let her alone. Oh, how she'd loved that man! How could he die so stupidly, doing something he was so good at?

But now she had to be glad, because it would be worse, so much worse, if he'd been arrested and dragged off to prison. And it would have been her fault, because if it hadn't been for her he wouldn't have had to do what he'd done. Matthew had been a gentle man, not given to violence. Stern sometimes, and not wishy-washy in his beliefs, but his quick temper cooled just as fast.

But that night... Oh, that night...

Shirley stared dully into space. She'd buried all this fear and guilt ten feet under, where it belonged, never thinking to meet it again. Matt and she had agreed that putting it out of their minds was the best thing they could do. What good would talking about it do? If they pretended none of it had happened, pretty soon it would be as if it hadn't.

The bad thing about their not having talked was that she only knew part of the story. Her part. She hadn't wanted to know any more, not then. What you don't know can't hurt you, the scared child inside her had whispered. Don't ask.

But if she knew what had really happened that night after Matt stormed out, before he came back splattered with blood, she would be able to handle this. The finding of the bones. That police officer, here asking questions.

What you didn't know could hurt you, she realized, and the child didn't try to argue. That part of her was gone. Dead. No, not dead, just all grown up. Mourning her husband, but glad he wasn't here to speak out. For above everything else, he'd been honest. He wouldn't let blame go where it didn't belong.

If she had asked, he would have told her.

Tears were running down her cheeks, blurring her vision, so the past was all she *could* see.

"Oh, Matt," she whispered. "What did you do?"

CHAPTER THREE

"WHAT HAPPENED fifteen years ago?" Shirley Barnard echoed Renee's question without so much as raising her eyebrows. Looking unnaturally calm, she sat primly on her living room sofa, her hair softly curled, her face made up, no trace of yesterday's distress to be seen. She'd made an effort today, replacing the everyday housedress with a going-to-town one. "As I said," she continued, "nothing in particular happened fifteen years ago that I can recall. Why, have you pinpointed the...death to that year?"

Renee wondered if she was imagining the tension that had crept into the older woman's voice with her last question.

"No." Renee glanced down at her notebook, where she'd written precisely nothing. She looked back up, expression suitably bland. "You were the one to mention that date. And you did seem quite agitated."

"Are you certain you wouldn't like a cup of coffee?" When Renee declined, Mrs. Barnard said with that same false calm, "I'm afraid I upset my son, too. Having bones found here, on our place—" She broke off. "It just brought it all back. I felt—I still feel responsible for my father-in-law's death."

"I understand, Mrs. Barnard." Although she didn't, Renee reflected, understand why a subject that had shattered Daniel's mother only yesterday could today be discussed as if it were less important than the weather. "But from what I read, it really wasn't your fault. You couldn't be expected…"

Mrs. Barnard lifted a hand. "Please, Officer Patton. You can't say anything that hasn't been said a thousand times before. My conscience doesn't believe any of it. I was alone with him. I let myself be distracted. He might have been gone as much as forty-five minutes before I noticed. If only I'd been able to call the police sooner…" She took a breath. "But that has nothing to do with your business here."

"Your father-in-law didn't disappear fifteen years ago."

"That's true." She went still. "I don't know what you're driving at."

Renee said conversationally, "I'm merely curious about why, when you became so upset, you specifically said 'fifteen years ago.' Not ten years ago, when your father-in-law died. Fifteen."

Now Mrs. Barnard did raise her eyebrows. "Wasn't it you who said fifteen years ago?"

"I gave a range. Ten to twenty."

"I'm certain you mentioned fifteen. I could only have been repeating the last thing you said."

Renee couldn't shake her. She also didn't believe her. Mrs. Barnard knew or suspected something that she had no intention of telling. At least, not telling Renee. Her son, however, might be another story.

She had already met and interviewed his sister, a

slender dark-haired woman who had left the house immediately thereafter with her toddler, destination undisclosed.

Mary Stevens—her married name—had been wearing no makeup, and dark circles under her eyes suggested she wasn't sleeping well.

She didn't offer apologies or explanations, merely answered Renee's questions succinctly. Ten years ago she'd been seventeen. Yes, she thought she would have noticed if any ranch hands had vanished unexpectedly.

A shadow of a smile touched Mary's pale lips. "I was at an age when I was all too aware of any young man in denim and cowboy boots."

"What about when you were twelve?"

She made a horrible face. "I was slow maturing. *Really* slow. At twelve, I was still hoping I wouldn't have to bother with breasts." Mary glanced ruefully down at her chest. If her bra wasn't a C cup, Renee missed her guess. "So the answer is no. I had no interest whatsoever in the help, with a few exceptions."

"Exceptions?"

"Oh…" She shrugged. "I barrel raced. Dreamed of doing the rodeo circuit, much to my parents' dismay. One guy who worked here had been a bronc rider. I don't remember his name, but there was something a little dangerous about him. Now, if I'd been sixteen, I'd have probably been in love. Instead, I pumped him for details about rodeo life."

"Any others?"

"There were a few who were willing to indulge me. I'd follow them around." Her blue eyes were as clear and penetrating as her brother's. "But I don't see how this helps you."

"I don't suppose it does," Renee admitted. "But I want to know the name of the man who died out there, apparently never missed by anybody. He might have been a drifter, but chances are he worked around here."

"Most likely at the Triple B," Mary said slowly. "That's what you mean, isn't it?"

"Or at a neighboring ranch. Or he might have been someone who came out here to drink with one of your hands."

"In which case, someone who worked here was a murderer."

"That's a possibility," Renee said evenly. "Anybody occur to you?"

Unlike her mother, Mary looked as if she was giving it some serious thought. But she ended up shaking her head. "I'm sorry. The idea of a murderer... The guys I remember... I just can't see any of them bashing a man's head in, or shooting him, or... How did it happen?"

"A knife, we think." Interesting that neither her mother nor brother had told her. Renee sidestepped to an earlier thought. "You said there was something 'dangerous' about the one fellow. What did you mean?"

Daniel's sister actually laughed at that point. "I suspect what my twelve-year-old self was trying to put into words is that he was sexy. You know, one of those guys who would raise a mother's warning flags. I know mine didn't like me spending time with him. Not that he'd have looked twice at me, even if

I had been interested. At that age, I could have stood in for a fence rail.''

"Me, too.'' Renee was momentarily surprised that the admission had slipped out. She rarely got personal with interview subjects. "Well,'' she said briskly, "I guess that's it. If you think of anything…''

"Of course.'' Mary stood, then hesitated. "You know, this is upsetting my mother dreadfully. Is it really necessary for you to talk to her again?''

So Daniel wasn't alone in feeling protective toward his mother.

"I'm afraid so,'' Renee said. "She's the only one still here who was an adult when the crime was committed. She would have seen things differently than you or your brother did.''

Mary accepted the answer, although she looked troubled when she left the living room. Yet she bundled up her boy and departed rather than staying to offer moral support to her mother.

Not that Mrs. Barnard appeared to need it. Today her facade never cracked. Renee wondered if she was as fragile as her children seemed to think.

Daniel was expecting her up at his house, Mrs. Barnard informed her at the end of the interview.

"His office is there. He has the boxes of old personnel records I'd stored in the attic.''

"Fine. Thank you. I'm sorry to have had to bother you again.''

Mrs. Barnard's dark eyes, so unlike her son's and daughter's, met Renee's with a kind of pleading. "This may have nothing to do with us.''

"That's true,'' Renee agreed, moved to both com-

passion and curiosity by the other woman's veiled
desperation. "But I have to start somewhere. You
understand."

"They—" she swallowed "—the bones...*he* was
found here. On Barnard land. Of course, I understand."

Renee didn't tell her that she would undoubtedly
be back. Nothing would convince her Shirley Barnard's terrified, grieving response to the news that a
murder had been committed here on the Triple B
fifteen years ago had a thing to do with the old man
who had chosen to die out in the wilderness rather
than in a recliner in front of the TV.

When she rang Daniel's doorbell, she had to wait
for several minutes before he opened the door.

"Sorry," he said curtly. "I was on the phone."

With his mother? Renee wondered.

His flannel shirt was unbuttoned over a faded blue
T-shirt. As she followed him, this time through the
living room, she saw that his dark hair was damp
and his jeans clean. Her uniform shoes clicked on
the wood floor; he padded silently in stocking feet.
Again his very presence, his height and sheer bulk,
moved her to uneasiness edged with something
she'd rather not identify.

Large and uncluttered, his office had the same feel
as the living room. Renee took in the gleaming birch
floors, ceiling-high bookcases, oak filing cabinets,
desk and computer, the screen glowing blue-white.
A dhurrie rug in rust and sage and desert sand added
just enough color. On the far side of the room, a big
leather chair faced the picture windows.

Once in the office, he stood to one side. Aware

of him behind her, she crossed the room and looked out. The expansive view explained why he'd built his house on the ridge. To the south, she could just see Rusty Butte, a small red cinder cone. Directly west were the barns and pastures laid out like a child's model. Beyond them was the dry gray-green high desert country, not beautiful like the mountains to the west, but compelling.

She made a sound and turned. "Wish we had a view like that from the station."

He didn't comment, only jerked his head toward the desk. "The files you asked for are right here."

"Thank you." Renee hesitated. "Will you be around if I have questions?"

He grunted. "I'm not going anywhere."

Oh, good. She could spend the whole afternoon with her nerves prickling from that uncomfortable awareness. Dismay drove her to say casually, "In that case, why don't I take these out to your kitchen table? So you can keep working."

"I'll bring a card table in here." He disappeared immediately, eager either to accommodate her or to keep his eye on her. She suspected the latter, considering the chill she'd felt from him today.

He set up the card table, pulled a straight-backed chair over from in front of his desk, and dragged the boxes to the table.

"Thank you," she said again.

Daniel nodded in acknowledgment, then bent to peel the tape from the flaps on one of the cartons. "These are payroll records. The other box has personnel files." Seeing her expression, he said, "Don't get excited. Basically, all we keep are the original applications, maybe a letter of recommendation, a few notes. We don't do written evaluations like a big company.''

To be thorough, she started back twenty years ago, taking notes when she came to anyone who fell in the right age range. No comments had been written when an employee left, although she discovered that sometimes a new hire started immediately, and sometimes several weeks passed before a new name and social security number appeared. From that, she could deduce when notice had been given and when someone had most likely quit unexpectedly. Or just flat out disappeared.

At first the records were all handwritten. The paper had yellowed and the ink faded. After scanning a couple years' worth, Renee took a break from the payroll ledgers and opened the box that held personnel files.

She had deliberately sat with her back to Daniel, at his desk. The intermittent clack of computer keys was sandwiched between long periods of silence.

When she stretched, he said immediately, ''Would you like a cup of coffee?''

''Do you have something cold?'' Renee asked without turning. ''Pop?''

He made a noncommital sound and went away, coming back after a few minutes with a glass of ice and a can of cola. ''This okay?''

''Wonderful.'' She smiled at him.

He didn't smile back. She was still in the doghouse. He also didn't return to his desk, however.

Renee asked idly, ''Is your sister here for a visit?''

"No." For a moment it appeared he would say no more. At last, looking reluctant, he continued, "She's having problems with her husband. They needed to cool off."

"I'm sorry. She seems very nice."

The groove in one cheek deepened. "Yeah. She is."

Still he stood there, towering over her. She wondered if he was making her feel small on purpose. Reminding her that he didn't think a woman should be a cop.

"Well," she said. "Back to work."

He took the hint and retreated, although she wasn't sure how far. He moved so quietly. And she was damned if she was going to turn to look. What if he were watching her? She wouldn't let him see that he made her self-conscious.

Damn it, she didn't know why he did.

The personnel files were marginally more interesting than the financial ledgers had been, although Daniel was right: they weren't a treasure trove of information. No photographs, just a bare application asking for a minimum of background data—previous jobs, education, two names for references. Age was asked, although a few had left the space blank. On the back of most, the date of employment and termination had been written.

"They don't stay long, do they?" Renee murmured.

Behind her, Daniel said, "Low pay, hard work."

She turned in her chair. He was leaning back in his, long legs stretched out, stocking feet on the desk. Hands clasped behind his head, he contemplated her. Had he been staring at her for the past hour?

"Is there any way of telling the ones who actually said goodbye from the ones who just upped and left?"

"Probably not." He didn't move. "I remember some of them."

"Your sister mentioned a cowboy she thought was 'dangerous.' Her word, not mine. She said your mother didn't like her talking to him."

He frowned and put his feet back on the floor. "Did she say how old she was?"

"Um…twelve, I think."

"Ah." His mouth tilted into a faint, crooked smile. "Yeah, I remember him. Let me think." He rubbed his jaw. "Seems like he went by initials. Uh, L.J., P.J.—no, T.J. Yeah, that was it. T. J. Baxter, though I might have the last name wrong."

Renee flipped back through the files. Baxter. There it was. She'd already glanced through it; T. J. Baxter was one of those who'd left abruptly, or so it appeared.

"Why didn't your mother like him?"

"He flirted with anything in skirts. Even Mom. Baxter liked Mary, though I never saw anything wrong in it. He was patient, indulgent…you know, as if she were a kid sister. But he made Mom nervous."

Renee could see why. Young Mary Barnard hadn't been far from physically developing. If T. J. Baxter, with his glamorous past as a rodeo bronc rider, had still been around when Mary did develop an interest in young cowboys in tight jeans, Baxter would have been a real danger.

"So, did he get fired?"

"Yeah, Dad lost patience. Baxter was good with horses but lazy. You couldn't trust him to keep working when no one was watching. Dad told him to clear out."

"You heard? Saw him packing?"

Daniel frowned. "No, his bunk was empty one morning, and Dad said he'd told him to go. You saying my father lied?"

Lying went hand-in-glove with murder. But Renee didn't remind him of that fact, since she had no reason at all to suspect the late Matthew Barnard of either offense.

"Just hoping to eliminate him as a possibility," she said neutrally.

He didn't comment, but the creases between his dark brows didn't smooth out.

"Thanks for the info," Renee said pointedly, opening the next file.

He gave only a brusque nod before picking up a pen and returning to work. Or to staring at her. She didn't know, since she didn't look over her shoulder to check.

She worked steadily from then on, her pile of notes growing. Given the social security numbers, she ought to be able to find out which of these men had started another job elsewhere after leaving the Triple B. And which one hadn't, because he'd never left Barnard land.

When Renee flipped the ledger closed, she glanced at her watch. Six o'clock. The shadows were dropping low in the sky. In another hour, the picture windows would frame a glorious spectacle.

She rotated her head, working some kinks out of her neck, then stole a surreptitious glance over her shoulder. She was alone in the office.

Returning everything to the boxes, she closed the tops and restuck the tape as best she could. Then she took her notes and made her way back through the quiet house. Had its owner left her alone altogether? At the front door, she called, "Mr. Barnard?"

He appeared from the direction of the kitchen before she could feel silly, shouting in an empty house.

"All done?" he asked.

"I think so. I appreciate your cooperation." She sounded wooden, worlds from how she felt. His magnetic blue eyes made her want to hang her head like a shy adolescent.

"I was about to put dinner on the table." He nodded back toward the kitchen.

Renee became consciously aware of the delicious aroma that had probably hurried her through those last files. Pot roast, she guessed. And biscuits? Was he expecting someone? Hinting that he'd be glad to see her backside?

Daniel rocked onto his heels and shoved his hands into the pockets of his jeans. "Can I talk you into staying? I get tired of eating by myself."

He wanted *her* to stay to dinner? Astonishment made her blurt, "Your mother would probably appreciate your company." Wasn't that graceless, even for her? she marveled.

One dark eyebrow rose, making her feel even

more gauche. Smoothly, Daniel said, "I'm sure she's sitting down to her own meal by now. We keep early hours."

"Oh. Um, I had plans for dinner." What lonely company pride could be.

His expression closed, becoming remote. "Ah. Well, enjoy yourself."

Exasperated, her stomach growled. Whatever he was making for dinner *did* smell awfully good. And he *had* asked her, which was something men rarely did. He undoubtedly wanted to know more about her investigation, or else he was just being polite, but it didn't hurt to be sociable, did it? He wasn't a suspect, for Pete's sake.

Impulsively, Renee admitted, "My plans were for a microwave dinner. Lasagna, I think. That's the best."

Daniel's mouth twitched. "Undoubtedly," he agreed.

"Your dinner smells better."

"Pot roast."

"I thought so." She took a deep breath. "If you really mean it…"

"I don't say things I don't mean."

Her father hadn't, either. Which was why he'd never given compliments. If Daniel Barnard hadn't said she was pretty, even implied she was as pretty as her sister Meg, Renee would have figured he was grudging with them, too. He didn't seem the slick kind to use flattery to disarm an opponent. But she had heard him say it, a mistruth so blatant that now she was suspicious. *You're not so bad-looking,* Renee might have bought. As pretty as Meg—never.

Except…there might be a man somewhere who thought she was. Men and women both had incomprehensible tastes sometimes, she'd seen that for herself. Fortunately, nature had the common sense to shield people's vision with blinders.

More likely Daniel Barnard had forgotten what Meg looked like, and the compliment had been an idle remark, the kind of thing people say without meaning much. Not a lie exactly, but not words to hold close to your heart, either.

Still, it wouldn't hurt to stay to dinner to see, would it?

"Well, then, thank you," Renee said. "A man who can really cook is a wonder I've got to behold."

A slow smile warmed his face, making her see it in a different light. That first time, she'd thought him plain except for those extraordinary eyes. But now, with a smile dipping the crease in his cheek deeper, creating tiny crinkles beside his blue, blue eyes, giving a sexy twist to his mouth, she knew she'd been wrong.

Or else nature was in the process of manufacturing a pair of blinders for her, custom fit.

Scary thought.

She followed him back to the kitchen, where her offer to help was refused. He poured her some wine and insisted she sit back and admire.

"Besides," he confessed, "it's ready. Not much else *to* do. Unless you want a salad?"

"Not if there are vegetables in with that meat. And potatoes. I never have potatoes anymore, except French fries."

Using quilted oven mitts, which were kind of cute on a man, Daniel carried the cast-iron pot to the table where he set it on a trivet. In the very spot the skull had sat, come to think of it. But she wouldn't let that bother her.

She blinked and realized he'd said something. "What?"

"I asked why you never have potatoes anymore."

"Because I'd have to cook 'em. I quit cooking after my father died."

Now, why had she told him that? He'd want to know how she'd felt about her father and what his death had meant to her. And she didn't know. Wouldn't want to say if she did know.

But Daniel surprised her. "Were they his favorite food?"

Renee blinked. "I guess so. Well, meat and potatoes."

"A man after my own heart."

Oh, she surely did hope not.

A basket of hot biscuits joined the main course on the table. Margarine in the wrapper—how typical of a man not to gussy it up. Then he joined her.

After the first bite, Renee gave an ecstatic sigh. "You can cook."

"Did you doubt me?"

His tone was serious enough to make her wonder if he was really talking about his ability in the kitchen. She looked up to find him regarding her with an expression just as grave.

"I have no reason to doubt you," she said after a moment, carefully.

Their eyes held. At last he nodded, as though satisfied, then picked up his fork. "Good."

She buttered her biscuit and discovered that it was melt-in-your-mouth perfection. Why wasn't a man who could cook like this married?

She didn't quite dare ask that.

"I hear your horses have quite a reputation," she said instead, almost at random. "Jack Murray says they've won national championships."

"That's the goal, if you really want to breed or train horses." Daniel savored a bite, then continued, "I rarely show them myself beyond the regional level. That's not what I want to do. I get them to a certain point, then sell 'em. The new owners make my reputation."

She tilted her head to one side. "Which means, I suppose, that you have to pick the new owners carefully."

"Right." He flashed a grin that almost stopped her heart. Definitely not plain. "I would, anyway, because I don't want to hear that one of my animals has been mistreated. But when I have a good horse, I'll only sell it to someone who has the ability to make it a champion. If Triple B horses aren't popping up in the top ten regularly, my asking prices would have to drop."

"Your father trained horses, too?"

"Yes, but on a smaller scale. He never made much money. I figured the business should be more than subsistence. Besides—" another quick smile "—when I do something, I want to be the best."

She contemplated what that said about him. "And your quarter horses are."

"I got lucky, to start with." He leaned his elbows comfortably on the table. "A colt my father almost sold turned out to be the smartest horse I've ever known. He went all the way, the one time I've competed at a national show. He's still standing stud here, along with one of his sons. That mare I was riding yesterday is a granddaughter. She's going to be the best."

"You love what you do," Renee said, amazed.

"Why else would I do it?" he said simply.

The answer came without thought. "Because you inherited this place. Because your father did it."

"Is that why you're a cop?" His eyes told her he'd see through any lie. "Because your father was?"

Renee looked down at her nearly empty plate. "Partly," she admitted. "It's...what I grew up with. Becoming a cop felt natural."

Instead of pursuing it, for which she was grateful, Daniel said mildly, "I suppose it's the same for me. I was put on a horse before I could walk. But that's not all of it. The same was true for my sister, but she's a nurse. Says she can't imagine spending her life on fun and games."

Amused at the outrage he couldn't hide, Renee smiled. "She has a point. Cutting horses aren't used much anymore on cattle ranches, I hear."

"The day an all-terrain vehicle can outthink Marian B Good is the day I hang it up."

"Marian be good," Renee mused. "Did you name her?"

Daniel sat back in his chair looking wary. "Yeah."

"Was it wishful thinking? Like, you could substitute any woman's name? Susan be good? Jennifer be good?" *Renee be good?* she couldn't help adding to herself.

"Her mom was Good Golly. Her grandma was Marian B."

"Oh, I see." Renee gazed innocently at him. "Strictly a family thing."

"Damn it," he growled, but with amusement narrowing his eyes "I'm as good in the kitchen as any woman. So don't accuse me of being a sexist pig."

She raised her eyebrows. "I seem to recall something about how a police uniform wasn't made to fit a woman. Care to comment?"

"It's ugly," he said bluntly. "It's not that I think a woman belongs in an apron. Or satin and lace. You, for example. I think you'd look fine in tight jeans. Or a doctor's coat. Don't read into my words what isn't there."

Not totally reassured, she asked, "Does Jack Murray look bad in this uniform?"

"I've never given a thought to how Jack looks. Now, you..." For the first time, he let his eyes blatantly caress her.

No man had ever hungered for her. She couldn't believe this one was. Stiffly, she said, "Well, give it a thought now."

"You're a tough nut to crack, aren't you?"

A tough nut. That was her. God forbid she be a desirable woman.

"That's right," she drawled. "So, what do you think? This—" she thumbed her lapel "—look okay on Jack?"

Now annoyance flickered in Daniel Barnard's eyes. "Yeah. The fabric is heavy, sturdy, utilitarian. Masculine."

It stung. She couldn't lie to herself. But she didn't have to let him know how much. "So," she said insolently, "the truth comes out."

A muscle in his jaw jerked. "The uniform is masculine. The job isn't necessarily."

She didn't back down. "The uniform's a symbol. Like the badge. It's all a package deal."

"Maybe so." He turned his wineglass without picking it up. "I like what's inside the package better than I do the wrapping paper."

She opened her mouth and closed it.

A smile appeared in his eyes. "Deflated all that righteous anger, didn't I?"

Renee struggled with the unpalatable fact that he was right. Oh, she did hate to admit that. "Yeah," she grumbled. "You took the fun out of my evening."

His gaze didn't leave her even as he sipped wine. "Now, why were you so all-fired sure I was a jerk? Didn't Meg like me?"

"Actually, she had a crush on you for a while. Before she and Jack started going out."

She'd expected him to look gratified. He only arched a brow. "Okay, then. Why the preconception?"

There had been no preconception. She'd taken his words wrong because she wanted to. Because disliking him was easier than wanting him.

"I guess I've just gotten prickly," Renee said. "I meet plenty of jerks who really think I have no business wearing a badge or a gun. The way you put it about the uniform…'' She shrugged. ''Like I said, I guess I'm too sensitive.''

Somehow she'd convinced him. He grimaced, nodded. ''I can see how that would happen. Okay. Can we start from square one?''

''You mean, I can't finish my dinner?''

His slow warm smile was just for her. ''We just jumped forward to square three real quick.''

''Square three being a display of hospitality.''

''No.'' Raw intent darkened his eyes. ''It's a woman and a man breaking bread together.''

Her heart felt as if it might bounce right out of her chest. She tried to sound insouciant, but her voice squeaked. ''I hate to think what square four is.''

''Well…'' Daniel's gaze touched her mouth. ''We might get there yet tonight, who knows?''

Lord Almighty, she thought. Was he talking about kissing? Did he *want* to kiss her?

CHAPTER FOUR

WELL, HE HADN'T GOTTEN so far as kissing her, but Daniel was otherwise satisfied with the evening. In that drab uniform, Renee Patton was like some neglected, winter-pastured horse, brought in with hip bones showing and coat dull. Given a month or two and the right care, that mare would become round and shiny and fit, an eyeful of magnificent horseflesh. Renee's spring hadn't come yet, he sensed; her father was dead, but she hadn't yet blossomed away from his harshness.

Or maybe, Daniel told himself, he was reading more into her few remarks about Patton than they deserved. For all he knew, she was mending from a heart broken by another man. But somehow he didn't think so. He remembered as a kid going to the movie *Cinderella*. He had never seen such innocence until he met Renee.

Sexual and romantic innocence, that is. Where her job was concerned, she was all too knowing. Young as she was, she already had cynicism in her eyes, an expectation that people would lie to her.

That his mother would lie.

God help them all, she was right. His mother was lying, although he thought it wasn't easy for her. But if she was concealing something that had happened fifteen years ago, she must have told plenty of lies in those years. Even to him.

Mary had tried to talk to their mother, too, with no more success.

"Maybe it is just thinking about Granddad that has her upset," his sister had said without much conviction. Her two-year-old son toddled toward Daniel's kitchen. Mary rose from the couch, corralled the boy and continued above his howls, "You know Mom. She wouldn't have…well, had anything to do with that dead body."

She couldn't say it either—Mom wouldn't have had anything to do with *murder*. Impossible. But then, why was she lying?

"Maybe not," he said. "But you know how much she loved Dad. And he had a temper."

Short-lived and never resulting in more than roars of displeasure, but if someone had hurt one of the horses or threatened his beloved family, he might have lashed out.

It was the knife part that had Daniel's imagination balking. Stabbing someone had to be planned. Feeling the blade bite flesh, sink in, scrape bone… Continuing to thrust every sickening inch. Hate, not temper, would lead you to do that. Or else no conscience at all.

"Not Dad," his sister said, as if she'd followed his thoughts as clearly as a trail through the high desert scrub.

"No," Daniel agreed, but he could see in her eyes that, same as him, she was thinking, *Then why is Mom lying?* Partly to distract her, he asked, "You been talking to Kurt?"

Tension quivered through his sister's fine-boned frame. "Yes. He says he misses me."

Not, he misses me, but he *says* he misses me.

She changed the subject immediately, so Daniel let it go. A few minutes later Mary hoisted her son onto her hip and left, looking pleased when he invited their mother and her and her son, Devon, to dinner that night. Renee's sharp little comment had reminded him he hadn't done so yet, and Mary had been home going on two weeks now, with no sign that she was thinking of returning to her husband.

Daniel had never liked Kurt Stevens, though for his sister's sake he'd hidden his feelings. Mary's husband was one of those men who seemed stuck knee-deep in adolescence. Daniel had been in the car with him once when he decided another driver had cut him off. Instead of shrugging and accepting that some folks had bad manners, Kurt had chased the other driver down, gotten out of his own car, stalked forward and slammed a booted foot into the door of a shiny red Subaru with a ski rack on top. Scared the hell out of someone. Kurt was lucky, Daniel thought, that the "someone" hadn't had a loaded gun under the front seat.

Daniel wasn't sure what had gone wrong with his sister's marriage. He'd been trying to find out, but she wasn't talking. It would be their business, he figured, unless his suspicions were right and the bastard had taken some of that rage out on his wife or son. Then it would become Daniel's concern. A sister had a right to her brother's protection.

As did a mother to her son's. There couldn't be any doubt, next time Renee Patton came calling, of

whose side he was on. He might want her with surprising fierceness, but his family still had to come
first.

He could only hope Renee didn't put him in the
position of having to choose. Wouldn't you think
she'd give up soon? The murder was an old one.
The present day had enough bloodshed and burglary
and car wrecks to occupy the small police force,
surely.

When his mother didn't call in a tizzy the next
day to let him know the policewoman had been
back, Daniel began to relax. Renee would follow up
on all those names she'd collected and get nowhere.
Find out that every one of the ranch hands had
moved on to work elsewhere or died natural if early
deaths like his father. With the social security numbers, it should to be easy, shouldn't it?

Yet another morning came with no police car
turning in through the ranch gates. He figured curiosity was a good enough excuse to call her by that
afternoon. When she came on the line promptly,
Daniel identified himself and asked if she was having any luck.

"Not as much as you'd think," Renee grumbled.
"The computers were down all morning, and I do
have other cases."

Good, Daniel thought. Maybe she'd let this one
go. Without answers, he might always wonder, but
sometimes that was better.

"Any chance you could have dinner with me tonight?" he asked. "I'll take you out for potatoes."

"You mean, you don't already have something
good cooking?"

"Day's been too busy."

"Mine, too." Weariness sounded in her voice. "Do I need to get dressed up?"

Itching to see her in a swirly skirt, Daniel was still gentleman enough to say, "Nah. We'll save fancy for some other night. How about Mario's?"

"Do they have potato pizza?" she teased. "You did promise me…"

He liked the picture he had of her rocking back in her chair, smiling.

Doing the same, he said, "We can always go to the Black Angus."

"No, pizza sounds good. Might as well eat there as often as we can before ski season opens."

Which was only two months away, he reflected; by Thanksgiving weekend, the population of Elk Springs would have doubled, and the wait for a table at the best restaurants would stretch to forty-five minutes or more. Locals tended to stay home during the winter.

To his disappointment, Renee suggested they meet there. "I don't know if I'll have time to go home first," was her excuse, although her tone was evasive. Well, he couldn't blame her if she was cautious on first dates—or even second ones, if you counted dinner the other night. Although he wasn't exactly a stranger; she'd said herself that her own sister had had a crush on him in high school. He remembered Meg Patton's little sisters often trailing behind her, skinny and blond, the both of them. Still, he shouldn't take it as a mortal insult that Renee didn't want him to know where she lived.

They agreed on a time. He settled all four legs of

the chair back on the floor, put down the cordless and reached for his phone book, flipping it open to the middle.

Patton. His finger moved down the listings. Two Pattons. One was nobody he knew; the other was Renee's father, whose name would disappear from the next directory, assuming someone let the phone company know about his death—2568 River Drive.

Had the house been sold? Renee might have a cozy condo somewhere. Maybe she and the younger sister lived together. But the way Renee had talked, it sounded as if she'd cooked for her father up to the end. So she might still be there.

Feeling low, he nonetheless chose a circuitous route to Mario's, one that happened to take him down River Drive. Idle curiosity, he justified his nosiness, as he glanced at house numbers. 2556. 2562. There it was ahead, a big white Colonial-style house, police car in the driveway. He put his foot down harder on the gas, even as he craned his neck to take in the mature shade trees, leaves golden and orange, the long sweep of grass, smooth as a putting green, the white picket fence, repainted in the recent past. She must hire someone to keep the place up, Daniel decided. She couldn't do all that raking and mowing and painting herself. Even so, it wasn't the house for a single woman. Kids should spill out of it. Or it could be a bed-and-breakfast.

Why wasn't a For Sale sign at the head of the driveway?

Hell, maybe she loved her home, Daniel thought, irritated at himself. Maybe her younger sister *was* married and had a brood, and they all lived in

Daddy's house. And maybe it was none of his damn business.

No surprise that Renee was five minutes behind him in arriving at Mario's, or that she had been home to change clothes. Not into a skirt, he was disappointed to see as she paused in the doorway, scanning the dimly lit room while shrugging off her coat. But black corduroy jeans fit as snugly as his hands itched to, and her juniper-green turtleneck sweater clung almost as closely, ending with a ribbed hem at her slender waist. She wore earrings tonight, too, he saw as she turned her head and silver shimmered. Hair still up, but maybe a little looser, a little more feminine. She'd made some effort for him, he thought, pleased.

He lifted a hand and she spotted him then, coming right over. When Daniel started to stand, she waved him back.

"Have you ordered?"

"Just the beer. Didn't know how you like your pizza."

She settled herself on the bench across from him and propped her elbows on the table. "Oh, I like anything. Well, almost."

They negotiated about the pizza and he went up to the counter to order. When he turned around, he saw that Renee had swiveled in her seat and was watching him. Though he wouldn't have sworn to a blush in this lighting, she swung back around mighty quick, embarrassed—he'd have been willing to bet—by being caught staring.

Daniel just hoped she liked what she saw.

She'd poured herself a glass of beer, but barely

touched it. Instead, with her fingertip she traced pictures in the condensation on the glass, not looking up until he'd sat down. Definitely a blush, he decided, contemplating her pretty face.

"I don't remember your little sister's name," he said, choosing an easy wedge to loosen any resistance she had to talking about her life.

"Abby."

"That's right." He sipped his beer. "She was—what?—a couple years younger than you? What's she doing these days?"

"Three years younger. And, believe it or not, she's a firefighter." His face must have showed his incredulity, because Renee continued in a defensive tone, "Abby's taller than I am, and more athletic. She passed all the tests with flying colors. Don't tell me you think a woman shouldn't be a firefighter, or we'll quit getting along."

Heaven forbid. He chose his words carefully. "Is she really strong enough to carry a two-hundred-pound man out of danger?"

Her eyes narrowed a flicker. "She wouldn't be doing the job if she couldn't."

Daniel raised one hand. "Whoa. Don't get testy on me. I was just asking."

"Why do men all assume…"

"Maybe because I can't picture you being able to sling me over *your* back," he said mildly.

Her gaze measured his shoulders, shifted to her own slender frame. She looked back at him, her nose scrunched. "Why do you always have to take the wind out of my sails?"

"Because I'm such a reasonable guy, I don't deserve all that anger a bunch of jerks have stirred up in you. That's why.''

"Oh, all right.'' She pretended to grumble, then gave him a sunny smile that snatched his breath right out of his lungs. "Did your mom sit you in a corner every time you told your sister she couldn't do something as well as you did?"

Suppressing his gut-level reaction to her, Daniel thought back. "Mom didn't have to. Even though Mary's younger than I am, she was always better at school, which shut me up. She's a gifted horse-woman, too. I never did understand how she could reject the ranch as a way of life."

Renee didn't say anything immediately, and he wasn't sure she was really seeing him for a second there. Then she gave her head a small shake. "Funny, isn't it,'' she said, tone faraway, "how you can grow up with sisters and never really know them?"

He reached out and gripped her hand. "You're thinking about Meg, aren't you?"

She looked at where their hands met and color blossomed in her cheeks again, a blush of wild rose. But she didn't try to pull free. "Sometimes I go weeks or months on end without thinking about her, and then for a stretch I can't get her out of my head. I guess this is one of those stretches."

"Do you know why she left?"

A tiny breath puffed out and her eyes became unseeing again as she gazed into the past. "Oh, sure. She and Dad fought all the time. Over boys or makeup or how clean the house was, or if dinner was a few minutes late... Over us, too—Abby and me. She'd defend us, you see.

"All I know is they had a really awful fight, the worst ever. The school called because she'd slipped away at lunchtime—it was a closed campus in those days—and somebody saw her. I think she had a friend over to the house, maybe a boy. I don't know. I just know that I got home from school and she was packing. Dad had—" Renee caught herself. "Well, her face was bruised and puffy from crying, and she had the most terrible look in her eyes. I've never forgotten." After a silent moment she shivered. "She kissed me goodbye, and hugged me so hard it hurt, and promised to call or write."

"Did she?" he asked quietly.

"No." For an instant Renee could have been a little girl, eyes pleading with him for an answer that he didn't have. *Why?* she asked silently. "Not once. She just...went."

He rubbed his thumb over the back of her hand. "You've never looked for her?"

"No." She averted her gaze. "I figure she needed to make a clean break. Meg was too young to have as much responsibility as Dad dumped on her. Maybe she got so she hated us, too."

What a son of a bitch Ed Patton had been. Daniel had guessed at some of it, but this story still came as a shock.

Grittily, he said, "And then he dumped it on you."

"Yes. But that's not Meg's fault."

"She was old enough to know that's what would happen."

"She was sixteen. That's all. Was she supposed to sacrifice herself for her little sisters?"

He heard too much passion in Renee's voice. She'd had this argument before. With herself?

"Maybe. Weren't you angry?"

Her eyes flashed. "Yes. Yes, I was angry! But I was a kid, too, then. Now I understand why she had to do what she did!"

"Do you." He didn't make it a question; the unintended curl of his lip said what he thought.

Renee wrenched her hand free from his. "What do you want me to say?" she demanded. "Yes, I'm still mad as all get-out? I'd spit in her face if she walked in this door? Fine. Consider it said. Yes, sometimes I hate her for leaving me the way she did. But that doesn't mean I can't understand."

"No." Daniel gave a crooked smile that held anything but amusement. "You're right. I just wanted to hear you admit how you really feel. I figured we might as well have honesty from the start."

She stiffened. "The start of what?"

"Who knows?" Daniel made his tone easy, as if he were soothing a spooked horse. "Whatever we make of it."

"There is no 'it.'"

"We're having dinner together," he said. "For the second time."

She gazed at him with her brow crinkled and what seemed like genuine perplexity in her eyes. "Why are we?"

He set down his beer glass. "What the hell does that mean? Are you asking why I *wanted* to have dinner with you?"

She took to tracing patterns on her glass again, attention on the swirly lines and not him. "I guess I am. I just thought we should get it straight from the first. Are you wanting to keep up on the investigation? I don't mind, but you don't have to buy me dinner to get a report."

His jaw almost dropped. Yeah, okay, he'd used a question about her progress as an excuse, but what woman couldn't tell when a man was in hot pursuit of her?

This one, apparently, and he knew who to blame. Too bad the bastard was in the grave and beyond Daniel's reach.

"I called for a report," he said evenly. "I asked you to dinner in hopes I'd get to know you and the evening might even end with a kiss. There. I'm laying my cards on the table."

Her eyes were huge and dark. "I'm a cop."

"Yeah. And a woman. Or so's my impression."

"And not all that pretty."

"I could argue with that. I will, at the right time and place." He let her absorb that. "I'm not much to look at myself."

"I didn't think so, either, until—" She stopped so fast, she should have had air bags. The rose in her cheeks deepened to scarlet.

Until. He savored the suggestion that she'd changed her mind.

"Until when?" Daniel prodded, his male ego, if not yet his heart, on the line.

She seemed unable to look away from him. "Until you smiled."

Maybe he'd been wrong about his heart. It damn

near stopped, the result of one too many electrical jolts.

Renee's expression changed to pretend or real affront. "You're doing it now."

"Doing it?"

"Smiling."

She was right. He was grinning like a kid who just knew what he'd find under the tree on Christmas morning. A kiss. *That's all I want, Santa,* he thought, even as he knew better. Christmas was a while away yet; by then he hoped her sweet kisses would have him putting a much bigger present on his list.

"You know," she said, "I think that must be our number they're calling. Over and over again."

"What?" He jerked back from dreams of sugar plums and a naked woman sprawled on his bed. Swearing under his breath, he slid off the bench. "It's probably cold."

Renee gave a saucy smile of her own. "Fortunately for you, I like cold pizza."

Not pretty. How could she think that for a second? Didn't the woman ever look in a mirror? Maybe the pain when she yanked her hair back so tight distorted what she saw.

Not pretty. He was still marveling when he brought the pizza back.

"Ouch," she said, reaching for a piece. "It's not stone-cold yet."

"Nope," he conceded, dishing up his own. "Would you like a soda instead of that beer?" He nodded toward her glass.

"No." Renee took a deep swallow, as if to show

him. "I was just a little nervous. I didn't want to…well, let my tongue get too loose. Now I guess I've said so much, why worry?"

"I like honesty," Daniel reminded her.

"Well, good." She sniffed the pizza appreciatively. "Because I'm lousy at hiding what I think."

"I didn't get that impression when you were talking to my mother."

Her eyes met his, wary again. "It's my job. I'm a cop."

"So you said."

"You don't seem to want to believe it."

If he were to be honest, the way he claimed to want, now was the moment to admit he wished she were anything but. Because, if she kept doing her job out on the Triple B, she'd soon discover that he'd chosen sides, and it wasn't hers. Coming from her background, would she understand? Didn't seem like either of her parents or even her big sister had put family first. How could Renee have learned that's how it ought to be?

So he lied—no, prevaricated. "I'm just trying to reconcile the cop with the woman sitting here eating pizza. Which one is the closest to who you are inside?"

Her laugh was a little uneasy. "Well, that's a deep question. Even if I knew the answer, I'm not sure I'd want to tell you."

"I'll find out on my own."

"You do that," she suggested without any sign of discomposure, then bit into her pizza with apparent relish.

He'd deserved that. A second date, and he was

trying to figure her out the way he did a new horse. A little more subtlety was called for with a woman, he guessed.

They chatted after that, like two people getting to know each other ought to. About the changes coming to Elk Springs with the new ski area, about why they'd stayed when most of their high school classmates had long since shaken the gritty soil of eastern Oregon from their heels. About movies and books and cats. Not about family, or jobs, or weathered bones. But Renee laughed a few times, and smiled often. Daniel began wishing even harder that he'd picked her up at her house. How was he going to kiss her good night out on the sidewalk?

The weather hadn't cooperated, either, he discovered as they stepped out of the restaurant. The night was dark and cold, with the smell of rain in the air. She wouldn't want to linger.

Renee shivered right away. "I'm already looking forward to spring."

"I thought you said you were a skier."

"A fair-weather skier." She struggled with the zipper on her coat. "I hate being cold or wet."

"Where's your car?"

"Around the side." Renee nodded toward the narrow parking lot tucked between Mario's and the two-story brick building next door. "What about you?"

"I'm the other way, but I'll walk you to your car."

"You don't need..."

As if a firm hand on the small of her back wasn't enough to silence her, he said mildly, "I want to."

She walked fast. Daniel had to stretch his legs to keep up. Renee stopped at the bumper of a red 4x4 not so different from what she drove on the job. A man's vehicle, he would have said, which was sexist as hell of him and better left unspoken. The truth was, it was practical transportation for a woman who didn't intend to stay in front of her fire knitting when bad weather hit. His mother had always had a man to depend on, first her husband and then her son. Renee was on her own now, and he guessed she always had been in most ways that count.

"Thank you for dinner," she said almost as quickly as she'd walked. "I enjoyed myself. I'll call you as soon as I know anything about the investigation…"

He withdrew his free hand from his pocket and wrapped it around her nape, tangling his fingers in her hair. "I enjoyed dinner, too," he said huskily. "I'm hoping you won't mind if I kiss you."

His heart sank when she stayed still and silent for a long moment. Maybe he shouldn't have asked; maybe he should have kissed first and let her protest after. But that wasn't the way he did things.

"I guess I don't mind," she conceded, voice low and grudging, just when he was about to release her.

"Well, there's a welcome a man could warm his hands over," Daniel murmured, though he hadn't taken offense—he knew shyness when he heard it.

He moved closer, liking the way she lifted her face, the back of her head nesting in his cupped hand. A car passed on the street, its headlights momentarily illuminating her, eyes closed, lashes fanned on her cheeks, her warm breath puffing a small cloud in the chilly night air. He made a sound and bent his head, his mouth finding hers.

Her cold lips warmed under the pressure of his. They softened when he nibbled. She didn't so much kiss him back as…accept. But his other hand had found her throat and felt the leap of her pulse, and he heard the vibration of a whimper when he lifted his head. She was as innocent as he'd imagined, as uncertain how to respond, but, oh, she wanted to. He felt it.

"I'll call you tomorrow," Daniel said. "Do you have your keys?"

"Keys?" Her immobility lasted long enough for awareness to return. "Oh. Of course I do. Right here in my pocket." She groped for them, dangled them under his nose. "There. I can make it home. Good night, Daniel."

"Good night," he said, amused and satisfied. Her snippiness, he figured, was in direct proportion to how swept away she'd been.

She unlocked the door and hopped in to start the engine.

Daniel stepped out of the way and watched as she backed out, lifted a hand and drove away.

Next time he'd definitely pick her up at her house.

DANIEL'S GENERAL STATE of smugness lasted for exactly twelve hours. Long enough to lie in bed having some nice fantasies that drifted into better dreams. Long enough to awaken with a glow of anticipation as he wondered whether he ought to call first thing or wait until lunchtime. Even long enough so that he could convincingly reassure his mother when she stopped by the barn midmorning, new lines beside her mouth and a tremble to her hands.

Hell, he wasn't even bothered by the mixed snow and rain falling. Well, this was October 2, a little early, but with El Niño and La Niña and all their cousins, you didn't know what to expect these days.

He'd worn a rain slicker to the barn, then hung it over a stall door. A heavy sweater and fingerless wool gloves were enough to keep him comfortable as long as he worked the horses in the smaller indoor arena.

At eleven o'clock on the nose—he knew, because he looked at his watch—one of the hands leaned against the gate and announced, ''Hey, boss. That cop's here again. She's heading for your mom's house.''

CHAPTER FIVE

SHIRLEY BARNARD came to the door herself, wrapped in an apron. Flour coated her hands as if she were breading them to go in the oven. Alarm sparked in her eyes when she saw who the caller was, but the next second her expression held only polite inquiry. "Yes?"

"Mrs. Barnard? I wonder if I might come in." Renee always liked to phrase it as a question, although it wasn't really. Most law-abiding citizens wouldn't dream of refusing admittance to a police officer.

"Why, yes, of course." For a moment the other woman didn't move, which was undoubtedly a more accurate reflection of how she felt than her conventional response. She did finally, grudgingly, inch back.

Renee stepped inside. With a nod at Shirley's white hands, Renee asked, "You're baking?"

Dumbly, Daniel's mother followed her gaze, as though her own hands were unfamiliar to her. "Oh. Yes! Yes, I'm kneading bread." Her mouth pinched. "I suppose you'll have to come back to the kitchen."

"I don't mind," Renee said mildly, although she could tell that Shirley did. The front parlor was probably for outsiders, for the enemy; only friends and family would normally be welcome in the kitchen. It seemed that Shirley was between a rock and a hard place. Let the partially kneaded bread go to waste, or sully the warm heart of the house with that irritating police officer's presence?

The bread won.

"I'd like to get my dough to rising, so if we can talk while I'm working, I'd be grateful," she said stiffly.

"Of course," Renee agreed.

The kitchen was big and old-fashioned. A chrome-trimmed wood cooking stove for winter heat shared space with a modern gas range. A long oak table filled the tiled expanse. A timer ticked beside the pale lump of dough resting on a flour-dusted breadboard.

"Tea or coffee?" Shirley Barnard asked with automatic courtesy.

"I'd love some tea." Renee waved her away from the stove. "Just tell me where everything is. You don't want the dough to decide not to rise."

Her hostess settled her hands as gently and firmly around that dough as if it were a baby. "Mugs in the cupboard to the right of the sink, tea bags in that copper canister. Water in the kettle was boiling just a minute ago."

Renee poured herself a cup of tea, found the sugar and added a spoonful, then took it around to the table. "You don't like the bread machine?" she asked, nodding toward the appliance sitting on the counter.

Shirley leaned on the dough, flattening it, then

with practiced hands pulled it toward her. The rhythm seemed to loosen her up, and her talk flowed as though they were friends, not adversaries.

"Oh, I use it once in a while, but the bread just isn't as good, though you can argue with me if you want. Daniel does. He says I'm wearing myself out for no reason, just sheer stubbornness. But I like my own home-baked bread, and with my daughter and grandson staying here, we're going through plenty."

"Kneading makes for strong hands." Renee smiled. "Besides, it's relaxing. I always find it frees my thoughts."

A hitch in the even motion—shove, ball the dough in her hands, pull it back, start over—showed Shirley's surprise. "You make your own?"

"When I have time. My father liked it."

He'd grunted with approval when fresh hot bread appeared on the table. Renee hadn't baked bread since he died, but she didn't say that.

"Daniel doesn't understand. This is time to myself," Shirley said. The timer went off, but she ignored it, having lost several minutes to let Renee in. "I can daydream without feeling guilty."

"Sometimes I wonder if men do," Renee said on impulse. "Daydream, I mean. They always seem to be thinking about something practical."

Shirley looked startled, then thoughtful. "Matt—my husband—never did. You know that song? The one that says you can't have a dream come true if you don't have a dream in the first place? He used to laugh and say if you waste too much time dreaming, you never get anything done and not a single one would come true. He wanted simple things, and usually got them. I thought it was just him, but maybe all men are like that.''

Renee opened her mouth to respond, although what could she say? She didn't want to use the same yardstick to measure her father and Matthew Barnard, who by all accounts had been a decent man. And she didn't know any other men all that well.

She didn't get a chance to say a word, anyway, because the sound of the front door opening and slamming was followed by heavy footsteps. Daniel burst into the kitchen. His wet hair clung to his head and he shook water and melting snowflakes from his wool sweater as if he were a dog giving up on a swim.

Frowning thunderously, he demanded, ''What's going on here?''

His mother kept kneading. ''You usually knock.''

''Someone told me he'd seen a police car.''

His narrowed gaze rested on Renee, who returned it as expressionlessly as she could, considering how her heart was pounding. She should have called him, but she'd feared he might think she was making an excuse to talk to him, or even angling for another invitation. And, how she wanted one, even after seeing him wet and angry, his presence filling the big kitchen.

Shirley glanced at the clock and stopped kneading. ''Pour yourself a cup of coffee,'' she suggested. ''You know where the towels are if you want to dry off.'' After draping a cloth over the dough, she went to the sink to wash her hands.

Daniel swung on his heel to face Renee. ''What do you want?'' he asked bluntly.

"Help from your mother."

"She's told you everything she knows."

Renee seriously doubted that, but she wasn't here to cross-examine his mother today, anyway. "I've run across some problems with your personnel records. A couple social security numbers were fakes, or the names the men gave were. I'm just following up. That's all."

His mother gave him a look that said, *See?* "Who?" she asked with apparent willingness, pulling up a chair at the table. "Daniel, don't tower over me that way. If you're going to stay, sit down."

Still glowering, he tugged off fingerless wool gloves and tossed them down, then went to the stove. Focusing on his mother, Renee tried not to be so damned conscious of his every move.

After a glance at her notes, she said, "Bill Hodgkins was one. He worked here from May 1978 to July '80. Longer than some. But the social security number I got from the files belongs to a ninety-year-old woman named Pearl Bishop who lives in Atlanta, Georgia."

"Well, now." Shirley gazed reflectively into space, seemingly unaware when her son thumped a mug of coffee onto the table, yanked a chair back and sat, his dark stare still pinning Renee. "Bill. I remember him because he was black." Her tone became apologetic. "I don't mean that in a bad way. It's just that we don't see many. The boys who come out here looking for work are usually white. He had a Southern accent, too. Not strong. Texan, maybe. He did know horses. But he was trouble. He'd steal money from the other hands. That kind of thing.

Petty, but it made for bad feelings. Matt finally let him go, even though he could ride like no one since, my husband thought.''

Renee concentrated on her notebook. She jotted down "black" with a question mark. Could the coroner tell race from those few bones? Had he said in his report?

"You never heard about him afterward?"

Shirley's eyes widened. "Why, I do seem to remember Matt saying something. Bill was riding in a cutting competition somewhere. Let me think.'' Her brow crinkled. "For someone we know. Up near Pendleton is where Matt saw him, seems to me.'' Her face cleared. "John Randall. That's who. He had a spread up that way. I don't think Matt said anything to him about Bill. He always hoped for the best, you see. He thought maybe Bill would have turned over a new leaf after losing this job. But I'm sure that was it.'' She gave a nod. "John Randall.'' She turned to her son. "Has John retired?''

"His daughter mostly trains their horses now, but he hasn't let up on the reins completely.'' His mouth closed tight; he'd answered his mother, but he wouldn't willingly go any further.

Although she would have liked to ignore him, irritation and the knowledge of how much time he could save her made Renee ask, "Would you happen to have his phone number?''

"I might.''

"I'd appreciate it if you could find it.'' Only an idiot wouldn't hear sarcasm in her syrupy tones.

Daniel wasn't an idiot. His hand tightened on his mug as if he wished it was her neck.

Shirley's amusement let Renee see that she might be just a flat-out *nice* woman when she wasn't scared.

"You said a couple numbers were wrong?"

Renee didn't have to glance back at her notes on the ranch hand whose employment at the Triple B had ended, one way or another, exactly fifteen years ago. She looked Shirley right in the eye and said, "Yes. T. J. Baxter."

Daniel's mother shot up from her seat. "I think I'll get myself some tea. Do you need a freshener, Officer?"

Renee found herself looking at Shirley's back as the older woman reached into a cupboard. Coincidence she'd chosen that precise moment to fuss in the kitchen? Frowning, Renee said, "Thank you. No."

"Now, what was that name?" Shirley asked as vaguely as if she really hadn't heard Renee in the first place.

Renee repeated the name.

"Now that one…" Shirley stopped as if thinking, the teakettle poised above her cup. "How long did he work here? I don't know that I recall him."

"Sure you do, Mom." Daniel intervened unexpectedly. "He was that bronc rider Mary worshiped when she was, oh, twelve or thirteen. Handsome devil."

"Oh, yes." Shirley came back from the stove, mug in hand. "I was glad Mary was young for her age. T.J.? Is that what his name was? I don't recall why he left."

Renee didn't buy it. Daniel and Mary had both

remembered this one particular ranch hand instantly. He'd made an impression. He'd have made just as much of one on Shirley, the mother of a pretty twelve-year-old girl. And hadn't Daniel even remarked that T. J. Baxter flirted with all women, including his mother? Surely that would have startled the wife of T. J. Baxter's employer. Especially since Shirley would have been in her late thirties. Men couldn't have been flirting with her every day.

But Shirley was gazing at her now with an air of pleasant inquiry. "And his social security number wasn't right?"

"Apparently not. You have no idea where he went when he left here?"

"No, I don't." The tone of finality was unmistakable. "Was there anyone else?"

"No, just those two." Renee had already heard Daniel's remembrance of why Baxter had left, but she turned to him, anyway. "If somebody had called or written for a reference, would your father have made a note?"

Daniel shook his head. "Not if it was a call. But I'm sure Dad fired him. This'd be the last place Baxter would give for a reference."

Unfortunately, that was probably true.

"He didn't have a nickname? Something that might have suggested another name?"

Daniel frowned. "Far as I know, T.J. was what he went by. I never even knew what it stood for. Mom?"

The pleasant, vague expression on her face didn't change one iota. "I didn't even remember him. How would I know if he had a nickname?"

Keeping a surreptitious eye on Shirley, Renee closed her notebook. "Well, it sounds like a dead end where T. J. Baxter is concerned."

Some emotion welled in Shirley so high she blinked several times, quick and hard. Relief?

"Unless he left any possessions behind?" Renee ventured.

Shirley bowed her head.

"If he had, we wouldn't have kept them long." Daniel shrugged. "After a few months, Dad would have taken anything to the Salvation Army."

"Well, then—" Renee pushed back her chair and rose to her feet "—if you can find that phone number for me, I'd appreciate it. Thank you both for your help."

"I didn't mind a bit." All smiles—damn it, *nice* again, relaxed—Shirley started to stand.

"*I'll* walk her out," her son said in a voice that had his mother's mouth opening in an O of surprise even as she sank docilely back into her seat.

Renee didn't think she cared for that voice. But it lacked the plain meanness her father would have imbued it with, so she didn't say a word as she preceded Daniel to the front door and out onto the porch, where Lotto waited with tail thumping. There she stopped dead. Hail pelted the ground and drummed off the top of her 4x4. She'd have to make a run for it. But first... Renee shivered and reluctantly turned to face Daniel.

His expression was harder than a basalt outcropping. "You said you'd keep me updated. Why didn't you call me?"

"I didn't see any reason to bother you." How weak that sounded!

A muscle worked in his jaw. "I thought I made it pretty clear last night that you aren't a bother to me."

He meant the kiss, she knew he did. She hadn't been able to think of much else since. The way his big hand had lifted her jaw, the tenderness of his mouth on hers, her own befuddlement... But it scared her, too, knowing she would have done anything he asked right then.

And how did she know he wasn't angry today because he'd figured he'd solved any problem she posed? Hey, the cop was a woman. Wine her, dine her and kiss her, was probably his strategy. He'd said himself she was a tough nut to crack. That wasn't what you thought about a woman you wanted.

Temper and deep-rooted insecurity flared. "Not a bother? What you mean is, you romanced me in the hopes it'd keep me away from your mother."

He took a step closer, crowding her. "Damn it, you know that isn't what I meant!"

"Do I?" Renee held her chin high.

He swore under his breath, making his yellow Lab whimper. "You think I'm that calculating?"

"I didn't," she said coolly. "But after the way you came roaring in here today just because I had the gall to knock on your mother's door, I have to wonder."

His eyes glittered. "Just like I have to wonder if you didn't call ahead because you hoped you could sneak by and corner my mother alone."

Renee opened her mouth to snap back, but guilt stopped the words. She *should* have phoned him. He was the one who'd found the bones in the first place. He'd been decent about this, even though it was upsetting his mother and Renee hadn't hidden the fact that she thought Shirley was lying about what she knew. Just last night at dinner she'd agreed to report to him when she knew anything. And then today...

Oh, Lord. How could she admit she'd felt *shy?*

"No." She fixed her gaze on the collar of his sweater. "Really. I wasn't sneaking. I just wanted some information. I wasn't trying to put her on the spot."

"Then why *didn't* you call first?"

Renee didn't know whether his expression had softened. She'd lifted her gaze only as far as his throat, strong and tanned. If he ever kissed her again, she'd put her hand there, feel the pulse beating, the smooth skin on his neck and the rough up above where he shaved.

"I..." She licked her lips. "Well, I thought your mother could answer my questions as well as you could. And I don't want to keep pulling you away from work for every little thing."

"A murder isn't 'every little thing.'"

"An investigation can take a long time. You don't want me calling constantly."

His voice had an odd intonation. "You sure about that?"

Oh, she was sure enough. Though she remembered that kiss again and trembled a little inside.

With incredulity, she heard herself declaring,

"Maybe it's a mistake to have any kind of personal relationship until this investigation is brought to a close."

Quicker than a blink, Daniel closed the small distance left between them. Lifting her chin, just as she'd remembered—though his fingers hadn't been so cold last night—he asked, "Do you think I murdered whoever the hell this guy was?"

"I... No," Renee faltered.

His head bent; his mouth hovered just above hers. "Are you attracted to me?"

She tried frantically to think of an out. "This isn't the time or place..."

"Okay, how about dinner tonight?"

Her mind was fogging just like the windshield had on her way out here. "I can't let you influence how I conduct an investigation..."

She thought he swore before he kissed her, but it didn't really register. She was too busy flinching from the icy touch of his lips, then reveling in the way they warmed, and at last in the heat her whole being tried to soak up. This kiss was simply erotic: he nibbled and suckled on her lower lip, stroked her tongue with his, pressed her hips up against him, making it impossible for her to pretend unawareness of the hard ridge under the fly of his jeans.

By the time Daniel lifted his head, she was shaking and weak-kneed. And angry, once understanding flooded her.

"You're doing it again!" she snapped in a voice too tremulous for a cop's. "Using—" her hand waved, encompassing them "—*this* to influence me!"

"This?" His brows drew together. "You mean sex?"

"We haven't *had* sex!"

"But we're working our way toward it, aren't we?"

They were?

But even to herself she couldn't pretend ignorance that complete. Wasn't sex exactly what she'd been thinking about all the way home last night? What had kept her awake, made her too shy to phone him in a business-like manner this morning?

"Just tell me," she pleaded, "why you're doing this. Even if you get me in bed, it won't make me softer toward your mother..."

He backed well away from her, his hands balled into fists. "Is it just me, or do you distrust all men?"

All men. The answer came, swift and shocking. Oh, she'd known distantly that she was looking for her father in the men she dealt with, and not in a nostalgic way. But this...this instant certainty that Daniel Barnard couldn't be treating her nicely because he liked her... If nothing else, it made her understand why she was alone when the friends her age from high school were wives and mothers, or at least girlfriends. She wasn't beautiful, she knew that, but she wasn't ugly, either. She could have had a man if she'd wanted one.

But it appeared that she'd been so certain they were all like her father, she hadn't let them get to first base.

Until this week.

Question was, why now? Why this man?

"Say something."

She realized abruptly that Daniel had stepped forward again and was gripping her upper arms, giving her a little shake. She must have been staring at him like an idiot.

"All men," she said.

"What?" Now he stared.

"I guess maybe I'm not inclined to trust men."

He had her in his arms in a heartbeat, just cuddled close as though she needed shelter. His voice held a growl of rage that vibrated deep through his chest. "That bastard," he said clearly.

Renee soaked up the bliss, his warmth and strength and anger, the fact that he still *wanted* to hold her. But finally she tugged herself free.

"Yes, he was," she said straight out. "Assuming you meant my father."

Daniel's mouth was tight; his hands automatically gripped her upper arms again, as though he were unwilling to let her go far. "Did he hit you?"

"Sometimes," she admitted, the first time she'd ever let herself say that to anyone but her sisters. "But mostly not. He just…froze me with his disapproval. Nothing was ever right. I couldn't come home and tell him about an unfair grade or a friend who'd snubbed me. He'd be mad, I'd screwed up again. If I got an A or won the science fair, he'd grunt. And I learned early on that if I told him anything, he'd use it against me. Or against Meg or Abby, if I'd been stupid enough to admit something about one of them."

She'd always thought it a cliché when someone wanted to drown in a pair of eyes. But right this minute Daniel's were like that, so blue she couldn't look away. Blue should be a cold color, bringing to mind one of the high mountain lakes nestled up in the bosom of the Sisters, but his eyes were more like the lick of blue in a fire: warmer than the hot springs or the glowing coals in a stove.

"Your mother?" he asked, voice low and rough.

Renee gave a small helpless shrug. "She was scared of him, too. I don't blame her for leaving him. If that's what she did." Another shock; she'd expressed a secret fear that she had only just told Abby.

"You think she might be dead?" He processed that, took the next logical step with startling speed. "Those bones..."

"I wondered for a minute," Renee admitted.

"Do you have any reason to think she's dead?"

"No. Just that she's gone so completely. She and Meg both. I've never heard another word from either of them. Of course, my father would have destroyed any letters. He had the mail delivered to the post office, not the house, so it would have been easy. Maybe that's why he did it."

"The SOB must have realized what it would mean to a kid to get a letter from her mother—" Daniel broke off. "We're standing here freezing our butts off. Let's go to my place."

She was shivering and hadn't even noticed. But panic set in. She'd said too much, too fast. They hadn't settled anything; he was a good listener, but that didn't mean he hadn't been using her attraction to him to manipulate her. She was cold, but the heater in her Bronco would unthaw her hands and feet.

"No," she said quickly. "No, I've got to get back. This isn't my only case."

"Then what about dinner?"

She owed him that, didn't she? After not calling this morning, and accusing him of…well, of kissing her in cold blood, which he might still have done, but then what if he hadn't? What if he really did want her?

That thought warmed her belly, if not her numb hands. Dinner wouldn't hurt. She'd find out sooner or later what his motive was. Once he noticed that his kisses didn't result in the investigation being shelved, well, then she'd know, wouldn't she?

"Dinner," she agreed.

His kiss was brief and cold, but it still affected her. Enough so that she had a revelation when she walked into the station twenty minutes later to find Jack Murray in her office stripping off a wet button-down shirt and yanking on a dry sweatshirt, giving her a front-seat view of well-developed muscles and soft, dark chest hair that trailed on down his belly to the belt of his pants. In other words, to a sight that would have induced some wild if hopeless fantasies not so long ago. In fact, just a few days ago. Before Daniel Barnard.

Only, now it was After. A.D.B., she told herself frivolously. And now her admiration of Jack's fine physique was purely aesthetic. Her heart didn't flutter; her blood pressure didn't shoot dangerously high, and no desire curled in her stomach.

In fact, Renee thought, she was cured.

Too bad the cure was only a symptom of a new disease.

While Jack's head was buried in the sweatshirt, she strolled in and perched on the edge of her desk. "You going to change your pants, too?"

His head emerged. "In your dreams."

Just a few days ago, that would have hurt. She could only be grateful that he had no idea she ever *had* dreamed about him. Or curdled inside every time she thought about him wanting both her sisters but never her.

"Oh, yeah, that one keeps me awake," she mocked.

He grinned, then let it go. "You were out at the Triple B?"

"Yup," she agreed. She gave him an update. "Daniel promised to call me with a phone number so I can follow up on Bill Hodgkins. This Baxter…well, I'm at a dead end right now. I'm going to keep putting pressure on Shirley Barnard. Baxter's the one who makes her nervous."

Jack ran his fingers through wet, dark hair. "Damn it, Renee, you might be making a mountain out of a molehill. Maybe she had an affair with him!"

"You don't get hysterical remembering an ancient affair," she retorted. "She could have even privately admitted it to me. Her husband's dead; I wouldn't have told her son or daughter. No, it's more than that. Murder's good at causing hysteria."

"That's an easy answer." Jack frowned at her for a long abstracted moment. "You don't really think that nice lady stuck a knife in somebody."

"Nice ladies do sometimes."

His mouth tilted in acknowledgment. "Usually their husbands. Not some drifter or ranch hand."

"Anyway," she said, "I don't think Shirley stabbed anyone. I just think she knows who did."

"You're guessing her husband."

She looked coolly back at him. "I'll wait till she tells me."

Jack ruminated, frowning the whole while. "Okay," he finally agreed. "You stick with it for a little longer. But I do mean 'a little.' These bones are old news. We can't waste too many man-hours on something as cold as this trail."

Her stomach churned, as if he were on the edge of firing her. This mattered that much. "In other words, make progress or forget it."

Jack lifted an eyebrow. "Ten more mailboxes were bashed in last night. People are getting mad."

"Let the post office handle it themselves," Renee snapped. "Or tell people to pick up their mail in town!"

"Oh, that'll be a popular proposition in the dead of winter." Jack grabbed his wet shirt from the back of her chair. In the doorway of her office, he glanced back. "Keep me current."

"Oh, sure."

Once alone, she sank into her chair and put her feet on the desk.

How much time was a little? One day? Two? A week, if she was lucky?

How, in one week or less, was she going to find out who the handsome, ex-rodeo bronc rider had been? The one who flirted with every woman and lied about his social security number? T. J. Baxter, whose very name scared a nice woman like Shirley Barnard?

T. J. Baxter, who had left no clues behind to his existence.

Aloud, softly, she put into words her suspicion. "Except maybe his bones."

CHAPTER SIX

RENEE HADN'T LIED to Daniel; she did have other cases. In fact, she'd intended to spend the afternoon visiting pawnshops in hopes of tracking down several items stolen from a house in the Heights. A phone message had been left on her desk this morning, reminding her that the homeowner was waiting to hear from her.

But she didn't have a deadline on that one. And she suddenly, passionately, didn't care who'd broken the window and stolen jewelry and antique clocks as well as the ever popular electronic equipment. It'd turn out to be the usual—teens out for a thrill and the bucks to let them indulge in some high-risk activity. Maybe drugs. Maybe just snowboarding, if they came from the wrong side of the river and Mom and Dad couldn't afford the lift tickets.

Renee would get them. For the Elk Springs P.D., the clearance rate on crimes like this was eighty percent or better. This side of Portland, there just weren't that many places to fence stolen property. Teenagers in particular would be unwilling to sit on the stuff for a while, which would have been safer. Instead, they'd choose some seedy pawnshop, take a fraction of what the VCR or diamond ring was worth, and never guess that the pawnshop owner would willingly ID them.

Tomorrow would do just as well, she decided, putting her feet back on the floor. Today, she'd return to the R & R, the cattle ranch bordering the Triple B. She wanted to ask Marjorie Rosler about her son's friend, the one who'd dropped out of sight only a couple years after T. J. Baxter vanished from the Triple B.

In comparison to the Barnard ranch, the R & R looked run-down. Fence posts needed replacing, barbed wire was rusting, and the siding on the barns was weathered instead of freshly painted. On the other hand, running cattle wasn't the same kind of operation as raising world-class quarter horses. Dick Rosler culled his herd and shipped the cattle to market; buyers didn't come to him. And who knew? Maybe he'd lost heart when his son opted for a life that didn't include ranching with his father. The other day, Renee had asked about the ranch name.

"I'm former military," Dick Rosler said. "It was a joke."

But his wife had bowed her head, and Renee guessed the R & R had been intended to stand for father and son.

Mounting the front porch steps of the white farmhouse, Renee wondered about the son who'd disappeared so abruptly only to surface in San Francisco. Talk about culture shock. Why San Francisco? Did he have a buddy there? Say, Les Greene? And what had precipitated his flight?

It wasn't Gabe Rosler she was interested in, but Renee couldn't get him out of her mind. Unlike her mother and sister, Gabe did write to his parents. But he'd never come home, either.

Would his mother tell Renee why he'd gone if she asked? Of course, it wasn't any of her business, Renee admitted, so long as the Roslers weren't lying about those letters.

Drying her hands on a dish towel, Marjorie came to the door alone to answer the bell. She didn't open the screen. Her face was a blur through it. "Officer Patton! Are you looking for Dick?"

"No, I just had some questions about a boy your son would have gone to school with. I figured you'd know the answers better than your husband would, unless Gabe was given to talking to him."

Her laugh had a bitter ring. "No, they never did get along. You know how it is sometimes, with a father and son. Sure, you come on in." She pushed open the screen and stepped back.

This front room looked lived in, unlike the Barnard's, yet oddly sterile. His and hers recliners, showing their age, were planted in front of a TV. Renee would have been willing to bet nobody ever sat on the couch. The oil paintings and knickknacks somehow weren't personal; it was as if someone had filled the empty space twenty years ago and had never really thought about what was there since, except to dust. Only the framed photos on the fireplace mantel gave any real clues to this family.

Renee crossed the room to look at them more carefully than she had the last time she was here.

"Your son looks like you," she observed.

Marjorie Rosler stayed beside her recliner. "Yes, he does," she agreed, sadness and warmth both in her voice. "He especially looks like my father did as a boy."

Gabe was blond and blue-eyed like his mother. Fine-boned, like her. Almost pretty, when he was about twelve. How he must have hated that!

"Do you hear from him often?" she asked casually.

Marjorie was wringing her hands. "No. Only about once a year. At Christmas time he always writes. Just to let us know how he's doing. He's an E.M.T.," she said, pride warring with her grief. "You know, an emergency medical technician? He always did love to watch an ambulance go by."

"Yeah, I'm pretty fond of those guys," Renee said with a smile. "I don't know where we'd be without 'em. Some of them are real heroes."

"Well." Still an attractive woman despite the grief worn like makeup she never washed off, Marjorie said, "Why don't you have a seat?"

Renee chose the couch. The recliners didn't seem to welcome anyone but their owners. Marjorie perched uncomfortably at the other end.

"Who was it you wanted to know about?" she asked.

"Your son had a friend named Les Greene." Renee knew because the two had been arrested together as teenagers and neither had ever acted to have their criminal records sealed. "I understand he disappeared about the same time your son moved to San Francisco."

"That poor boy." She sighed. "I never did like him. That sounds awful to admit, doesn't it? I know it wasn't his fault, the way he was. He didn't have a father, and his mother was a drunk. He had a couple of cigarette burns on his back. I saw them once. I mean, they were scars by then, but I could tell what they were. He made some excuse, but it just gave me the willies. You know? Sometimes his mother had some man living there.''

''Were the boys friends for a long time?''

''Oh, I think maybe it was sixth or seventh grade when they got to be friends.'' She frowned, thinking back. ''I don't know how they hooked up. Having such different backgrounds, I mean. Les wasn't a very good influence on Gabe. At first I thought maybe it would work the other way around, but it didn't. Gabe was going through a difficult stage right then—mostly just adolescence, but he and his father fought a lot, too. Sometimes I'd swear he would go out of his way to provoke Dick.'' She shook her head. ''Then I'd see Les, standing there in the background smirking. I swear, I could almost hate him.''

Because she couldn't afford to let herself hate the man who was helping make all their lives a misery?

Renee had no trouble disliking Dick Rosler, though she hardly knew him. It was no stretch to see her father in him.

As a teenager, she'd been the one to go out of the way to push her father's buttons. Some of it was just blind anger. She hated him, and she wanted to yell and scream and maybe even nurse a bruised cheek, because then she could hate him even more. But now she thought that wasn't all there was to it. Stupid as it sounded, every time she picked a fight she hoped for a grain of understanding or patience or affection. She had to test him, over and over.

Her guess was, Gabe Rosler had been testing his dad, too. And maybe getting madder and madder. More and more hurt. Until one day he finally saw there was no point in wasting hope, because his father wasn't going to change.

The difference was, Gabe Rosler had had one parent who did love him, unless Renee missed her guess. And that was a big difference. However angry at his father, how could he never come home again to see his mother?

Well, that wasn't her business, Renee reminded herself. Les Greene was.

"Do you remember whether Les went away before or after your son left home?" she asked.

"Later, because when Gabe disappeared I went to see Les, to find out if he knew anything. I thought he might have gone, too, but he was home. He was working on his car, I remember. You know, feet sticking out from under it, but when I said, 'Les, is that you?' he wheeled out on one of those little trolleys. He had grease on his face and his hands. He looked surprised when I asked if he knew where Gabe was. He claimed he hadn't known my son had run away. It was strange." She fell silent.

"Did you ever see him again?"

"What?" Seemingly lost in the past, Marjorie looked blankly at Renee, who repeated her question.

Marjorie shook her head. "After Gabe called—and then I got a letter from him—I went to tell Les, in case he was worried. His mother was the only one there. She'd been drinking, and she just shrugged and said he was gone for good and she didn't know where he was. Didn't care, either.'' She paused, amazed by the very notion. ''Can you imagine?''

''There are a lot of parents out there like that,'' Renee said gently. ''Gabe was lucky to have you.''

She looked away. ''Well, I guess he doesn't think so. Though he does write.''

''You're the one who reported Les missing to the police.''

''Yes.'' She stared down at her hands, folded so tightly in her lap they must hurt. ''I knew his mother wouldn't. If his car had been gone, I wouldn't have, but I couldn't believe he'd left that Chevy. He loved it so. I think it was the only thing he did love.''

Renee made a note. She'd known boys like Les Greene. Ones who spent half their lives under the hoods of their cars. Like Marjorie Rosler, Renee couldn't imagine a boy like Les leaving his behind to rust in his mother's driveway, or for her to sell to buy jugs of wine. Even if something unexpected or traumatic happened, why would he have taken a bus or hitchhiked when he could have driven?

The investigation had been cursory, as far as she could tell from the notes. Les had been seventeen. The officer didn't find it surprising that a poor student hadn't hung around to graduate. Les hadn't bought a Greyhound bus ticket, at least that anybody recalled, but a wild kid like him was more likely to have hitchhiked, anyway. His mother had no idea whether he'd taken some clothes or not. In the end, the officer concluded that he'd packed a duffel bag and gone out to the highway to stick out his thumb.

There was no reason to suspect foul play, nor any reason to track him down, given his age. The file was closed.

"One last question," Renee said thoughtfully. "Do you happen to know what dentist his mother took him to?"

"His mother?" Marjorie snorted. "You mean, the social workers. I don't know, but they must keep records, don't they?"

Yes, they did, Renee discovered shortly thereafter. Within an hour a young woman returned her call with the name of the dentist Les Greene had seen several times. The man had retired, but Dr. Clifford, who'd bought the practice, still had records of former patients. Renee took over photographs and X rays of the skull's upper teeth, and within another hour had her answer.

"Nope," said Dr. Clifford, shaking his shaggy hair regretfully. "Whoever you've got there, it isn't Les Greene."

Peering at the X rays, hung side by side in one of those light boxes, Renee had no trouble concurring. "I don't suppose you can tell me anything more from these. Age, say."

He frowned and leaned closer. "With the weathering that's taken place—and of course I'm used to judging a mouth by the health of the gums, too... No. I'm afraid not. I'd agree that this was a young man. Could have been as young as Les Greene when he disappeared. Could be a man ten years older, too." He switched off the light and unclipped the X ray, handing it to her. "Sorry."

"Don't be. I appreciate your time."

Okay, forget Les Greene. Although she surely would love to know where he'd disappeared to. It occurred to her, as she drove, to wonder if he'd held any summer jobs as a teenager. Maybe she could get his social security number, run a check on him.

Quietly, she cautioned herself. If he caught wind, Jack would tell her to drop it. Bad enough she was wasting time on a case that had no fresher clues than a long-scattered skeleton. Never mind an ancient missing persons report unconnected even to that case.

And he had a point. For Pete's sake, Les Greene would be—she had to think—twenty-nine years old now, a year older than she was. That required a mental adjustment on her part. She'd been thinking of both Les and Gabe Rosler as teenagers still, looking about like they had in that mug shot taken fourteen years ago.

She did stop at two pawnshops on her way back to the station, and hit a row of little red cherries at the second one. Shown photographs of the antique clocks, the owner slapped his hand down hard on the countertop. "God damn it. I bought the story hook, line and sinker."

"What story?" Renee asked, leaning against the glass-topped counter.

"Inherited them from his mom." He made a sound of disgust. "Didn't know what they were worth. Said all he knew was the damn things used to tick, tick, tick all over the house. Drove him crazy. Then come midnight, every damn night, it was New Year's Eve in Times Square all over again. I've never had anyone admit they hated something they were pawning. Usually they want to claim how valuable the stuff is.''

Now, that was interesting. The name on the pawn ticket he produced didn't ring any bells, but who gave a real name anyway?

"What'd the guy look like?" Renee asked.

The answer was exactly what she'd expected to hear. Half an hour later, she handed the homeowner a box containing most of his missing possessions. Along with it, she broke the news that his nineteen-year-old son had faked the burglary and pawned Daddy's precious clocks along with Mommy's beloved diamond jewelry.

Daddy went through the usual stages of disbelief, shock, rage, and finally hurt. He declined to press charges, not at all to her surprise, thanked her profusely and hurried her out the door.

The crime had turned out to be a little more interesting than usual. You had to wonder why a kid from a family this wealthy had felt he needed the money. Or maybe money never had been the point. Maybe hurting his parents had been the kid's sole motivation.

She'd agreed to have dinner again with Daniel, so she went straight home to change clothes. He'd pressed until she also agreed to let him pick her up here.

Renee didn't even totally understand why she'd been reluctant, or why she hustled out the moment he rang the bell, making him back up quick to allow her room to lock the door. She just knew she didn't want him inside. Didn't want him to see that living room and realize it was some kind of morbid museum, untouched except for cleaning since the day her father had died.

Daniel quirked an eyebrow. "Uh…hello. I'm glad you're eager."

"The phone was ringing," she lied. "I didn't want to answer it."

"Don't you have a machine?"

"Yes, but I feel guilty and can't ignore a voice. If we leave, I won't feel obligated."

"Ah." He seemed satisfied with her explanation. Escorting her to his truck and holding open the door, he added, "Pretty big place to live in all by yourself."

"Too big," she agreed, scrambling in. "I inhabit a few corners and ignore the rest."

He went around to the driver's side and slid in behind the wheel, starting the engine. "Are you thinking about selling?"

"Yes." How bald the one little word sounded, not suggesting in any way how conflicted she felt over the whole thing.

Sell. Walk away, common sense insisted. But another part of her felt obligated to keep the home fires burning, or something equally ridiculous. As if Meg and her mother wouldn't be able to find her if strangers occupied the house. As if the only hope of them ever coming home was for her to keep the house intact, untouched. A museum.

"You lived there your whole life?"

She'd almost forgotten Daniel's presence. Renee blinked and pulled herself together.

"Mmm-hmm. I guess that's why I've put it off.

Abby keeps urging me, but…oh, it's only been six months. I just didn't want to jump. You know?''

He gave her a peculiar look, but said agreeably, "Sure. Makes sense."

Renee was grateful when he didn't pursue it. Probably he hadn't because it *did* make sense not to make any hasty decisions after a loved one had died. Which meant that she was only being sensible. Taking into account, of course, the one hundred percent wrong assumption that she'd loved her father.

Over dinner—tonight at a Chinese restaurant—she and Daniel tacitly agreed to stay away from the subject of his mother and the investigation of the bones his dog had brought home.

Instead she told him—without naming names, of course—about the rich kid who'd ripped off his parents' valued possessions.

"What I can't figure out," she said, "is whether we'll see the kid again. I mean, will he start breaking and entering as a regular habit? Maybe move on over to his parents' friends' houses? Or will the fact that he got caught so easily this time scare him?''

"Scare him?" Daniel popped a bite of spring roll in his mouth. "Depends on how his parents handle this. If they don't do anything more than have a little talk with him, scared is the last thing he's going to be.''

"Um." She frowned, imagining herself in that father's shoes. "Hard to know what they should do. Prosecuting your own son—that'd be hard. But grounding him doesn't somehow quite cover it.''

"Reform school hits the right note." Daniel didn't sound sympathetic. "But, yeah, you're right.

I wouldn't want to be in that spot. Family should take care of family. Question is, why does the kid hate his parents so much?"

Renee sighed. "I thought I'd call children's services tomorrow. See if they've been involved before."

He stirred a sugar into his tea. "Otherwise?"

"What can I do?" She spread her hands.

Daniel grunted. "You must face this a lot."

"Not being able to fix a problem? Yeah. If we had time, and better ties to social services, we could do more. We try."

"Here." He handed her the bowl of sweet-and-sour prawns. "Have you had any of these?"

She had, but she took a couple more anyway. "How was *your* day?"

Lousy, it turned out. He'd gone into the barn that afternoon to find a colt down in his stall, hind leg shattered.

"It happens." His jaw set. "It's just one of those freak things. Somehow he got tangled up, or kicked the wall wrong. It was a messy break. We had to put him down."

"I'm sorry," Renee said softly. "Was he...was he a favorite of yours?"

"He had promise." Daniel didn't sound expansive. A typical male, not wanting to admit to emotion?

"Are you trying to tell me you don't get attached to your horses?"

"It's a business," he said stolidly. "I sell horses. I'd be a fool to make 'em all pets. That doesn't mean it doesn't hurt when they suffer or die."

"Of course you're right." She made a face. "I have a feeling I wouldn't be very good at shutting myself off that way."

"Are you sure?" His eyes, unnervingly perceptive, zeroed in on her face. "You're philosophical about the people you wish you could help but can't. Isn't that the same thing? You know what you can let yourself care about and what you can't." He shrugged. "It's reality."

Renee held up both hands in defeat. "Okay! You're right again. Darn it, are you ever *wrong?*"

"Hell, yes."

"Yeah? When was the last time you were wrong?" she challenged.

His expression became shuttered. "When I figured you'd give up on the case once you realized how long those bones had been out there."

Their pact had ended. A little tartly, she said, "Are you sure you've admitted to being wrong? You're not still hoping I'll hang it up?"

He met her stare straight-on. "What I'm hoping now is that you find out this guy had nothing to do with the Triple B."

"You must have known Gabe Rosler," Renee said on impulse. Funny, until this moment it hadn't occurred to her that the neighboring rancher's son was near to Daniel's age, too.

"Yeah, sure." Daniel frowned. "He was a year or two behind me in school. What's this got to do with anything?"

She wrinkled her nose. "As it turns out, nothing. Gabe had a friend named Les Greene..."

"I remember him. Tough kid."

"Well, around the time Gabe took off, so did Les Greene. Only he left behind his car which according to Mrs. Rosler, was the only thing in the world he loved. She filed a missing person's report. The kid's mother apparently didn't care enough to bother. Anyway, because of his age, the investigating officer took a cursory look around, couldn't find any trace of him, but also no evidence of foul play, and closed the file. I tracked down his dental records."

She had his attention now. Without moving a muscle, he still crackled with sudden tension. "And?"

"Your skeleton isn't Les Greene. So much for that brainstorm."

Daniel's shoulders relaxed. "Maybe he found out the damn car needed a new engine that he couldn't afford. Maybe he sold the car's guts for parts and used the money to start over."

It wasn't a bad explanation. Marjorie Rosler's whole case had rested on Les Greene's abandonment of the beloved car. Heck, it probably *had* been a heap of junk he kept going by sheer willpower. Maybe the thing had died the same day he had a final, ugly fight with his mother. Why not hit the road?

"I didn't think of that," she admitted. "It makes sense."

Daniel pushed away his plate and poured himself another cup of the fragrant, pale amber tea without which a meal couldn't be eaten at any bona fide Chinese restaurant. "Did his mother tell you why Gabe ran away?"

"She hinted at trouble with his father. That's the closest she got to an explanation. Do you know?"

"No, but I have my suspicions."

When he didn't go on, Renee leveled a look at him. "You're planning to leave it at that?"

He raised an eyebrow in what appeared to be genuine bewilderment. "Why would you care about Gabe's troubles?"

"Because I'm nosy!" she said in exasperation. "I like to hear every detail connected to a case. You never know what little tangent will turn out to be important."

Daniel grinned, the slow sweet smile that set her heart to thumping once it got over a missed beat or two.

"Okay, okay." Amusement still played in his eyes, although he tried to look grave. "Heaven forbid I frustrate you."

"Did I say you would?" Why did she suddenly have a feeling they weren't talking about Gabe Rosler anymore?

His gaze swept over her, slow and sensuous. "I'll do my best to be sure I don't."

Renee felt her cheeks warm. "You're flirting with me."

"Yup."

"I wish you wouldn't."

She'd wiped that *knowing* smile from his face. "Why? Damn it, I thought we were getting along well."

"We are. I just…" She looked down. "I don't know how to flirt back. You embarrass me."

He reached across the table and gripped her hand,

his thumb circling on her palm. "The way you blush gets to me a lot faster than a little flirting would. I...like knowing you haven't had too much practice at this."

Her head shot up. "Why?"

"Why what?"

"Why are women supposed to want an experienced man, but men think a woman should be a..." The word stuck in her throat.

"Sweet innocent?"

"Yeah. Why?"

Brows drawing together, he said, "I don't know what men *should* want. I don't even know what my ideal is. All I do know is that I'd rather not think of you in bed with another man. If you haven't had a lot of practice at batting your eyes, I have to figure you haven't had much practice at bedding men, either."

Well! Renee felt as if she ought to be outraged. Wasn't it the same old stereotype? A woman should "save" herself for one man, while he could do anything he damn well pleased?

On the other hand, she *had* saved herself. Shouldn't she be glad Daniel wasn't hoping for an experienced bed partner?

Feeling the blush rise again at the idea, Renee hastily amended her thought. She should be glad, *assuming* she and Daniel ended up going to bed together. Assuming he really wanted to, and that she worked up her nerve.

"I'd give more than a penny to know what you're thinking about right now," he said softly, eyes narrowed.

Her cheeks must be flame-red. "What if I told you I was wandering down memory lane?"

"I'd say you were lying."

How she would have liked to argue! Considering, however, that he was right, dignity seemed to call for retreat without admission either way.

"Why don't you just tell me," she suggested, "why Gabe Rosler had to run away from home before he graduated from high school?"

"Chicken," Daniel murmured.

"I refuse to discuss my sexual experience on a second date."

"Third."

"What?" she asked, startled.

"Third date. You had dinner at my house."

"I thought we were 'breaking bread' together. Quote unquote. You didn't describe it as a date."

"You don't really think I work that hard on dinner for myself, do you?"

Ridiculous to feel so flattered. But she couldn't help it. He'd gone to all that work without even knowing whether she'd stay? And then he'd schemed to persuade her?

"Really?" she asked shyly.

"The first time I saw you, I knew I'd ask you out." He searched her face. "That so hard to believe?"

Yes. Yes, it was. But she'd already admitted more of her insecurities to him than she should have. So she raised her eyebrows, trying to suggest a hint of disbelief, and said, "The day I came out to the ranch to look through your records, you didn't act as if you liked me very much. In fact, I thought you were mad as all get-out.''

His expression changed, a subtle shift, but she felt as though he'd just closed a door in her face. "My mother had just called, upset. She's had a tough enough time without all this happening.''

Yes, but why was this so upsetting to her? Renee wanted to ask. Discretion won.

"You've managed to evade my question again.''

"Question?'' Daniel's eyebrows rose before understanding resettled the lines of his face. "Gabe Rosler. Yeah, okay. This is just between you, me and the fence post, though.''

"Understood.''

"I think he was gay. Papa Rosler would not have been sympathetic.''

She almost shuddered, picturing Dick Rosler, square-jawed westerner whose wife quivered into silence at a look from him. If his son, his only child, had come to him and admitted to being homosexual... No, the kid was better off taking a long hike and not coming back.

As if he'd followed her thoughts, Daniel added, "And remember, this was some years ago. No ski area here, no espresso stands, no yuppies telecommuting from Elk Springs. I mean, Dick wouldn't have been alone. Not many folks hereabouts would have accepted Gabe.''

"Did he *tell* you...?''

Daniel shook his head decisively. "There was just something about him. And something about his friendship with that Greene kid.''

"You mean, you think...'' Why so amazed? she

asked herself. It was logical. Gabe's father found out. Maybe the boy went to tell Les and couldn't find him, so he split on his own. When Les found out Gabe had gone, he packed up and left town, too. Maybe they'd even arranged to meet, if their secret ever came out. Renee pursed her lips. "I wonder if Marjorie Rosler knows?"

"I have no idea," Daniel said flatly. "Now, how about if we forget Gabe and talk about something more relevant. Like whether you're going to let me beyond your doorstep tonight."

Oh, God. Did he mean for a cup of coffee, or to join her in bed?

She took a deep breath. He'd asked for honesty, hadn't he?

"No," she said. "I'm not. This is only the second—okay, the third—date. I have to work tomorrow, so I don't want to have a cup of coffee or a glass of wine. And...I don't know about anything else."

"Fair enough." He lifted her hand and kissed it, just a brush of his lips, but enough to send shock waves up her arm. "But it's damned cold out there tonight. We're going to freeze on that porch while I kiss you."

She batted her lashes—hey, maybe she could do this after all!—and murmured sweetly, "We could skip the kiss."

"Hell, no."

"Well, okay," she conceded. "One step inside, just to stay thawed. I'll give you two minutes."

That warm smile made her feel as limp as if she'd

just crawled from a hot spring. "And I'll raise you to three."

Something told her he was right. Again. But she wouldn't admit it. She'd win tonight's contest if he didn't get beyond the front hall. If he didn't discover how bleak and empty her father's house was inside.

The thought came insidiously: if, by extension, Daniel didn't also discover the places *she* had inside that were just as bleak, just as lonely.

Or did he already suspect they were there?

CHAPTER SEVEN

"SO," HER SISTER SAID, turning casually away to pull aside the lace curtain and peer out the kitchen window, "why *do* you care what happened to Les Greene?"

"It's my job..." Renee began.

"Oh, come on." Abby swung back impatiently, letting the curtain drop. "It's not like you can save him now! I mean, he either made a new life for himself, or he didn't. Whichever, no one cares anymore but you. Well—" she made a face "—I suppose Les Greene does, if he's alive."

From her comfortable seat at the table, Renee watched her sister's restless prowling. Maturity and a job that required peak physical condition kept Abby looking like some kind of Norse goddess: tall, sleek, blond and blue-eyed. Maybe, if Meg were here now, she'd find she had lost her position as the prettiest Patton sister.

In answer to the question, Renee said honestly, "I don't know. I have to keep reminding myself he's not a seventeen-year-old kid anymore. Did I tell you what Daniel thinks?"

"'Daniel' now, eh?" Her sister threw a quick grin over her shoulder before she opened the freezer compartment and inspected its contents. "Jeez.

You've won the title as Ms. Frozen Food Queen.'' She closed the freezer. "And, yes, you told me. Sure, it's sad the kid's own mother couldn't be bothered to file a missing persons report. And, wow, it would have been hard to be gay in good old Elk Springs back in those days—truthfully, it's probably still hard if you're in high school. That jock attitude prevails. Still, the bones aren't his. Good idea. Didn't pan out. You should move on. If you don't, Jack's going to think of something more useful for you to be doing.''

Renee groaned and let her head fall back. "Such as picking up some twelve-year-old who's shoplifted a candy bar at the 7-Eleven.''

"A hardened criminal in the making,'' her sister said with mock reproof. ''It's important to intervene early.''

"Yeah. Right.'' Renee grimaced. "Let me tell you about today's big excitement. We got this hysterical phone call. A teenage girl was home alone. Someone was trying to break in. I'm the closest, so I go over there, gun drawn, heart pounding, but whoever it was is gone. We call her parents home from work, everyone is all worked up over it, and I pin her down on what she actually heard.''

Abby boosted herself onto the kitchen counter, eyes bright. "Yeah? What'd she hear?''

"The screen door on the enclosed back porch. It creaks and slams. Footsteps. Loud. Not somebody sneaking.''

"*I'd* be scared.''

"So I interview neighbors. A woman three doors down says gosh, no, the only person she's seen all day is the meter reader. Was just there, maybe half an hour ago.''

Her sister had begun to laugh.

''Back to the house. Gee whiz, the meter *is* on the back porch. I check with the utility. Yeah, he had just been there. The parents look at the girl, she bursts into tears. Mystery solved.''

When Abby quit laughing, she said, ''I still don't blame her.''

''No. I guess I don't, either.''

A small silence fell. Abby tapped her fingers on the countertop, the nervous gesture reminding Renee of how energetic her little sister had always been. She'd never napped the way other toddlers did. Once she reached school age, she would burst in the door at the end of the day as fresh and ready to go as she had when she woke up in the morning. Meg used to groan and say, ''Why didn't God share some of that get-up-and-go between the three of us? Why did *she* get all of it?''

''Hey,'' Abby said suddenly. ''The snow's really coming down out there, you know.''

Renee knew. Given that Halloween hadn't even arrived yet, how could she be oblivious to snow falling outside? Maybe that's why it felt so cozy in here.

''Let's go out and make a snowman.''

''What?''

''Come on.'' Abby jumped down from the countertop. ''Don't be a party pooper.''

''But there isn't enough snow!'' Renee protested, even as she knew she'd lose this argument.

''We can *try*.''

Renee rolled her eyes, but got to her feet. "Do we have to?" she mumbled, but obediently hunted for her gloves and hat and took her parka from the closet. Abby, of course, was ready and impatiently waiting for her.

On the porch, Renee surveyed the front yard. More snow had fallen than she'd realized; perhaps two inches of white blanketed the smooth sweep of lawn. Fat wet flakes floated down from a pale sky that would deepen toward dusk in another half hour.

Abby bounced down the steps and threw herself onto the ground, flapping her arms and legs to make a snow angel. She opened her mouth to catch some flakes, an expression of childish abandon on her face. "Come on. You do it, too."

"Maybe we should go down to the park," Renee suggested. "Like we used to."

Her sister sat up and stared at her. "Ding, ding. Dad isn't here anymore."

"I know, but…" His ghost was. How did she say that?

Their father had never let them play in the yard. When Abby was pitcher for the softball team, she couldn't practice at home; she might wear down the grass. Pets weren't allowed; they might poop in Dad's flowerbeds. He once trapped a neighbor's cat because it dared to use the soil on his side of the fence. The neighbor, thank God, retrieved her big orange tabby from the pound before it was euthanized, but she refused to speak to Renee's father ever again. Who could blame her?

And the girls had never been allowed to have snowball fights or build forts or snowmen in their own yard. The snow, just like the grass, must be pristine. "You tromp all over it," he'd growl, "it'll look like hell."

Still she hovered on the porch steps. "I know he's gone. This just seems…disrespectful."

Her sister hooted. "Excuse me? Who was the disrespectful one around here? What's gotten into you? You suddenly give a care what he thinks?"

"I always did." There it was: truth she'd always sidled away from. Not profound; kids had a way of wanting love and approval even from parents they thought they hated. But not her, Renee had always told herself. How could you hate someone as passionately as she hated her father, and still want him to love you? It didn't make any sense.

It still didn't make any sense. It just was. She'd spent a lifetime fighting her father, all the while desperately needing his love and approval.

And she was still trying to get it.

"Well, here's a tip," Abby said without of a hint of sympathy. "Quit. He's dead. If he were alive, you'd be the first one to tramp all over his snowy lawn, and to hell with him."

"*You're* a fine one to give advice," Renee said bitterly. "Daddy's little girl, always sucking up."

"You mean, *I* figured out how to get along with him." Abby picked herself up, only to bend over and pack a snowball in her gloved hands. "*I* didn't always talk back. *I* knew how to make him approve of me. You're just jealous."

Horribly. Renee ducked the snowball when Abby let it fly. Within seconds, she was down on the lawn, packing some snow into a firm ball. Abby ran, but the snowball smacked her right at her nape and slid down inside her jacket.

Shrieking, she made another and threw with that pitcher's arm. It splattered on Renee's chest, icy shards hitting her chin and bare neck.

The war was on.

By the time they collapsed, giggling, the snowy expanse looked as if a Cub Scout troop had held a rally on it, one interrupted by a bomb threat that had sent little boys scattering in panic.

"Too bad Dad already had a heart attack," Renee muttered. "Just think, we could have given him one."

"You really did hate him, didn't you?" Abby rose to her knees. "Come on. Let's make that snowman."

"Okay." Renee made a snowball, then gently set it down to roll. "Yeah. I hated him. Didn't you?"

"Nope." Abby had begun her own part of the snowman's fat body. "But I didn't especially love him, either. Not the way you did."

Renee digested that. She could see it now, so why hadn't she realized before that her little sister, the one Dad had indulged, didn't care about what she'd won so easily? Maybe that was natural; maybe you wanted most desperately that which you *didn't* have. Maybe anything achieved easily was to be despised.

"You're right. I'm jealous," she said, but Abby didn't hear her. She was rolling her ball in the other direction, leaving a grassy trail in her wake. If Renee didn't hurry, Abby's snowball would be the biggest, and therefore the base. Renee had been scrunched in the middle for too many years. The symbolism seemed suddenly important. *Hers* would be the biggest, the foundation.

Well, really the snowman's hips, but she wasn't about to let her little sister beat her.

Renee bent over and gave her ball of snow a shove to start it moving.

"SO BILL HODGKINS definitely did work for you after he left the Triple B." Phone wedged between ear and shoulder, Renee doodled on her pad of paper as the old man rambled on, repeating what he'd already told her. "For ten years?" she echoed politely. "And he has a ranch of his own down in Oklahoma now. Yes, I'm glad to hear he's done so well. I'll surely watch for his name in cutting competitions."

Renee glanced up to see Jack lounging in her office doorway. She rolled her eyes and tried again to end the conversation. "Thank you, Mr. Randall. You've been a big help. His phone number? Oh, I don't think I need it... Well, sure." She wrote it down. "Again, thanks. I'll certainly call if I need more information." He was still talking when she firmly set down the receiver.

Jack grinned. "Chatty?"

"Reminds me of Abby when she was about four. She'd never shut up."

"Learn anything?" he asked.

She tensed inwardly. "Just eliminated another possibility."

"Sounds like you've eliminated all of them."

"You know these things are slow."

"It's looking like an early ski season." For the

Elk Springs P.D., having the ski lifts start running was like opening day of the hunting season was for wildlife agents.

"This snow won't stay on the ground."

"Not in town. It may on the slopes."

They were starting to sound like two competing weather forecasters, Renee thought ruefully. Channels four and seven.

"Jack," she said, "it's October. We have a month to go, minimum, before ski season. You know that. I'm here when you need me. We don't exactly have a crime wave going on at the moment. This matters to me."

A frown gathered between his dark brows. "Law enforcement isn't supposed to be personal."

Uh-oh. She had to open her big mouth. "It's not that I have any stake in one person being guilty or innocent. I didn't know any of these people! I just don't want to let this one go. The more I dig, the more I'm convinced this wasn't just a drifter."

He still frowned, his dark eyes searching her face.

"Come on, Jack. What's so important I should be doing instead?"

"The gym wall at the high school got spray painted with obscenities last night."

She didn't have to say anything.

His grin flashed again. "Okay, our community won't crumble at the foundations if we don't catch the punks."

"Before we know it," Renee said, "they'll graduate—or not—from high school and be off to the big city."

"And another generation of punks will take their place. Yeah. I know."

"I'll tell you what, though," she said. "I'll go up to the high school today. Nose around a little. Heck, maybe I can scare 'em, if nothing else."

He nodded. "Go for it. As far as the other… Fine. Just don't step on too many toes. I've already heard from Dick Rosler. He didn't like having you up there."

That one came from left field. "Why?" she asked blankly.

"Didn't like you upsetting his wife."

Renee rocked back in her chair. "Funny," she said thoughtfully, "how this seems to be upsetting several people. You wouldn't expect that, considering what old news it is."

"Don't put words in my mouth." But his tone was mild. "And, yeah, I thought it was interesting, too. It's one reason I'm not ordering you to drop the investigation."

"Okay," Renee said. "I'm heading out to talk to Shirley Barnard again. I should warn you, Daniel won't like it."

"I hear you've had dinner a couple times."

Irritation brought her out of her chair. "Informers everywhere?"

"You know what this town's like."

"Well, if you're worried he's succeeded in bribing me, you can forget it. My price is higher than dinner."

"I wasn't worried—"

She cut him off. "Once I press his mother a little, I can kiss the dinners goodbye, anyway." She shrugged as if it didn't matter, even as she cursed herself for choosing the word "kiss." No more kisses, sweet, erotic, mind-drugging. No next step. No chance to find out what it would feel like to have Daniel's weight on hers, his hands on places no hands had ever touched, his... Never mind, she told herself hastily, about the time she noticed Jack's intrigued contemplation.

"Busybodies," she muttered.

"Yup." He tried to hide his amusement. "We're usually grateful for those same folks who notice everything."

"Well, I didn't commit a crime."

"Romance is just as interesting."

She mumbled an unprintable comment. He just laughed and disappeared from her doorway.

Renee dropped back in her squeaky office chair and stared at the telephone on her desk. Call Daniel and tell him she was coming back out to question his mother again? Or blindside Shirley Barnard, knowing full well how angry Daniel would be?

She closed her eyes, panic and depression weighting her chest in equal measure. She didn't need Daniel's smiles or kisses. Truth be known, they scared her some. It might be better this way.

So why, she asked herself as she quietly closed her office door behind her on the way out, did she feel like she had when her father's coffin had been lowered into the ground?

PROPELLED BY A SLAP on her rump, a cow burst through the gate, head swinging as she searched for a herd or escape back the way she'd come. The colt

Daniel rode quivered at the sight of her, his skin rippling in fright or excitement. His ears swiveled like small radar antennae as he waited for a signal telling him what to do about this strange creature that now trotted toward them, following the fence in the round pen.

Daniel waited until the cow came abreast, then neck-reined the three-year-old in place just off the bony left flank of the cow. When the colt wanted to speed up, he eased back on the reins; when he lagged, Daniel tightened his legs.

The cow wheeled suddenly and took a few running steps in the other direction, still following the fence. With Daniel's guidance, the colt mirrored her movements. With no corner for the cow to hole up in, the round pen was best for an inexperienced horse.

Starting a colt like this wasn't demanding work, and someone else could have done it. But Daniel enjoyed this part, and he found he could make decent predictions about how far a young horse would go by observing these initial reactions to cattle.

This colt was pleasantly surprising him. Sometimes lazy, he was responding today to the tiniest shift of weight or touch of the rein. The cow fascinated him; his ears were pricked, his attention exactly where it should be. Within minutes he seemed to understand what was wanted of him. That's what Daniel hoped to see. A good cutting horse had to rely on his own instincts, not just on commands from his rider.

When the cow, frustrated, came to a stop, Daniel gently backed the colt a step, then tipped the horse's nose toward the cow's hip. A couple of feet forward, and the cow became uneasy enough to resume her trot. Daniel could feel the horse's surprise and delight. He'd just discovered a new toy, and he was having fun.

Daniel didn't wait until the colt's interest diminished, ending the session even though he could feel reluctance in the powerful muscles beneath him. He'd bring in another young horse and start with a fresh cow; a bored one was tougher to work and less likely to pique the horse's curiosity.

He was just dismounting and handing the reins to Stan, one of the ranch hands, when Lee called from the barn, "Hey, Barnard! Your mom called. She wants you to come by."

She didn't often interrupt in the middle of the day. His dad had hated keeping a horse standing around, and she took for granted that Daniel felt the same. Something must be wrong.

"Cool him," Daniel ordered. When he passed Lee, leading out the three-year-old filly he'd been planning to ride next, Daniel said, "You start here. Let me know how she does."

Lee flashed a grin. "You betcha."

With ground-eating strides Daniel covered the quarter mile to the homestead. No police car out front. He hadn't any trouble interpreting the depth of his relief. Choices that had looked simple early on weren't so simple anymore. Now that he was beginning to understand the deep-rooted fears that made Renee prickly, he was more drawn to her than ever.

Drawn to her, hell! He wanted her like he'd never

wanted a woman. The worst part was, he was dreaming about things that had nothing to do with his hunger to have her under him, her bare legs wrapped around his waist. No, he'd find himself imagining what she'd be like in five years, ten years, once he'd convinced her to trust him. How it would feel to know he'd healed her. He'd see her smile when she first opened her eyes in the morning. She'd laugh often, once she didn't have to guard herself from the world.

Except the one time he'd almost gotten married, Daniel had never thought more than a few weeks down the line where a woman was concerned. And that time—well, it was partly the fact he *couldn't* see ahead that had given him cold feet. By then, he'd been dating Carol Lynn for two years, sleeping with her for one. He hadn't so much asked her to marry him as they'd fallen into assuming they would get married.

Two *years*. He hadn't known Renee for two weeks and he was seeing her pregnant with his baby. He still didn't understand how he could be imagining a future with a woman he hardly knew.

But he couldn't deny that he was.

One of these days he'd have to tell his mother that he'd picked out a bride. Freely admitting to cowardice, he wasn't in any hurry to do it.

At her place, he knocked on the door. He waited, but heard no footsteps, no voice inviting him in. Mary wasn't here, either, he remembered, frowning. Taking her boy, she'd left this morning to go back over the mountains to Beaverton for either a reconciliation with Kurt or to collect more clothes—

whichever seemed like a better idea at the time, she'd told Daniel wryly.

Starting to feel some disquiet, he hammered again on the door. His mother wouldn't have waited for him if she was ill, would she? Like if she were having chest pains? Surely she had the sense to call an ambulance, or at least tell Lee what was wrong.

The door wasn't locked. He thrust it open and went in, calling, "Mom? You here?"

The parlor was empty. So was the kitchen. She wouldn't have asked him to come over, then driven off to town, would she? Urgency had him taking the stairs two at a time.

Her bedroom door stood ajar. His breath whooshed out of him when he saw her sitting on the edge of the bed, her jewelry box open beside her. Her head was bent over something she held.

"Mom?"

All in one motion, she looked up and shoved whatever she held back in the polished mahogany box, snapping it shut. She jumped to her feet and set the jewelry box back onto her dresser as he came the rest of the way into her room.

"Daniel," she said breathlessly. "I'm sorry. I didn't hear you."

The way she looked scared him. It was as if she'd suddenly aged ten years. She seemed stooped, frail, her skin crepey and blanched. What in hell had happened? he wondered.

"What were you looking at?" he asked, curious.

"Oh, nothing. I..." She tried to smile. "I was just thinking about your father."

"I'm sorry." He tried to take her hand, but she backed away.

"What did you want?" she asked.

Now he was really scared. "You told Lee you wanted to see me."

She stared at him for a heart-stopping moment, during which thoughts of Alzheimer's and senile dementia crossed his mind with lightning speed.

She blinked. "Oh. I...I did leave a message, didn't I?"

"Was it important?" he asked, even as he debated whether he should call an ambulance. Or put her in the car and take her straight to her doctor's office.

She took a shaky step backward and sank onto the edge of the bed. "No, I... It was that policewoman. But I shouldn't have interrupted you, should I? It could have waited."

His gut tightened. "Policewoman?"

"She was here again." His mother knotted her fingers together, and tension made her voice tremulous. "She kept asking the same questions. About...about that rodeo rider. And what happened fifteen years ago. She doesn't believe me. I can tell she doesn't."

Feeling sick, he said grimly, "Apparently not. You didn't know she was coming?"

"She seemed so nice the last time she was here." His mother pinched together trembling lips. "I feel like...like some kind of criminal!"

"I'll talk to her." He sounded far away to his own ears, as if someone else was talking in that stony voice. "We'll get a lawyer if we have to. She doesn't have any right to harass you like this."

Hope filled his mother's eyes and stilled her writhing fingers. "You can stop her? I don't have to keep answering her questions?"

"We might have to get a lawyer, but I think you've cooperated more than enough. So long as you've told her everything you know." He didn't phrase it as a question, but it hung there as if he had. Daniel didn't know what he wanted—that she'd tell him whatever it was she was keeping secret, or that she'd convince him he'd been imagining things.

Either way, she bent her head to avoid his eyes and nodded. "You've always been a good son, Daniel. Taking over when your father died, the way you did... He'd be proud of you. He always was."

His father would have expected him to protect his mother, no matter what. Daniel knew that. He'd lied to himself earlier; he wasn't wavering on where his loyalties lay. He might be falling in love with Renee, though right this minute his former certainty about that *was* tottering. Sneaking out here to upset his mother like this, without calling him first... That was low. It made him question whether he was seeing in her what he wanted to see, not what was really there.

The last time they'd gone through this, he'd convinced himself she'd just felt shy after their date the night before. And she had genuinely seemed to be seeking information his mother hadn't minded providing. But this time, there was no misinterpreting why Renee hadn't phoned ahead.

Well, never again. He'd talk to her boss. He'd hire the best attorney in Oregon. Whatever it took.

But first he'd give himself the satisfaction of telling her what he thought of her behavior.

Now, when he took his mother's hand, she squeezed back. "Mom," he said, "will you call on over to the barn? Tell Lee I've had to go to town. I ought to be back in an hour or two."

Every word seemed to strengthen her, returning color to her cheeks. She nodded. "I'll phone right away."

"You'll be all right?" Daniel asked.

"Yes." She sounded more like herself. "Of course I will. I shouldn't have let myself get so upset."

Unless, he thought, *you really are hiding something. Unless you're afraid.* But immediately he felt like a traitor.

All her agitation meant was that his mother was blowing something way out of proportion. Hell, Dad could get pretty steamed when he thought someone had been careless in a way that might have led to one of the horses being injured. Mom was remembering some incident where Dad had ranted and raved and shaken his fists, maybe claimed he was going to string up that so-and-so, and now Mom was thinking maybe he'd been serious and gone and done it.

Didn't she know Dad better than that? Matthew Barnard was an honest, upstanding man. If he'd killed a man in a fight, it would have been an accident and he would have gone straight to the telephone to call the police. But to sink a knife into a man's chest, then dump the body... Daniel shook his head in instinctive denial.

He'd admired his father more than anyone on earth. Daniel knew damn well he wouldn't be the man he was if his father hadn't been there as an example. There was no way on God's green earth that Matthew Barnard had died with murder on his conscience. Daniel would stake everything he had and was on his bone-deep belief in his father's integrity.

Now, if Renee had been on her way to trusting Daniel the way he'd have liked, his word for it would have been good enough for her. As it was, he was going to have to march into her office breathing fire to stop her from tormenting his mother.

He didn't kid himself that Renee would see it his way, or forgive him anytime soon. Maybe she wasn't the woman he'd thought she was. Somehow that didn't seem like a great comfort right now.

It was going to be even less comfort when he got in his big empty bed tonight—the one he'd dreamed of sharing—and thought about her kisses and her innocence and her shaky steps toward faith in him.

Would she understand why he couldn't let her hurt his mother? Or would she believe he was just one more man who didn't hesitate to hurt *her?*

CHAPTER EIGHT

THE ELK SPRINGS Police Department was housed in a bland modern edifice that would have been interchangeable with the elementary school built the same year if it weren't for the jail. The new public safety building was part of a complex that included city offices, the library and a fire station. It was a big improvement over the old building, built in the 20s to intimidate the average citizen. Gray granite blocks, imposing stairs, wire-caged windows and the obligatory lions guarding heavy double oak doors had been right out of a Gothic novel. That old police station, two blocks away, was now an antique mall. This summer, Daniel had noticed the flower wreaths the lions sported around their necks.

Today he parked his pickup in a slot marked for visitors in front of the low building, then strode in, rage still simmering.

Just inside, a kid who looked about ten but was probably thirteen or fourteen slumped sullenly on one of a row of padded chairs, his expression imitating those on the faces that sneered from the Wanted posters hung above his head. A few feet away, a woman who was most likely the kid's mother stood talking to a uniformed officer behind a long counter. Her voice was rising, and although the boy was pretending indifference, his knuckles showed white where he gripped the arms of the chair.

Another uniformed officer approached him. "May I help you?"

"I'm here to see Renee Patton," Daniel said.

"I'll check on whether Lieutenant Patton is in." The policeman disappeared down the hall that led to rows of individual offices, a change from the old squad room where each desk had been separated by no more than a wastebasket and a chair to seat suspects.

Daniel knew. At fifteen, he'd been with a friend who shoplifted a pack of cigarettes. Both boys had been hauled down to the station. Daniel's genuine shock at his buddy's dishonesty must have showed, because his innocence was accepted and he walked out with his parents. His friend had stayed behind, his dad looking about like the kid's mother did today. As Daniel waited, he could hear her behind him.

"You stole a car? What were you thinking of?" The kid mumbled a brief reply Daniel couldn't make out. "Oh, God," his mother cried, "what did I do wrong?"

Daniel had been lucky. His parents had believed him. Of course, he hadn't had the cigarettes in his pocket. Or been sitting behind the wheel of a hot-wired car.

"Daniel!"

He quit eavesdropping in a hurry when Renee hurried toward him.

"What's up?" An open, inquiring expression didn't quite disguise her wariness.

"I want to talk to you."

"Well... I was about to go to lunch. Join me?"

"Fine," he said tersely.

Damn it, why had he agreed to make their talk social? he asked himself, irritated, as he waited while Renee let somebody know she was leaving. What he'd wanted to do was flatten his hands on her desk, bend menacingly forward and say, "Get a warrant if you plan to come out to the Triple B again. Otherwise, you're not welcome." After which he'd stalk out.

Instead he found himself walking beside her and amicably debating where they'd eat—they agreed on the deli down the block. On the way, he kept sneaking sidelong glances, bothered afresh by her uniform and the holstered gun bumping on her hip. He had trouble seeing in her the woman he'd kissed. Yet he couldn't help noticing the delicate line of her cheek, the way her uniform shirt was rounded out, never mind the awkward fit of that holster because of the curves beneath. Even like this, she was pretty. Sexy. Daniel resented the fact that his anger didn't turn off his reaction to her.

The deli was a nice little place: antique tables and chairs, wallpaper with voluptuous roses and pink bows, an oak-and-iron coatrack in the entry and an old oak-and-glass case where pies were displayed and orders taken. The big disadvantage, he saw immediately, was that the tables were placed close enough together to eliminate any possibility of a completely private conversation.

Renee went for the special—minestrone soup with fresh-baked bread and a plate of fruit. Not hungry, Daniel ordered a sandwich and coffee.

She led him to a corner table, where between lacy curtains they could see down the riverfront park. They sat with their backs to the other diners.

The waitress brought his coffee and Renee's lemonade. Renee thanked her, then seemed to take a deep breath. Her eyes met his candidly. "I suppose this is about my having gone to see your mother this morning."

Jaws tight, he said, "I thought we'd come to an understanding."

Her eyes narrowed. "Really. And just what was that?"

"That you'd call me if you were coming out. Give me a chance to be there."

"And deflect my questions?"

He fought to keep his voice down. "Hear what the hell you're up to."

"And *I* thought I'd made it clear that our personal relationship wouldn't influence how I do my job."

"All I asked for was common courtesy," he growled.

"No," she said passionately, "you're asking me to dump this one in the unsolved files, because you don't want your mother bothered. Think about it for a minute. Every citizen in this country has the duty to cooperate…"

"You're accusing her of something without any evidence at all!"

He felt the stir as other diners turned. Well, let them listen.

"I haven't accused your mother of anything, and I don't expect I will. But you know as well as I do that she's hiding something. I want to know what it is."

"Thinking about the past upsets her. That doesn't mean she's lying."

"Don't kid yourself." Her voice was scathing. "You can't possibly believe she'd forgotten who T. J. Baxter was."

No, he didn't believe that. But his mother's conveniently poor memory didn't necessarily have anything to do with murder. His mother, a killer? His father? Never!

He opened his mouth to say something he probably would have regretted, but was prevented by the arrival of the waitress with their food.

After depositing their lunches in front of them, she caroled, "Enjoy!" and trotted away.

Renee ignored her steaming bowl of soup. "Can you?" she repeated.

"Why the hell does this matter so much?" he heard himself asking. "Is it your first murder case? Are you afraid if you don't solve it, it'll show as a failure in your file?"

Her face was unreadable, her voice steady. "Maybe it matters to me because nobody else seems to care. Even you, and those bones came from *your* land. I want to know who he was more than I want to find out who killed him. I want a name on his gravestone."

"And you think my mother can put it there."

"That's right." Her gaze dared him to be honest.

"And you think she can, too. You're just afraid to find out what she's hiding."

She'd nicked a vein with her accusation. It felt like rusty barbed wire biting deep.

"Maybe you're talking about yourself," he said, acid in his mouth. "Your father hid a hell of a lot, and you've spent a lifetime being afraid to find out what it was."

He was sorry the minute the words were out; fear and hurt pride were no excuse for striking where she was most vulnerable.

Her face paled.

He swore. "I shouldn't have said that…"

Color rose in her cheeks, vivid spots against the white. "No, you shouldn't have. But then, I guess you're willing to use any weapon to stop me, aren't you? Sweet words and kisses didn't work, so you're moving right along. Well, save it," she said bitterly. "Maybe you'd better go the legal route. Get your mom an attorney, why don't you? Admit she might need a defense."

She was in the act of rising to her feet, but he beat her to it. "Maybe I will," he snapped, "since you're obviously on a witch-hunt!" He yanked his wallet from his back pocket and tossed some bills on the table. "Enjoy your lunch." He walked out without looking back.

HUNCHED IN MISERY, Renee sat in her easy chair in the kitchen, knees drawn up and arms hugging herself.

Stupid, she thought. *Stupid, stupid, stupid.* She'd known all along why Daniel was interested in her.

Of course he hadn't fallen madly in love with her at first sight! All she had to do was look in a mirror, especially when she was wearing her uniform. Helen of Troy, she was not. Heck, she probably had more in common with one of those Greek warriors. Achilles, maybe. Lord knew she'd discovered she possessed an unexpected weakness.

Not Daniel, she told herself. Vanity. All these years, she'd been the tough one. Abby charmed Daddy, and Renee refused even to try. Instead she tried to prove she could do everything as well as he did. Better. She wasn't soft; she didn't need or want anything that a woman had to coax from a man.

So, here she was, twenty-eight years old, and she was just discovering she'd lied to herself. *She* wanted tender words and flowers and passion, just like every other woman. She could become weak in the knees, too. No, weak in the head, Renee told herself in disgust. How could she have let herself crave approval from some man, to the point where she was tempted to surrender her convictions to get it?

"Which just goes to show," she muttered, "why I can't."

Because Daniel was right about that part, anyway; she *had* spent a lifetime being afraid. Not afraid of her father, exactly; rather, of who he was. Of what he might have done. Of finding out that her mother and sister hadn't just gone away.

What a mealymouth! She couldn't even put it into words. She was afraid of finding out that...

"He killed them." Throat thick, she felt the words lingering, as if they'd taken on bodily form.

What if she'd spent years desperately seeking approval from the man who had murdered her mother?

Renee shuddered and burrowed deeper in her own embrace. A grown woman trying with all her might to return to the womb. *Pathetic.*

Some sound made her lift her head. Was it...? Yes. The doorbell was ringing.

A kid trying to sell Girl Scout cookies. No. That was spring, wasn't it? Abby? But she had a key.

Whoever was there had abandoned the doorbell and was knocking now. She'd ignore it. Her. *Him.* Because she knew who it had to be.

He felt guilty. Or else he figured he could still string her along. Either way, she didn't want to hear it.

But he kept hammering, and after a while she heard his muffled voice, "Renee! I know you're home. Answer the door!"

Her father would have had a fit. She could just hear him bellowing, "God damn it, Renee, answer the door!"

"All right!" In her bare feet, she hurried to the front hall and flung the door open. "What do you want?"

"To talk to you." He glowered at her, dark brows drawn together. "I was getting worried."

To protect herself—ah, pride!—she tried for flippant. "What, you thought I committed suicide because you're mad at me? Well, sorry. I just wasn't in the mood for company. Especially yours."

In bulky parka and boots, Daniel looked even bigger than usual. Solid and sexy and scary, because

It's fun, and we're giving away *FREE GIFTS* to all players!

PLAY ROULETTE!

Scratch the silver to see that the ball has landed on 7 RED, making you eligible for TWO FREE romance novels!

PLAY TWENTY-ONE!

Scratch the silver to reveal a winning hand! Congratulations, you have Twenty-One. Return this card promptly and you'll receive a fabulous free mystery gift, along with your free books!

YES!

Please send me all the free Harlequin Superromance® books and the gift for which I qualify! I understand that I am under no obligation to purchase any books, as explained on the back of this card.

Name: _____
(PLEASE PRINT)

Address: _____ Apt.#: _____

City: _____ State: _____ Zip: _____

Offer limited to one per household and not valid to current Harlequin Superromance® subscribers. All orders subject to approval.   PRINTED IN U.S.A.

336 HDL CQX5   **135 HDL CQXK**

(H-SR-08/99)

The Harlequin Reader Service® — Here's how it works:

Accepting your 2 free books and mystery gift places you under no obligation to buy anything. You may keep the books and gift and return the shipping statement marked "cancel." If you do not cancel, about a month later we'll send you 6 additional novels and bill you just $3.57 each in the U.S., or $3.96 each in Canada, plus 25¢ delivery per book and applicable taxes if any.* That's the complete price and — compared to the cover price of $4.25 in the U.S. and $4.75 in Canada — it's quite a bargain! You may cancel at any time, but if you choose to continue, every month we'll send you 6 more books, which you may either purchase at the discount price or return to us and cancel your subscription.

*Terms and prices subject to change without notice. Sales tax applicable in N.Y. Canadian residents will be charged applicable provincial taxes and GST.

he knew her too well. He could hurt her easily now, just as he had earlier.

"You're making it hard for me to apologize," he growled.

Renee crossed her arms. "Which part are you apologizing for?"

"That dig..."

"Fine. Consider your apology accepted."

His hand shot out, preventing her from closing the door.

"I want to talk to you."

"Come to my office tomorrow." Renee shoved at the door, gaining a few inches until he pushed back and regained every one of them plus more.

"Now," he said implacably.

A minor spurt of humor came to her rescue. To anyone else, they'd look as childish as she and Abby had the day before, each rolling bigger and bigger balls of snow until they couldn't make a snowman because both were too heavy to be lifted atop the other.

"All right." She let go of the door and stepped aside so suddenly he staggered and almost went down, a sight as gratifying in her current mood as she'd hoped. "Come in."

Daniel muttered something under his breath that she was just as glad she couldn't make out, then stalked ahead of her into the living room.

"Not here," she said hurriedly when he made a beeline for her father's recliner. *Not there.* She fancied it gave a small irritated rock. "Let's go into the kitchen."

Daniel stopped, but stood looking around. "You don't use this room, do you?"

"No. I told you the house was too big." *And this is* his *room.* She closed her eyes, for a moment fearing that she'd spoken aloud.

"It doesn't fit you."

Daniel had gone over to the bookcase, where he perused the titles, all true crime. Dad had loved that stuff, the gorier and sicker the better. He'd been known to muse aloud that it was too bad Elk Springs didn't have a *real* case like these.

Maybe he'd committed his own. The thought came unbidden, more readily than it once would have. It was getting easier to think of her father as the monster he'd been, whether he had also been a murderer or not.

"No," Renee said levelly. "This house doesn't fit me. But it's mine until I work up the energy to clean it out and sell it. So, can we go to the kitchen?"

"Cheery reading." Daniel shook his head. "Yeah, okay."

The minute he walked into the kitchen behind her, it came to her that she'd rather not have had him here, either. She felt like Shirley must have at the police intrusion. She'd gotten it wrong that day. It wasn't the presence of the enemy that made her uncomfortable, but rather the knowledge that this room revealed more about her than she wanted him to know.

His gaze went immediately to the dining nook, where the meager reality of her life was on display. There was the well-worn easy chair, the TV, the remains of her microwave dinner, the single piece of mail that had arrived today: a bill. Through his eyes, she saw it all and cringed. The lonely cell of a spinster.

"Were you watching something?" In his gentler voice, she heard pity.

"No." She'd forgotten the TV was even on; sunk in unhappiness as she'd been, she had no idea even what show it was tuned to. She stabbed the power button, bringing instant silence to the kitchen.

"All right." She didn't care if she sounded rude. "What did you want to say?"

He faced her, and she was confounded. The emotions in his electric-blue eyes were too complex to be labeled "pity." "I shouldn't have said what I did about your father. It had nothing to do with anything. I was angry. Trying to hurt you."

"I was getting personal, too," Renee felt compelled to admit. "Accusing you of being afraid to find out what your mother knows."

He swallowed hard. "But you were right."

She lifted her gaze to his. In a voice just above a whisper, she said, "You were, too."

"We all want to believe the best of our parents."

"I've never been able to do that."

"But you've tried."

"Yes." She gave a sharp, humorless laugh. "I've tried. Do you know, after that first day I never once asked Dad where my mother was? I still don't know whether I was scared of him, afraid of what he'd tell me, or trying to please him by implying that I didn't need her, that he was enough."

"And you're ashamed of yourself now." Somehow he'd moved. His hands clasped her upper arms, squeezing gently, massaging, comforting.

"Sure I am." Truer words had never been spoken. Her chest felt as if it might split open with the pain. "All these years I've hated my mother for deserting us, but I deserted her, too."

He swore and gave her a small shake. "You were a child!"

"Still. I could have hung on to her memory a little harder. Not gone along with pretending that she never existed, because that's what *he* wanted."

"Why not? He was here. She wasn't."

Irrational anger exploded. "And you think that was her fault? Did you ever meet him? He was...he was..." Oh, God. She pressed hands to her cheeks, finding them wet with tears.

Daniel pulled her into his arms. She went passively. Against her hair, he said roughly, "A son of a bitch. Yeah. I know. He was still your dad."

Anger and turmoil played tug-of-war in her chest, spilling those hated tears down her cheeks. She tried to wrench free. "Damn it! Why are you always so understanding?"

He wouldn't let her go, though his grip never hurt her. "Because I know you well enough to despise the bastard."

She let out a choked sound. "Am I that messed up?"

"No. God." He closed his eyes briefly. "No. I just don't like to think about what you had to deal with. It's a miracle you came through whole."

"Whole?" Now, that *was* funny.

He scowled, not liking her laughter. "You did. You are."

Her bitter humor died. "You call this 'whole'?" Renee swept an arm in a gesture encompassing the kitchen, the living room behind them, the nook, her cocoon from the world. "It's weird. Why am I here? Why don't I have a nice condo like my sister does?"

Tone reasonable, he said, "Plenty of people live at home until they're twenty-eight. It's free."

"Oh, no." Her stomach clenched. "Not free. Believe me, nothing from my father was ever free. He extracted his price."

"He's dead. Gone." The compassion in his voice soothed, made promises. *Trust me,* he seemed to be saying.

Renee let herself believe, just for this minute. Still, she backed away from Daniel until she came up against the kitchen counter, needing the support, the distance. "Do you know—" the words just came, though she tried to say them lightly "—I'm not so sure he is."

He stared at her in open shock. "You're serious."

"Do you believe in ghosts?"

"No." His mouth closed tight.

"Well, I don't, either. I never did. But this house has just…soaked him up. Except out here. He only came in the kitchen to grab something from the refrigerator."

"So you hide here."

Her mouth twisted. "Something like that."

Pure rage flared in Daniel's eyes. "All right. Where is he?"

"Where…?" She gaped.

"Right now. Where is the bastard?"

"Do you plan to exorcise him?" Renee asked sarcastically. *If only it were possible.*

He stalked toward her. "Where is he?"

She threw up her hands. "It's my imagination! You know it is. He can't be here."

Daniel didn't hesitate. "But you feel him."

"I...yes."

"Where?"

Was he going to punch a ghost? she wondered wildly. What if she said, *Everywhere*? Would he burn the house down? She wouldn't mind; she'd been tempted herself. If she'd thought she could get away with it, walk away with the insurance money...

Her damned mouth opened itself. "Did you see the recliner rock when you went toward it?"

Daniel spun on one heel and went through the swinging door into the living room. Renee hurried after him. "What are you..."

Without a word, he grabbed the recliner and headed for the front door.

Sickening fear washed up in her throat. "Daniel! Where are you going with that? What are you *doing?*"

Her father... Oh, God, what would he say? The time she'd rearranged the living room and moved his chair ten feet to accommodate a pretty little antique chest she'd spotted in a store downtown, he had gone out to the garage, come back with an ax and chopped the chest into firewood. Then he'd looked at her and said coldly, "Clean this up and put the furniture where it's supposed to be."

That was when any illusion this was her home, too, had died stillborn.

"I'm throwing the damn chair out." Daniel set it down long enough to open the front door. He stopped its violent rocking by snatching it back up and wrestling it through the doorway. The muscles in his arms and shoulders bunched as he lifted the recliner and flung it off the porch. Renee heard a crunch.

Daniel turned to face her. His expression changed. "For God's sake, Renee! It's not some kind of altar." He stopped. "Or is it?"

Brushing past him, she clutched the porch railing and stared down at the chair, lying on its side on the wet lawn so that the mechanism beneath showed. A long wicked branch of the climbing rose had entangled it on the way down. Stuffing popped through one of the new tears. The branch was broken, its celery green heart showing. She would have to prune it at the base.

"No," she said slowly. "Not an altar. It was just…his."

"I'll load it in my truck when I go. Take it to the solid waste station."

She'd actually considered burning down the house, but it had never occurred to her to get rid of the chair. Giddily she thought, *I could strip the whole living room. Buy new carpet—something* he *would have hated. Teal. Periwinkle. Flowery, overstuffed sofa and chairs. Paint the heavy dark mantel white or cream. Have a dainty coffee table, instead of that ponderous mission oak he'd loved. Burn those horrible books. Fill the shelves with romances, fantasy, humor.*

Make this *her* room.

Do it now, an inner voice said. *Now, before you chicken out. Start thinking it's sacrilege.*

Feeling weirdly numb, Renee went back into the living room and scooped up an armful of her father's favorite reading. "Take these, too," she said, rushing out to throw them from the porch, watch them tumble and flutter to the soggy grass. She went back for more. "And these."

Without a word, Daniel helped her. When the bookcase was empty, she looked around. "And this. I hate it." The gun cabinet was too heavy for her. Daniel broke the glass and she dropped the row of rifles uncaringly on the brown carpet. She watched the cabinet crunch and splinter when Daniel flung it after the recliner. She remembered her pretty antique chest and thought, *What goes around comes around.*

The destruction was unexpectedly exhilarating, which worried her. Did she have a criminal bent? But, no—all she was doing was taking possession of what was hers. Dispossessing her father.

She and Daniel emptied the living room, moving a few pieces of furniture into the dining room or front hall, throwing out the rest. When Renee dropped to her knees and began wrenching up the carpet, Daniel went out to his pickup and came back with a hammer and screwdrivers.

"Get some big scissors," he said.

The stuff rolled up, revealing thin padding that she tore into shreds and heaped in a pile. Daniel pried up the carpet tacks and the staples that had held the padding. Renee cut up the carpet into manageable strips. They loaded what they could into plastic garbage sacks, carrying the rest out and shoving it into the back of his pickup. He obviously wouldn't be able to get all the furniture tonight, but she was glad when he loaded the recliner.

"Have you had dinner?" Renee asked recklessly. "I could make something."

"Actually, I have." Daniel sounded apologetic. "How about you?"

She remembered that microwave dinner and felt deflated. She'd wanted to cook something her father would have hated. Use the wok that had sat untouched in a lower cabinet since she'd bought it in a brave moment that didn't last long enough. Eat the dinner at the mahogany dining room table, where she hadn't sat since he died.

Not that she would have had the right ingredients. When was the last time she'd bought staples, the stuff you needed when you really cooked? She knew, of course—six months ago.

"I've eaten, too," she admitted. "Daniel..."

He forestalled her gratitude. Taking her arm, he said, "Let's go see what we've wrought."

Furniture and carpet gone, the living room was an alien landscape. *He* wasn't gone altogether, but his presence was fainter, and she knew suddenly that it would be gone completely when she painted the mantel and bookcases on each side of the fireplace, tore down the heavy drapes, let in sunshine and light and color.

"Too bad Abby wasn't here," she said.

"She would have enjoyed it, too, huh?"

"She'd have loved throwing out his things," Renee said fiercely. "She can help me with his bedroom. Or maybe I should do it right now."

She'd taken no more than a step toward the staircase when Daniel's hand stopped her. "Tomorrow. You've done enough for one day."

He was right, she thought reluctantly, feeling the ache in her shoulders and back. The exhilaration was fading, leaving her drained. Not having second thoughts—oh, no, still glorying in the echoing emptiness that could be a beautiful room, a *new* room, but definitely weary.

"Yes. Okay." She turned to face him, wondering with sudden apprehension whether now he did think she was crazy.

He was watching her, worry in his eyes. Worry and tenderness and patience.

It was the patience that got to her. They were adults; why wait? She was in just the mood to do something *really* reckless.

She ought to go slowly, seduce him, let him think it was his idea. But tonight, she was taking charge of her own destiny.

Before she even opened her mouth, his expression changed. His eyes narrowed, the air became charged, as if he were so sensitive to her moods, he'd felt her decision before she could speak it aloud.

"Will you stay tonight?" She'd wanted to sound provocative, bold, but her voice squeaked. "I want you to make love to me."

Her fantasy man would have come to her in two long strides, kissed her passionately, then lifted her into his arms and carried her up the stairs to her bedroom.

The real man stayed stolidly put. A muscle jerked in his cheek, and he made a rough sound that might have been a groan. But his tone was controlled, even cool.

"That depends on whether you want me just because it would tick your father off royally."

Her miniscule store of confidence in her sexual appeal rushed out, as if someone had pulled the plug on it.

"Never mind." She shrugged as if his answer didn't matter, as if her impulsive invitation had been as trivial as a suggested lunch date. "We're both tired."

"Not that tired." Now he did take those two steps, and his big hand lifted her chin. "You know damn well I want you, Renee. I'm probably an idiot not to take what you're offering, no questions asked. Trouble is, I'd like sex between us to be about us. Not a dead man."

"I…" She stared up at Daniel, seeing the banked desire, the desperate honesty.

Was it about her father? He'd sneered at her every small effort to make herself look pretty. "Why would you put that crap on?" he'd asked when she tried mascara and blush. "A little paint doesn't turn a plow horse into a high-stepper." Oh, how he would tumble in his grave at the knowledge that a handsome man wanted her, that she was making love upstairs in this very house!

Suddenly shaky, weak-kneed, she had to lift her

hands to Daniel's chest to brace herself. The answer came to her, searing, unexpected.

"No," she whispered. "No, it's not about my father. I was just using my anger to…to bolster my courage."

His big hands framed her face, and she felt the faintest trembling in them. His voice was gruff. "You're afraid of me?"

"No." Renee couldn't look above his throat. "Not you. I'm afraid of *this*. You see, I…" She had to stop, take a deep breath, finish in a rush. "Well, I've never done it."

CHAPTER NINE

STUNNED, Daniel froze. Dear God, she was a virgin. Twenty-eight years old, and she'd never had sex. Never, he had to guess, trusted any man or boy enough to let herself be that vulnerable. Or maybe, never believed anyone would want her.

This time the surge of rage was violent. So easy-going he'd never totally understood even his father's quick but short-lived temper, Daniel had never before wanted to hurt anyone. Not so seriously that he might have shoved a fist down her bastard of a father's throat if he could.

Now he knew what it felt like.

But she was still waiting.

"You're a virgin," he said aloud. *Brilliant.*

She flushed deep pink. "That sounds so…so Medieval. I just thought you should know that I'm not very experienced. I mean, I'll probably disappoint you…"

His fingers bit into her arms and that edge of violence honed his voice. "Disappoint me? Don't you know what a gift you're offering?"

Renee stiffened under his hands. Tone combative, she asked, "Why a gift? Don't tell me you think it's okay for guys to play around, but girls should save themselves for their 'true love.' That's *worse* than Medieval! It's..."

Daniel kissed her into silence. Drugged by her softness, the tremor of her lips, the hitch in her breath, it was all he could do to raise his head.

"You always want to misunderstand me, don't you?"

Eyes wide and shimmery golden-green, Renee stared up at him.

"And I think we had this discussion before. No, I don't believe a woman should 'save herself.' But when she does give herself for the first time, the man she chooses ought to feel honored." He cupped her face, his thumbs moving in slow circles, teasing the corners of her mouth. "As I do."

"Oh," she whispered.

He kissed her again, lingering, nibbling gently, sucking on her bottom lip. "Is it okay," he murmured against her mouth, "if I delude myself that you must feel something special for me?"

"I..." Her head fell back against the support of his hand; her lashes swept down as she lifted her face to his. "I suppose," she said on a release of breath.

She loved him. She couldn't say the words, but she did. She must. The knowledge roared through him like an earthquake that could ripple tons of earth as if it were a sheet of cloth.

He groaned and took her mouth again, this time with savage need. That innocence... He had felt it, and now understood it. Even—though he would never admit to emotion so primitive—gloried in it. He was first. She was his.

Daniel bent, wrapped an arm under her thighs and lifted her up.

Renee gasped and clutched at his shoulders as though afraid to trust that he wouldn't drop her. Stiffening, she cried, "Daniel!"

"Indulge me," he said roughly. She might think she was tough, but she was a featherweight, all legs and fine bones and big eyes like a newborn colt. Despite her slenderness, however, she had plenty of curves, including a nicely rounded bottom nestled against him right where it tormented him the most.

Two or three stairs up, she relaxed and kissed his neck, a tiny shy peck that wrung a groan from him. Despite her inexperience, she apparently recognized pleasure when she heard it, because her mouth touched his throat again, more lingeringly this time. She trailed tiny kisses down to the hollow at the base. When her tongue flicked his skin, a warm damp taste, it was all he could do not to strip her right there, on the landing, and take her on the floor, to hell with gentle, patient foreplay.

Daniel reined himself in with a painful effort. *She's not ready,* he told himself grimly. *She can't be.* This was her first time, and he had to be sure it was good. He'd scare the hell out of her if she had any idea how close he was to breaking.

"Which is your bedroom?" he asked hoarsely.

"I..." She lifted her head and looked around, dazed, as if she had no idea where they were. "Oh. It's... Mine's the one on the right."

The white-painted, paneled door stood open. With an elbow he nudged the light switch. Inside was about what he'd expected, and feared: a room as innocent as she was. Walls a pale aqua, woodwork white, pastel rag rugs on the gleaming hardwood floor. White dresser, beveled mirror above. Stuffed animals lined up atop a tall bookcase, also white. Lacy curtains. Silver-framed photos on the bedside stand.

And a twin bed, covered with a pink and blue-green quilt that looked old, in a good way: gently faded, frayed, but all the prettier for that.

He bit back a word that didn't belong in this room. Any more than hot sex did.

She began to stiffen again. "Is something wrong?"

"No. Nothing." He *had* to make love to her here, on her bed. If she knew that *he* was suddenly scared, she'd chicken out. Decide she was what was wrong.

And what was bothering him, anyway? She was an innocent; he knew that, he'd known it all along. This wouldn't be hot sex—it would be lovemaking.

And, God help him, he loved the girl who'd made this room and the woman who still felt at home here.

So what if his feet dangled off the foot of the bed?

"It's too short, isn't it?" As he let her slide to her feet, Renee looked at the bed. "And…and too narrow."

Husky amusement in his voice, Daniel said, "Definitely not too narrow. The short part doesn't matter. If, um, a man and a woman can have great sex in the front seat of a car, you don't need to worry about your bed being too small."

"Not very long ago, when I was out on patrol, I interrupted a couple of teenagers." She was blushing fiercely. "I shone the flashlight right in and…"

"And?" He quirked an eyebrow.

"The boy was on his knees and…" Her courage ran out.

"That works," Daniel said.

Shoot. He was getting randier by the minute. He wanted to try that with her. Her skirt—the one he had yet to see her wearing—up around her waist. Bare silky thighs, breasts pale in the moonlight, his pickup truck groaning as they rocked it…

"I went to a drive-in with a boy once." Musing aloud, she didn't seem to have a clue what she was doing to him. "But we didn't…you know."

Daniel couldn't stand it another minute. He peeled off her sweatshirt and tossed it aside. The static he'd created fluffed tiny hairs around her face. And her bra… God help him, it was as pretty and sweet as her bedroom. Dainty, with scalloped edges and the hooks in back. His breath rasped out.

The pink on her cheeks crept down her neck. "I'm not very big…"

"You're perfect." He didn't sound like himself. His hands shook as he reached out and cupped her breasts, gently squeezed, ran his thumbs over the hardening nubs still hidden from his hungry gaze.

"Oh-hh," she sighed.

He turned her around and with hands that still trembled unhooked her bra. He slipped the straps from her shoulders, feeling the satiny skin, the fragility of her collarbone, the quick shaky breath she drew. And then he turned her back to face him.

She tried to cover her breasts with her hands; he pried them away. She was so pretty, with the snow-white skin that went with her pale gold hair. Pink nipples as petite as he'd imagined. He swallowed, touched her breasts. Her head bent as she watched, took in the contrast of his big, dark hands against her tender skin.

She swayed, then reached out and grabbed his shirt in two fists. "I don't think my legs want to hold me up," she whispered.

"Good," he said hoarsely. He lifted her and laid her on the bed. The sight of her sprawled there, half naked, was better than any fantasy he'd ever dreamed up.

He put one knee between her thighs.

"No fair," she murmured. "Your shirt has to go, too."

He fumbled with the damn buttons, popping one off before the shirt joined hers on the floor. He kicked off his boots, too, and peeled off the heavy socks he wore underneath. She'd already dropped her Swedish clogs on the floor, but he took care of her socks. Her feet were narrow with a high arch, and her toes curled in shyness.

He was smiling when he kneeled atop Renee. "You have sexy feet."

"They're…they're skinny!" she protested.

"At least you don't have hairs on your toes, like I do."

She giggled, then sighed when he nuzzled her breast. By the time he drew it into his mouth, she was arching up and whimpering. She didn't even seem to notice when he unsnapped the waistband of her jeans and eased down the zipper.

Her stomach quivered as his hand slipped inside her cotton panties, and her legs tried to tighten once she realized what he was up to, but then she had to cry out when he cupped her and rubbed gently.

He didn't dare take off his own jeans; he'd have been on her like a stallion on a mare in heat. The tight denim curbed him, kept him sane. Let him caress her and tell her how gorgeous she was and taste her breasts and kiss her smooth flat belly, and finally pull down her jeans and panties to reveal narrow hips and a silky vee of golden hair. She tried to cover herself there, too, but he only set her hand on his chest and stroked her thighs and tried not to picture himself between them.

She either didn't have the nerve to touch him, or didn't know he might like it, for which he was thankful. If she'd run her fingers down the painful bulge in the front of his jeans, he'd have reacted like a sixteen-year-old during his first sexual experience. And, damn, he wanted to be inside her before he lost it.

He teased and played and rubbed until her thighs parted and her hips rose and fell and she made urgent sounds that included his name.

"Daniel. Oh, Daniel! Oh, please." Her voice rose in what seemed a bewildered question. "Daniel?"

He pulled away from her just long enough to unbutton his jeans and rip them off. Renee came back to herself, rolling her eyes like a spooked horse, and he had to grit his teeth and hold on a little longer as he soothed her back to mindless wanting.

The next time she arched upward, he pushed inside her. Slowly, a fraction of an inch at a time, easing back, then forward. Nothing in his life had ever felt as good as this did, or as exquisitely frustrating. Damn near every muscle in his body locked with the effort not to thrust hard and fast, as deep as her lost memories.

Don't scare her. Don't hurt her.

He pulled back, waited until her hands clutched at him and she pushed upward herself.

She trusted him. He could endure anything.

"That's it, love," he whispered. "That's it. Just like that."

Her glazed eyes held his. "Daniel."

"You feel so good."

"Please."

He thrust. Felt the resistance, heard the rattle of her breath. But at last, at last, he was buried completely, part of her.

"I'm sorry, I'm sorry, I'm sorry," he groaned, even as he couldn't stop moving, had to retreat, push back, do it all over again.

She gave a hiccuping sigh, then, incredibly, smiled. "Don't be. Oh, Daniel."

She was there, moving with him, whimpering again, saying his name as if he could give her the world.

Slowly. Wait.

Her voice became puzzled, then frantic, as the need built and built and she didn't know what to do with it. But he did, moving as deliberately as he could make himself, holding back, waiting. Until her body squeezed around him and she cried his name one more time with all the wonder and joy a man in love needed. And then he convulsed inside her, pleasure blinding him and deafening him. It was like dying and being reborn.

Not sex. Love.

RENEE LAY CUDDLED against Daniel, her head on his shoulder, his arm wrapped snugly around her. His heartbeat drummed, slow and heavy, beneath her ear. One of her legs tangled wantonly with his, which felt coarse with hair. She'd dreamed of this, without knowing what it would really be like. It was…so *physical,* so sensual, so sweaty. And, oh, so glorious.

But scary, too. She didn't know him that well. And yet she'd let him see parts of her she'd never even taken a good look at herself. He'd touched her in shocking ways.

What was worse, she'd been noisy, she knew she had. The embarrassing knowledge prickled on her nerve endings.

Panic edged its way into her consciousness. Oh, Lord, what had she done? What must he think of her now? She'd practically thrown herself at him.

Had he really wanted her, or had it all been a big act to keep her away from the Triple B? Her humiliation reached a peak when she thought about how she'd put him on the spot. *Make love to me,* she'd said. *Will you stay tonight?* What could he do?

Her cheeks felt so hot, it was a wonder she wasn't burning him. Sizzling those tiny chest hairs that tickled at her nose. She prayed he couldn't see her face.

Before, she'd always been secure in her dignity. Now she felt stupidly vulnerable, stripped bare in more than one way. She hated knowing she'd made a fool of herself. Begging him to stay. Screeching like…like some cat in heat, just because what he was doing felt good.

He probably hadn't even enjoyed himself.

An image flickered into her mind, and she backed off. Well, she guessed he had enjoyed himself, sort of; she knew at least that he'd…*satisfied himself.*

Mealymouth, Renee thought scornfully, not for the first time. Some tough cop she was. She couldn't even use the words so common every thirteen-year-old used them without a second thought!

Daniel's hand moved, sliding up her back in a long, slow caress. Renee stiffened.

"Hey," he said softly. "I thought you were asleep."

Good excuse. "Mmm," she murmured. Could she turn away from him as if it were a natural shift, something a sleeping person did unconsciously? He wouldn't feel as if he could leave as long as she was hanging on him like a leech.

Renee lay still, breathing slow and deep, until she felt his muscles go lax again. He must have lifted his head from the pillow to look at her, and now he was lying back again. She gave it a minute or two, then sighed and burrowed her head as if seeking a more comfortable position. Finally, she just rolled away, hoping he would release her.

Smooth move, except she rolled herself right off the bed. Renee hit the floor with a bump and a shriek.

Daniel jackknifed up. "Are you all right?"

Renee stared up at him, horribly aware of how ridiculous she looked sitting naked on the floor.

"I'm not hurt, if that's what you mean!" she snapped.

His face worked. Had she offended him? Then, indignant, she realized he was trying hard not to laugh. "I guess—" his voice was muffled with the effort "—I was wrong. Your bed is too narrow."

He looked good, lying there on his side, dark hair ruffled, blue eyes bright with laughter, a grin warming a face that was often too impassive. His shoulders were sleek, smooth skin over muscles that rippled as he laughed. Hips narrow, belly flat, thighs powerful. And what lay in between… Renee gulped. She hadn't really looked earlier. In fact, she'd squeezed her eyes shut tight so that she wouldn't!

It wasn't as if she didn't know what a man had between his legs. She and Abby had even gone to a porno movie once, feeling embarrassed but daring. It had been kind of disgusting, but…interesting.

Something up on the movie screen was one thing, though, and in real life another. It suddenly struck her: there was a naked man in her bedroom. In her *bed*. Right before having wild sex with him, she'd gutted the living room. Flung her father's books out in the slushy snow. Splintered his gun cabinet. If she went downstairs right this minute, she'd be walking on plywood.

Had she gone completely nuts?

"Learned anything?" Daniel asked.

She came to. "What?"

Humor and something more sensual roughened his voice. "You've been studying me real hard."

Studying? Oh, God. She'd been staring this whole time right at him. At his…

She swallowed. His penis wasn't limp anymore. Before her very eyes, it was changing. Thickening, lengthening.

"I…" Her throat clogged. "You're…"

He glanced down. "Yes. I am."

"Why?"

"I like you looking at me," he said simply.

"Oh." Now she felt even more foolish. "But we just…"

"Yeah. We did."

Was he laughing at her? she wondered suspiciously.

But his voice stayed grave. "We could again. If you'd like."

Warmth blossomed in her belly even as her mouth went dry. The first time, she hadn't been thinking. She'd been swept along by her sense of triumph, of freedom, of empowerment. But now…well, it was like waking up with a hangover. Totally stone-cold sober. Afterward, she'd have no excuse for her behavior.

"You can't stay the night," she blurted. "There's not enough room for both of us in my bed."

His mouth quirked. "No kidding."

She remembered that she was still sitting on the floor. But standing in front of him would be even more embarrassing.

"I'm not sure…"

His smile vanished. "That you want me here?"

"No! I didn't mean that!" Yes, she did, but at the same time, she didn't. A normally resolute person, she'd never been so rattled in her life.

"No?" The grooves in his cheeks deepened. "Then why don't you come back up here?"

"I..." She stared at his outstretched hand, frozen in indecision.

Into her mind flashed, *Oh, why not?* At least this time *he* was the one doing the asking. And, heck, if this turned out to be her only fling, she might as well make it a good one.

Eyes locked with his, she rose slowly to her feet. His gaze lowered, traveled slowly over her body, and her skin shivered at the passage as if the touch was physical.

"You're beautiful," he said hoarsely. "Wondering what you looked like without clothes has been driving me crazy."

She wanted to believe him wholeheartedly. His eyes said she could, but he was basically a kind man, one who'd lie under these circumstances. She'd never driven any man crazy before. Why would her effect on him be any different?

But tonight, just tonight, she would pretend. She would stretch, and revel in the hot awareness in his eyes. She would smile—yes, just like that—and sit next to him on the bed and wriggle her hips a little and pretend she didn't know she was pressing against him *there*. And maybe, oh, maybe, she would even wrap her hand around him, see if the skin felt as satiny as it looked, feel him quiver, those thick blood veins pulse.

"You don't look so bad yourself," she said throatily, like Rita Hayworth in an old movie, and curled one foot under herself as she sat on the bed. She stroked his chest, just for starters, and felt the groan rising from deep inside him. Hey, she wasn't doing half-bad.

Even if it was just pretend.

ABBY STOOD in the middle of the living room and stared, rotating slowly as if to take in the magnitude of what she was seeing. Finally she shook her head. "When did you do this?"

"Last night."

Seeing it through her sister's eyes, Renee was shocked afresh at what she'd done. She had lived in this house all her life, and the basic decor had never changed. Now she felt as if she'd wandered into a house under construction: raw, unfamiliar, uninhabited.

"Why?" her sister asked in genuine puzzlement.

It was fun was one possible explanation. *I was exorcising Dad's ghost* was another.

Renee took a breath. "I'm going to remodel. Paint all the woodwork white. Buy a new couch. New carpet." She gestured. "Teal, I think. Wouldn't that be pretty?"

Now Abby swung to face her. "But...are you planning to stay in the house?"

She had every right to want her share of the money from the sale of the house. To her credit, she'd been patient with Renee, and now she sounded disturbed, not angry.

"No-o," Renee said slowly. "I thought...well, that this would make it sell faster. And maybe make it easier for me to leave. It won't be *home* the same way. Does that make sense?"

"No." Abby's voice was flat. "Nothing you've

done lately has made sense. You hated Dad—so why didn't you move out years ago? You hate the house, and we should have sold it this summer while the market was decent. It's not vacation house material, so it won't appeal to the skiers. Now we might as well not bother to put it on the market until May! You're irritating your boss because you can't get a few dirty old bones off your mind. You don't date, you don't have friends…'' Abby gave her a look. "And it's not hard to see why. I mean, jeez, Renee, move on."

A sickening sense of betrayal hit Renee in the stomach, a fist of disbelief. "You don't like me very well, do you?"

Abby gave a careless shrug. "Don't be ridiculous. I'm your sister. Can't I tell you what I really think?"

Struggling to keep her voice even, Renee said, "Obviously, you can. You just did."

Abby cocked her head to one side. "You're mad, aren't you?"

"No." Hurt, not mad. Stunned. And chilled by her sister's emotionless expression. Either Abby didn't realize how much she'd revealed, or she didn't care.

"Good." Abby turned away to survey the bare room again. "Do you want company when you go shopping for carpet and furniture?"

"I suppose. I don't know. Maybe Saturday."

"Well…call me. Okay?"

Renee didn't say anything. Abby took one last look around, shook her head, rolled her eyes, and left. Renee fled into the kitchen to curl up in her easy chair in the dining nook. Her refuge.

Her sense of triumph was flattened. She'd wanted Abby to laugh and rejoice in what she'd done. She'd wanted to tell her sister about last night, about Daniel and the way he'd made her feel. About her cowardice afterward, when she'd pretended to be asleep when he got dressed and departed, about ignoring his phone messages today, about letting the phone ring only half an hour ago, though she knew it must be him.

But now she knew that her sister—her only remaining family—wouldn't have sympathized, wouldn't have understood. Inside, she would have scorned. She would have believed there was something wrong with Renee, who had never been able to deal with either their father or boys with Abby's insouciance.

Renee squeezed her eyes shut and hugged her knees. Was she so terribly neurotic?

She'd been doing fine until recently. Until Lotto brought home those bones, and they came to symbolize all the losses, all the mysteries, in her life. So many emotions had surfaced since then: grief and anger most of all.

She'd never let herself feel them before. Not until now, when it was safe. When she wouldn't be punished with her father's heavy hand or by being shut out emotionally.

Maybe she *needed* to feel all these extremes, everything she'd shut down all these years. Maybe the fact that she was letting herself meant that she was healing.

Maybe Abby didn't understand because she had

grieved. After all, she'd been much younger when their mother left.

Or maybe, Renee thought with a twinge of unease, Abby, who didn't seem to let herself feel much of anything, was the one who needed help.

The phone shrilled again. Renee's head jerked up. As the ring stabbed at her, over and over again, she stared at the wall-hung telephone, fighting the urge to pick up the receiver, wanting to and afraid to at the same time.

Tomorrow, she promised herself. She'd talk to him then. When she decided what tack to take. How to be casual, friendly, flirtatious. How to hide what she really felt.

Because she'd discovered that among her tumult of emotions was love. She wasn't a casual person. She'd never made love with a man before because she'd never felt what she did now. And she had no idea how Daniel felt about *her*.

And she had no idea what would happen when he discovered that she wouldn't give up, that she had to find out who those bones had belonged to. As confused as she was, she understood this much: her quest was part of putting herself back together. She couldn't "move on," as her sister had so disdainfully put it, until she'd accomplished this one thing.

The one Daniel had begged her to let go.

The answering machine picked up at last. The caller didn't leave a message. Dry-eyed, Renee bowed her head against her knees.

It wasn't fair. How could he ask this of her? Why couldn't she have fallen in love with some other man? Why did it all have to happen now, before she was ready?

CHAPTER TEN

AFTER SENDING DANIEL on his way, Shirley started in on the dirty dishes. It had been nice having Mary and Caleb here, she reflected, but it was good to have the house to herself again. Daniel and she, they hadn't used that many dishes. Think of the pile if there'd been two more at the table tonight!

She paused, hands in hot soapy dishwater, and looked at her reflection through the steam fogging the window above the sink.

She almost wished she hadn't suggested Daniel come for dinner tonight. First he'd said he had other plans, then tersely declared that he didn't after all.

Shirley could see her son's unhappiness and even knew some of the cause. Thanks to those bones, his faith in his father's worth was crumbling. *Like hers,* she'd been about to think, but that wasn't true. She knew why Matt had committed murder, if he had.

Oh, if only there was some way to find out for sure, without betraying him! But as far as she could see, there wasn't, so no point in thinking about it.

Daniel had more on his mind than just his father, though. Shirley could tell. It was that lady police officer. He'd fallen for her, and hard. Once upon a time he'd have told his own mother, but circumstances being what they were, he was keeping his mouth shut. But she knew. For one thing, Mary had mentioned that he was taking the policewoman to dinner.

Over the kitchen table this evening they'd talked about Lieutenant Renee Patton and her investigation. His voice caressed her name, but unhappiness showed bleakly in his eyes at the same time.

Last night Shirley hadn't been able to sleep, which was why she'd been up to see the headlights of his truck so late. Must've been two, three in the morning. She hadn't looked at the clock. Her Daniel never stayed out drinking to all hours, and he hadn't had a girlfriend in a while. He'd stomped out so darn mad yesterday, Shirley had known who he was after.

At the time she'd been hopeful he would talk Renee Patton into looking somewhere else for the killer. But at dinner Daniel hadn't sounded as if that was so. He'd suggested Shirley not talk to the police again without him there.

"And maybe an attorney," he'd suggested.

"An attorney?" Shirley repeated, not sure whether to be outraged or comforted by the idea. "They don't think *I* had anything to do with that man dying?"

"They think you know who did," he said bluntly, and she'd felt him waiting.

She *wanted* to tell him what had happened, but silence was a hard road to quit. And she still felt such shame and horror. Every time the memory of what had happened tried to slither up from the depth of her consciousness, her mind battled it back down, out of sight. She couldn't even bear to face the memory herself! How could she put it all into words?

But she hated to see Daniel so unhappy. What she didn't know was whether she'd make anything better by telling. She wanted to do what was right for her son, and for Matthew. She didn't care so much about herself; she'd face anything if she had to—and if it was the right thing to do. But what was right? she worried.

What would Matthew want her to do?

Tonight she'd pretended that she hadn't noticed her son was waiting for an answer. She chattered about some other thing and ignored the searching look he gave her and the small frown between his dark brows. He was near the spitting image of his father! Sometimes that resemblance gave her a turn, letting her think for just a moment...

But of course Matthew wasn't back, wouldn't ever come back. She was on her own now, so far as this kind of decision went. Shirley almost wished she was crazy enough to believe that Matthew could answer her questions.

Tonight, looking at her misty reflection in the kitchen window, she felt a stir of painful humor. Heck, maybe she could *make* herself that crazy! Maybe Matt's voice would come to her, if she begged him loud and long enough.

She shut her eyes, so as not to see her own face looking back at her.

Voice as insubstantial as the steam rising from the hot dishwater, Shirley murmured, "Oh, Matthew, tell me how to do what's right for Daniel."

WEARING ONLY JEANS, Daniel toweled his hair dry as he walked barefoot down the hall to the kitchen. More crappy weather. He'd been working horses for a couple hours before his foul mood and numb fingers sent him back up to the house. Ten minutes under the hot spray in the shower had brought painful feeling back to his fingers without doing a thing for his mood.

Why the hell wouldn't Renee return his phone calls? Had she hankered to experiment sexually, and now that she'd gotten what she wanted, she didn't know how to tell him *adios?*

But he just couldn't believe that. She was shy; that had to be it. He latched onto this explanation, though he wouldn't be able to hold on to it long. These past two days, his mind wouldn't stop worrying the problem of what had gone wrong, like a dog nipping at a horse's heels. Every time he satisfied himself that he understood her, his certainty would bounce loose, as if that horse had kicked him good and hard.

Coffee bubbled gently in the pot. Daniel tossed the towel over the back of a chair and grabbed a mug from the cupboard. He was taking the first sip when his gaze encountered the answering machine. The red light blinked once, hesitated, blinked again, and his heart went still.

Daniel swore aloud. She'd called while he was in the shower. Didn't it figure? Why hadn't he taken the cordless phone into the bathroom where he could hear it?

Almost reluctantly, he pressed the play button.

Probably wasn't her at all, he told himself without believing it for a second.

"Daniel, this is Renee." She sounded as if she were right there in the kitchen. He even heard the breath she took next. "I'm sorry I haven't called. Things at work…" She trailed off, as though even she realized how weak an explanation she was concocting. Then her voice strengthened, became formal. "I'm planning to come out and talk to your mother this morning. About eleven o'clock, in case you want to be there. Or you want an attorney representing her." Another pause, before she said in a rush, "This is something I have to do," and hung up.

Rage whistled through him like an icy north wind, and he wheeled to look at the clock. Ten-fifteen. If her call had come when he first got in the shower, she'd given exactly one hour's notice.

No wonder she hadn't called before! She'd been avoiding him because she wanted to spring another little surprise. She'd known damn well he would ask what her intentions were, and she hadn't wanted to lie. She'd probably hoped he wouldn't get this message until she'd been and gone, his mother in handcuffs if Renee had her way, he thought viciously.

Well, she'd made a big mistake, Daniel vowed. He wasn't letting her near his mother.

Coffee forgotten, he stalked back down the hall. In his bedroom he yanked on thick socks and boots, buttoned up a flannel shirt and grabbed a wool fisherman's sweater. He knew damn well she wouldn't take his call if he phoned, and he didn't dare set out to town to intercept her, in case she was early and took a different route than he guessed at.

He turned the heater in his pickup on full blast, and roared down the curving driveway from his place to meet the main ranch road. No sign of a police car yet in front of his mother's; Renee hadn't jumped the gun that much. Without stopping he turned right and sped the half mile to the Triple B gates, where he abruptly swerved and slammed on the brakes. The pickup bucked and slithered on the cinders, but came to a stop sideways. Blocking the way onto his property.

She'd better have a warrant if she thought she was going to get by him.

He waited, leaving the engine running for the heat and regretting the mug of coffee left sitting on the kitchen counter. 10:30 came and went. 10:40. He turned on the radio and George Strait's twangy voice came on, singing about love and loss and memories. With a muttered curse Daniel punched the button and cut George off mid-word.

10:55. What if she didn't come? He'd feel like a fool sitting here in the middle of his driveway. He hadn't called his mother and hadn't checked to see if her car was here. She wouldn't have gone to town to meet Renee without telling him, would she?

11:02. Daniel drummed his fingers on the steering wheel. Simmering anger was all that held boredom at bay. Anger, and the memories of her that kept playing in his mind: the long milk-pale line of her body as she arched her back in pleasure; the soft round weight of her breasts; her throaty cries; her hesitant kisses; the desperate need to tear out and throw away every physical manifestation of her father.

His fingers wrapped around the steering wheel so tightly his knuckles showed white. Nothing he knew or remembered about her, no touches, no doe-eyed looks, would weaken him today. By God, he *wanted* her to show up so he could tell her what he thought.

11:05. He lifted his head, and there was the 4x4 just turning into the Triple B, braking a nose away from his pickup.

He turned off the engine and shoved open his door. Jumping down, Daniel circled the bed of his pickup, strode to within a few feet of her door and waited, arms crossed.

Fiddling with something in there, she took her time before she climbed out to face him. Hell, for all he cared she'd called for backup. Uniformed, controlled, she said coolly, ''What's the meaning of this?''

''You have a warrant?'' he challenged.

''Your mother is not a suspect. She's helping me with my inquiries.''

''She's done helping.''

''She sent you out here?''

The way she looked at him with her gaze steady, not a flicker of remembrance or guilt or regret in her eyes, ate away at him. He didn't mean a damned thing to her. She was a cop, first and foremost; he'd apparently been a little fling, a boy-toy.

The answering ice in his voice was less slick; he wasn't as good at this. His voice could have scraped bare skin raw.

''This is my spread. I decide who's welcome.''

Her eyes narrowed. "You've decided not to cooperate in a murder investigation. Is that what you're telling me?"

He widened his stance, not looking away. "We've cooperated. My mother has told you everything she knows. You can't figure out who that poor bastard was, so you're harassing her. I can't let you do that."

Her nose was turning pink from the cold and she stamped her feet to keep the blood circulating. "She's my best source..."

"She's told you everything she knows," he said inflexibly.

He'd gotten to her. The icy veneer of a law enforcement officer cracked. Temper spotted her cheeks with red. "Come on! You don't believe that any more than I do! Your mother is lying through her teeth. She has been from day one!"

A scene flickered before his eyes: his mother keening in despair or grief, all because unidentified bones had been found on their land. Then her denial that they meant anything to her, that anything special had happened fifteen years before.

With a shake of his head, he shut down the projector. He had to believe his mother, protect her. She'd have told him the truth if she knew anything.

The doubt he couldn't quite suppress lent whip to his voice. "You *want* to think she's lying to excuse your incompetence!"

Renee thrust out her chin, hurt buried quickly beneath fury. "Maybe you're lying, too. Is that it? So tell me. Why'd you call us in the first place if you're hiding something?"

"Because I didn't know my local police department conducted witch hunts!" he snapped.

"Oh, that's the oldest excuse in the book!" she scoffed. "How can you live with yourself, shielding a murderer?"

Like George Strait's song, her words cut too close to the bone. The pressure in his chest became unbearable, and Daniel shouted, "My father's dead and buried! Why the hell are you so determined to brand him a murderer?"

The shock in her eyes could have been a reflection of his own. What had he just done? Maybe she never had suspected his father. If not, he'd opened a new door for her.

Sick with turmoil, he braced himself as she stared at him.

When Renee finally spoke, it was more quietly. Her tone held an odd note. Compassion?

"Do you really believe your father killed someone?"

Daniel kept his mouth clamped shut. Couldn't do anything else. Nothing in his life had ever seemed to matter as much as her question. And he was such a goddamned coward, he wouldn't answer it, even to himself.

He was afraid to.

Now the compassion, or maybe pity, was open on her face. She even reached out to him. "Wouldn't you really rather know?" she asked softly.

He closed his eyes to shut her out. "Why?" he asked gruffly. "Why can't you let it go?"

After the briefest of pauses, she said in a curiously flat voice, "I'm atoning for my sins."

He understood and despaired, because his most gut-wrenching fear had met head-on her most desperate need. Attraction, sex, friendship—God help him, *love*—had no place here.

Into the darkness came her voice. "You think about it." The touch on his cheek had no more substance than a snowflake, but was a hell of a lot warmer. "Call me," she said, and he heard her swallow. "This time, I'll pick up the phone."

Still he said nothing. After a moment he heard the crunch of her footsteps on the red cinders, the slam of the car door, the roar of the Bronco's engine. He opened his eyes at last, now that she was blurred by the windshield, and watched her back out.

He could not sacrifice his father's honor or his mother's peace of mind to further Renee's quest. What if Matthew Barnard was branded a murderer? He knew how his mother felt about his father—her love, and pride and constant, silent grief. What if everyone else condemned the man she'd spent her life loving?

Daniel let out a long ragged breath. Forget his mother. *He*'d spent his own life trying to live up to the man his father had been. If that had been a lie, it would be as if he'd spent years following the lines on a map, only to discover it was a fake, meant to deceive him; that all those years had been wasted.

He scrubbed his hands over his face. It felt…stiff. He didn't know how to move those muscles. How to smile or sneer. He was cold, down to his bones.

A groan rattled in his throat. He'd thought he could live with uncertainty, with the small quakes beneath the ground, so long as it didn't split open.

But now? Now, he wasn't so sure. Thanks to Renee Patton, he had a sickening feeling that he did need to know. One way or the other.

Whatever the cost.

RENEE MADE IT to the outskirts of town before a sob tore through her. Tears came in a hot, ugly cascade. She managed to pull over to the curb and yank on the emergency brake before she broke down completely.

She hadn't cried, not like this, in more years than she could remember. She didn't know how. The sobs just came, shaking her body, making it hard to breathe. Renee crossed her arms on the steering wheel, laid her forehead against them, and gave in to a force bigger than her.

New anguish and old piled atop each other. Looking in Daniel's eyes had been like seeing death. An end she'd brought on herself but would take back if she could. Why hadn't she known how much she loved him before it was too late?

Daniel! she cried. And then, *Meg, where are you? Why did you go?* And, *Mama, please stay!*

In as close to a fetal position as she could get, she cried for the emptiness in her life, for the people who'd left, and most of all for the man she'd driven away by her obsession with the past.

I love you. Come back! she begged, knowing she wouldn't get an answer, never had gotten one. Could she bear the loneliness?

With time the agony subsided, dulled, and the tears dried. Renee was left limp, face swollen, head aching, in emotional limbo. If she didn't open her eyes, she could imagine that she was floating in dark water. Utterly relaxed, almost peaceful, knowing only that she didn't want to be found.

But peace never lasted any more than tears did. A knock on the window jolted her back to life.

Renee lifted her head. Through puffy eyes she saw the fogged-up window and through it a face. A man with a red muffler wrapped around his neck was bent over peering in at her.

"Are you all right?" he called.

She stared stupidly. *Was* she all right? She thought that one over. Not really, she finally concluded. But, in a curious way, she was better than she'd been before the tears. All these years, she'd known a tight feeling in her chest, like a watch wound so much it quit working, the tension more than it—more than *she*—could bear.

The tightness was gone now. Instead, her chest hurt. But she also felt relaxed.

So... She rolled down her window a few inches. "Yeah. I'm okay. Thanks for asking."

The stranger's worried frown didn't go away. Her face must look like a drunkard's after a bar brawl.

"It was personal news," she explained reluctantly. "It just hit me. Nothing to do with the job. I hope you won't tell anyone that cops cry."

His frown eased; he almost smiled. "It'll be our secret. As long as you don't tell anyone that ambulance chasers do, too."

She watched him walk away, a tall man in a beautifully cut dark suit, the red muffler an incongruously human note. She imagined a wife winding it lovingly around his neck. Or maybe a daughter had knit it for him. She wondered what kind of law he practiced. If they met in court, she suspected he'd do no more than give her a small, acknowledging nod. *You're human. I'm human.*

The brief contact, the knowledge people did care, gave her the courage to look in the rearview mirror.

"Aagh!"

She had to go home before she went back to the station. A sink full of cold water, maybe a few ice cubes thrown in, might reduce the puffiness. A little makeup wouldn't hurt.

She turned up the defroster, released the emergency brake and checked for oncoming traffic. As she drove, the ache whispered at her—*Oh, Daniel!*—but she thought she could live with it, at least long enough to decide what was most important: settling with her past or working toward a future.

BACK AT THE STATION she found chaos. Members of the S.W.A.T. team had suited up in their dark uniforms and bulletproof vests and were running for their cars. The moment she stepped in the back door, she heard Jack bellowing down the hall.

"God damn it, you can't hesitate! What'd they teach you at the academy? To *negotiate?*" He spit out the last word as if it were loathsome.

Renee stopped in the door of his office, taking in the sight of Jack Murray, hands flat on his desk as he leaned menacingly forward. The young patrolman stood with his shoulders square, but a frightened tic played piano up and down his jaw. Though she could see only his back, Renee knew the guy: twenty-two years old, smart, shy and determined to be a good cop. What had he done that was so terrible?

"What's happening?" she asked.

Jack turned his glower onto her. "Where the hell have *you* been?"

"Triple B."

He swore. "You're still wasting time on that?"

He'd known perfectly well she was, but under the circumstances she forgave him the irritation.

"What happened?" she repeated.

"Domestic disturbance that's turned into a hostage situation." He cast a look of dislike at the patrolman. "Thanks to Keller here."

"Sir, I felt…"

"I don't give a damn what you felt. What you should have *done* was slapped the bastard in handcuffs."

Patrolman Keller tried again. "I thought I could calm him. Defuse his anger."

Jack smacked his desk. Renee winced along with Keller.

"Defuse, hell!" Jack snapped. "That's a woman's tactic. Patton here might have to try that if she was too outsized. But you…you're a man, remember?"

Keller opened his mouth, thought better of it, and said only, "Yes, sir."

"Ah, jeez." Jack gestured disgustedly. "Go on. Out of here."

Renee waited until the door shut behind the patrolman. "You were a little hard on him," she said mildly. "And what's this 'be a man' crap?"

He went still. "Who says it's crap?"

She leaned back against the door frame. "I do."

Jack's eyebrows shot up. He wasn't used to her challenging him. She'd been inhibited by the crush she'd had on him. By the fact that he held her father's job.

To her surprise, he thought about getting angry but chose not to. "You know I respect your police work," he said gruffly. "I'm just trying to build some spine in this kid. Situation's ugly from the get-go. The husband's throwing furniture, tells Keller to butt out, backhands the wife when she grabs his arm. So Keller decides to take up counseling." Jack shook his head. "Instead of the bastard being behind bars where he ought to be, he's got a gun to his wife's head and he's threatening to kill their baby, too."

Renee digested the story. Bulling in and making the arrest sounded easier, she knew from experience, than it would have been in practice. Usually talking helped. Killed time, until the anger cooled, the booze wore off. Maybe until the wife grabbed the baby and slipped out. But that was her style. Jack's was to bounce the husband around a little, smack him against the wall and cuff him. He didn't cross the line to brutality, but he believed in coming down hard on criminals.

This time... Well, she just didn't know.

"Did you call in a negotiator?" she asked.

He was shrugging into his own bulletproof vest. "Cunningham," he said with a grimace. "He ought to be able to distract the guy while we go in the back."

"He's had good training." Renee kept her tone

nonjudgmental, even amiable. "Give him a chance to work."

"If I see a chance to do *my* job, I'm going to take it," Jack said curtly. "You're in charge here." He brushed past her and was gone.

Renee stayed where she was, in the silence of his office, musing on the oddities of life. Man's man that he was, Jack and the drunken husband were flip sides of a coin. Both thought a man should act, be physical; that talk was a waste of time. Difference was, Jack acted in defense of the vulnerable instead of abusing them.

You could have said the same about her father. Except that at home, he *had* abused his wife and daughters. He'd only hidden his ugly side with the collusion of Renee and her sisters, who dreamed up excuses for every bruise and even a few broken bones. Too bad *they* hadn't had the guts to act. Maybe then Jack Murray wouldn't have spent his career trying to win Chief Patton's approval. Maybe then he'd give the hostage negotiator a chance today, instead of emulating how his predecessor would have handled the same situation.

Would she and her sisters have been believed? she wondered.

She left Jack's office and went down the hall to her own. Heck, she thought with a new feeling of liberation, maybe she should find out. Once Jack was back from proving how a "man" did his job, she just might tell him everything Meg apparently hadn't mentioned about her father all those years back, when she and Jack had been high school sweethearts. He might be real interested to know why Meg had left town and never come back.

Renee sank down in her chair and swiveled it so that she could stare moodily out the small window across ten feet of space to the brick building next door.

You never know, she thought. Jack might turn out to be man enough to rethink his life.

Question was, could she do the same for her own?

CHAPTER ELEVEN

DANIEL URGED his gelding into an easy lope. Lotto had disappeared ahead, although every now and again Daniel heard a deep woof or caught a glimpse of a yellow tail wagging furiously behind a rock. He'd trailered Keegan, a fiery bay, up to Blue Lake, nestled at the feet of the Sisters. The trail, which circled the crystal clear mountain lake, was a favorite of his, a good place to think.

At this time of year the small parking lot at the trailhead was deserted except for his rig. Patches of snow replaced wildflowers in the open meadows, but the pungent scent of the pines was the same, and under a cold blue sky the lake water was as startling an azure as always and as clear. Fish darted, shadows among the rocks he could see several feet down. Above the meadow of thin grass reared a talus, boulders strewn like a kid's blocks after little sister had destroyed his tower.

The gelding moved at an easy jog and obliged with a lope whenever the trail was clear of snow and Daniel squeezed his legs. This beat endlessly circling an arena any day.

His thoughts here were more direct, less repetitive. In the arena, his mind tended to circle the same way, over and over a problem until he was dizzy and no further ahead than he'd been to start with.

Could he face knowing the truth? Did he want to find out for sure that his father had killed someone? Daniel asked himself. He shook his head in disbelief. Thinking about the man his dad had been, Daniel couldn't see it any more than he'd been able to a week ago. Damn it, Matt Barnard had been a good man!

Maybe he'd killed because he had to. It could be that, if he'd done the unthinkable, it was for a reason Daniel could understand. Daniel's mother had continued to respect and love her husband despite fearing—or *knowing*—what he'd done.

The time Daniel was unjustly blamed for starting a fight at school, his dad had listened carefully to him before he came to any conclusions. He hadn't jumped based on someone else's word or his own anger or fears. He'd given his son the benefit of the doubt.

Put it that way, and Daniel figured he owed his father the same.

He wasn't even sure why he'd been running scared. Smugness, maybe; he didn't want to believe his family was less than perfect. The Barnards had a solid reputation. They were old-timers in this community, respected. He admitted to himself that he even irrationally resented his grandfather vanishing the way he had, because afterward there had been whispers mixed with the pity and compassion. He liked having people look up to him. Was that such a sin?

The real question was, would he somehow be less

of a man if it turned out his father had committed a terrible crime? Were the values Matt Barnard had taught his son any less worth living for, because the man who'd taught them had once violated his own beliefs?

Look at Renee, Daniel told himself. Her mother had deserted her kids, her father had been an animal. Renee wasn't like either of her parents.

The saddle leather creaked as Keegan gathered his haunches and scrambled up a rocky incline made slick by snow. Automatically Daniel shifted his weight to help the horse.

He felt stupid, having the most basic of self-knowledge seem like a revelation straight from heaven.

Because he'd finally figured out that he didn't have to be who his father was. He'd rather remember him with respect and admiration, but if it turned out he couldn't, that didn't have to diminish his own self-worth.

What he didn't know was whether his mother felt so tied to her husband that she wouldn't agree. Or had she only been trying to protect Daniel and Mary from having to know their father had done something awful?

He guessed there was only one way to find out.

She didn't look real happy to see him when he went by after unloading the gelding and rubbing him down. Daniel had knocked and gone right on in.

The vacuum cleaner was running, but his mother turned it off when she saw him. "Daniel! What are you doing here in the middle of the afternoon?"

She didn't sound annoyed or even scared. *Wary* was closer to the mark.

"I wanted to talk to you," he said. "Can we sit down?"

"Well..." She drew out the word, every inch grudging. "I suppose so." His mother straightened some books in the case, then bent to unplug the vacuum cleaner and slowly rewound the cord. "Is something wrong?"

"I don't know." Daniel made himself sit, though he itched to pace. "I want you to tell me."

She perched on a chair as if ready to spring up at any second. Her gaze met his with obvious reluctance. "What on earth are you talking about?" she asked, but without any real indignation or surprise.

"Mom..." He half rose, made himself settle back down. "What happened fifteen years ago? Did it have anything to do with Dad?"

He'd have sworn her cheeks blanched; he knew she swallowed.

But she marshaled herself enough to protest, "Are you going to start harping on this like that police officer, just because I was a fool and got upset at the idea of those bones out there? I thought you believed me."

"I *wanted* to believe you," he corrected her. "Probably for the same reasons you don't want to admit anything happened. But something did. I'm convinced of that. And I've decided I'd rather know what it was than spend the rest of my life wondering."

"Wondering," his mother said slowly, pure pain in her eyes, "is something you can put out of your head. Knowing..." Her mouth twisted. "Well, I'm not so sure once you *know* that you can ever forget. Maybe we're better off the way we are."

Not letting himself heed the lure she had thrown out, he leaned forward, seizing instead on the hope. "So you don't know for sure that Dad did anything."

The breath she released seemed to rack her body like a shudder contained for too long. "Daniel." With words and eyes both, she pleaded with him. "Are you sure you want to do this? Your father was a fine man. Can't we just leave it at that?"

"You're right. He was. And I have a hard time believing he would have done anything I couldn't understand or forgive him for."

"He was so angry..." Shivering again, she looked right through Daniel, seeing another man, another time.

Daniel moved swiftly, squatting in front of her and taking her hands. "Angry about what?"

"I..." She came back from the past and focused on him, though not without a struggle that squeezed his heart. "Are you going to tell that policewoman?"

"I think we should," he said carefully. "She's not going to let up until we do. She came again this morning. I headed her off, but I can't forever."

His mother's eyes searched his. "You like her, don't you?"

"Yes, but that's not why..." He stopped, wanting to be honest. A brief self-examination allowed him to continue more strongly. "Mom, you and I both know Dad would have been the first to cooperate with the police investigating a crime. How would he have felt about our covering up something that might be important? Anyway, who are we protecting? Dad's dead. Mostly Renee wants to know the name of the man who died. If we can help her find out, we should.''

He was ashamed that it had taken him this long to come to the ethical conclusion. Whether Renee and he had any future, he didn't know. But he should have been helping out, not setting up roadblocks.

His mother bowed her head. She'd be fifty-four next month, but right now she could have been ten years older. Her hair had been turning silver fast lately, either because it was time or because she'd quit doing something to it, he wasn't sure. Worry had leached the pink from her skin; sleeplessness had left crepey bags under her eyes and a tremor to her hands.

Daniel felt a quiver of fear. What was all this doing to her? Would it get better or worse once the whole story came out?

Ruefully he said, ''That was easy for me to decide, wasn't it? I'm sorry, Mom.''

She lifted her head, squared her shoulders and countered with surprising resolution, ''No, you were right. Even back then, I *was* the one who didn't want anybody to know. I wouldn't even talk about it with your father. He wanted to go to the police.''

That clutch of fear gripped harder and Daniel's voice became gritty. ''Mom... What didn't you want anybody to know? *What happened?*''

''If you don't mind,'' she said with dignity, gently

pulling her hands free from his, "I'd rather tell the story only once. Why don't you call your Officer Patton and see when she can come out here. Don't make her feel as though she has to rush." She rose to her feet. "It's not as if I'm going anywhere."

He stood, too. "Are you all right?"

"Why wouldn't I be?" She held herself straight, but resignation tugged at the lines of her face. She looked vaguely around. "Now, I really should finish the vacuuming. Especially with company coming."

"Yeah, okay." Daniel hesitated. "Mom, you could tell it all to me and I could pass the story on to Renee. That wouldn't be as hard on you."

"You know she wouldn't be satisfied with that. And—" her composure cracked "—I really don't think I can bear to do this more than once. Please." She turned blindly away. "Let me get back to… to…"

He touched her arm, but she shrank away, shutting him out. Her own son.

Daniel's fingers curled into a fist and he let his hand drop to his side. He stood there for a moment, feeling helpless, and then turned and abruptly left. She wanted to be alone. He had to respect that.

Striding along the ranch road toward the barn— no, he'd go home to make this call—Daniel hoped like hell Renee was free to come right out. He felt sick with the need to know what terrible thing his father had done and his mother had kept secret for half her son's lifetime.

And now that he'd done this, forced his mother to admit to something she hadn't been sure she could bear to bring to the light of day, he wanted it over with.

What scared the hell out of him was wondering whether they'd ever be able to go back to the way they'd been.

"I HOPE YOU DIDN'T MISS dinner," Shirley fussed. "I told Daniel there wasn't any hurry. And I suppose he insisted you turn on your siren and rush right out here, didn't he? I could throw together some soup or sandwiches..."

"Thank you, Mrs. Barnard," the young policewoman said. "But I'm not hungry yet. I had a late lunch."

She was pretty, this woman Daniel looked at with such hunger and pain. Thin and strong, but also fragile. But not like china that shattered if you even knocked it against a crystal glass. More like those racehorses capable of such thundering speed and power, but with long skinny legs so vulnerable to snapping under the force of their own momentum.

Of course, pretty was only what made a man look in the first place. To break his heart, a woman needed to have more.

Well, it worked the other way around, too. Matt's broad shoulders and blue eyes had caught Shirley's fancy right away, the first time he came into the library where she worked. And then his smile, and the way he frowned, intent but also puzzled, over the books. And the way his big hands seemed clumsy turning the pages, but were so precise and strong and sure when he handled a horse. Or when he touched her, once she was ready. What got to her was his kindness and his laughter and his gentleness.

She was never quite sure why he'd fallen in love with her, or loved her so single-mindedly all those years. Some men had a wandering eye when their wives were pregnant, but not her Matt. Oh, no! He never saw any woman but her once they met, not even when... Though she knew she had to think about it, that the time had come, she shied away from the memory.

Maybe, she told herself hurriedly, it was knowing she loved him so completely, no part of her held in reserve, that Matt couldn't resist. How often did a person have a chance to be loved like that? Some people never did, she guessed.

"Mom." Daniel sat on the arm of the couch, beside her, his hand resting on her shoulder. "I think Renee is ready."

"Coffee," Shirley suggested, starting to rise. "I could at least get you a cup of coffee. It would only take a minute."

Daniel frowned at her and said sternly, "Mom."

But Renee Patton smiled as if she understood. "That sounds good. Can I help?"

"No, no. You just sit here and chat to Daniel." Shirley ignored his hand, which fell away from her once she stood, although she could tell he wanted to push her back down and make her talk as if she were a child wanting to slip away from explaining why she'd lied to her parents about something or other.

From the kitchen she heard their voices, her son's sharp and aggressive, the woman's a hushed mur-

mur. The softness of Renee Patton's answers comforted Shirley, helping her feel she was doing the right thing by telling what happened. Matt would agree, she believed; Daniel had talked most about the morality of it, but if her telling cleared the way for him to win the woman he loved, that was what Shirley cared about.

Maybe that was a flaw in her, putting her family first, above any kind of noble truth, but it was a woman's flaw, she thought, and maybe not such a bad thing, because a mother had to want to protect her children no matter what, didn't she?

"Matt," she whispered, "you do understand, don't you?"

No ghostly hand patted her shoulder, no lips brushed her cheek, but she felt no sense of protest, either. If Matt was there, watching over her, he was leaving this one to her.

Shirley carried the tray of coffee cups along with the sugar and creamer back to the living room. Daniel ignored it, but Renee smiled her thanks and stirred a dash of cream and half a teaspoon of sugar into her cup. Shirley did the same to hers, although she had no real interest in drinking the stuff right now; a cup of warm milk might have suited her more under the circumstances!

The policewoman sipped the coffee, set it down on the coaster and placed her notebook on her knee. With a pen poised above it, she said, "Whenever you're ready, Mrs. Barnard."

"Shirley."

"Shirley," she repeated, smiling again, as

friendly as can be and with no sign that she was insincere.

"Well." Hand trembling, Shirley set down her cup before the hot liquid spilled over her legs. "I think it's possible that T. J. Baxter is the one who died here." She hated even saying his name!

Something flickered in Renee Patton's eyes. "And why do you believe that?" she asked.

How hard it was to say! Shirley looked away from them both, the worry on her son's face, the keen interest and compassion on the policewoman's. She took a deep breath and said baldly, "You see, he raped me."

Daniel swore and came to his feet; Renee motioned him to sit down again.

"So it wasn't Mary he was interested in."

Goose bumps rose on Shirley's arms at the very thought. "Afterward, that was the one thing that really scared me," she confessed, "but when I talked to her I could tell nothing had happened. She was only twelve, you know, and really still a little girl. She couldn't have hidden such a thing. Oh, if he'd done that...!" Why, she would have killed him herself, and suffered no guilt at all! she thought fiercely.

"I remember the way he looked at you and smiled," Daniel said suddenly, his voice raw. "I didn't like it."

"He was always polite and proper when Matt was around," Shirley said. "If Matt had seen him smiling and...well, he would have fired him just like that! But I thought it was just Mr. Baxter's way with all women. You know? There's a kind of man who doesn't know how to talk to a woman without flirting. He...he made me uncomfortable, but didn't scare me. I never dreamed..." She shuddered to a stop.

Daniel briefly squeezed her hand. "How could you?"

"You never told your husband?" Renee Patton asked.

With her eyes, Shirley begged for understanding from the other woman. "Matt couldn't believe that I hadn't complained about the flirting. But I knew my husband would fire him, and I thought he was harmless. He was good with horses, Matt kept saying he was one of the best, and I didn't like being responsible..." She tried again. "It didn't seem as though he should lose his job because he smiled a certain way at the boss's wife, or brushed against her." She felt Daniel stir restlessly and couldn't bring herself to look at him. "Afterward I knew I should have told, but..." Her fingernails bit painfully into her palms. "Oh, this is horrible to have to admit..."

"You were flattered." Renee spoke in a quiet voice that said she did understand. "Why is it horrible? He was a handsome man, you were in your thirties with teenage children. A woman likes to know she's attractive."

Shirley swallowed convulsively. Tears trickled down her cheeks. "It wasn't that he appealed to me. I never wanted any man but my Matthew. But it was nice to think I might still be pretty. Not that I encouraged him! I never did that!" She looked wildly from one to the other. They had to believe her; that was more important than anything!

"Of course you didn't, Mom." Daniel gripped her hand again, prying her fingernails away from her palm. "I know how you felt about Dad."

"Did Mr. Baxter ever make any advances?" Renee asked, tone gentle but clinical. "Did you ever have to say no?"

"He never…not once…" It was coming back to her now, the horror. She shut her eyes. "Not until that day."

"Will you tell us about it?"

She sighed. "Matt was away, trailering some horses he'd sold over to Springfield. I guess Mary and Daniel were at school. *He* came to the door. I opened it, never thinking a thing. He shoved the door open and just came in."

Shirley saw it, plain as day, her standing there with the door open a polite twelve inches, him putting a hand against it and pushing hard so she stumbled back. Once in, he shut the door behind him and locked it. At the solid *thunk* the dead bolt made, her blood had chilled.

"He said I was beautiful and he could tell my husband didn't appreciate me. He smiled and swaggered toward me—I'd backed up against the wall— and claimed I'd been smiling at him, too. He said, 'Today there's no jealous husband around.'" Terrified despite herself by something that was over and done with fifteen years ago, Shirley stared straight ahead and scarcely breathed.

She didn't see the policewoman move, but suddenly she was beside Shirley on the couch, holding her hand. "Would you like some water to drink?"

"No! No." Shirley squeezed Renee's hand. Her

son's comfort she couldn't accept right now, but another woman—well, that was different, although she didn't know why. She couldn't even look at Daniel. "I'd rather finish."

"Okay." Renee's smile was infinitely gentle. "Did you tell him to leave?"

"Over and over. He kept saying he knew I didn't mean it. He…he grabbed me and kissed me." She was shaking all over now, just remembering. "Not like Matt kissed me. Nothing like that. He hurt me. I could taste blood and…and whiskey, I think. He wasn't staggering drunk, but he'd been drinking, though it was the middle of the day."

"Alcohol may have given him courage to do something he'd only thought about until then," Renee suggested.

Her head had hurt, grinding against the wall; he'd mashed her lips with his and bitten them and thrust his tongue in… "And then he ripped my blouse off, just tore all the buttons, and my bra. I fought, but he hit me." Reliving the shock and pain, Shirley fell silent for a moment. "I couldn't even scream, he didn't let me. He just…threw me onto the floor and came down on top of me and…" Hot tears scalded her cheeks. She could not, would not, describe the terrible things that happened then. "Afterward," she said starkly, "he stood above me, buttoning his jeans, and said, 'That was good, baby,' and then he left."

Daniel made a convulsive movement beside her, but she still couldn't face him. A son shouldn't have to hear this kind of thing about his mother!

"What did you do?" Renee asked. "Did you call anyone?"

Shirley shook her head. "I just lay there for...I don't know, hours, I think. I was so cold, and I hurt so much, and I was so ashamed."

Renee's eyes held hers. "You were in shock. And all rape victims feel the shame, even though what happened isn't their fault."

"But I should have made it plainer I didn't like him looking at me the way he did." The tears were weaker now. "Or told Matt. If only I'd told my husband..." She clasped a hand across her mouth to hold in a sob.

Renee touched her cheek. "You know none of that's true, don't you?"

"Yes," Shirley whispered. "It was *him*. But still, I can't help thinking..."

"If I give you the address and phone number, will you go to a rape counselor? Let her talk to you about these feelings?"

"Her? It would be a woman?"

"Yes. Anne McWhirter. She's a friend of mine, though closer to your age. She was raped herself, as a teenager. Will you talk to her?"

Shirley nodded numbly.

"Good. Now, do you feel up to telling us the rest? What happened when your husband found out?"

"Yes." She felt drained, and almost peaceful. The worst was over. Though the blood on Matt had frightened her, part of her had hoped Mr. Baxter was dead. It was what had happened right out there in the front hall that she had been determined to forget.

A box of tissues appeared in front of her, held by

a man's hand. Daniel's. She took one and blew her nose. "Thank you."

He kissed the top of her head but said nothing, for which she was grateful.

She took a deep breath and continued. "It got dark and I crawled upstairs. I ran a bath and sat in it for a long time, until I was cold again. So I let the water out and ran more hot. I shampooed my hair and washed myself. I kept forgetting whether I already had and would do it again. The next day, I saw that I'd used half the bottle of shampoo. And my hair wasn't even dirty. But I *felt* dirty."

"Of course you did," Renee murmured.

"At last, because I was so cold, I put on long underwear beneath my nightgown and I got into bed. That's where Matt found me."

The front door had slammed and she'd started in terror. Where could she hide? He'd find her in the closet, under the bed...

And then she'd heard her husband's roar of anguish and fear. "Shirley!"

"My clothes were still strewn around, you see. And there was blood. Just smears, but he was scared."

"Of course he was." She had such a soft voice, this woman Daniel loved.

"He...he made sure I was all right, and we talked about calling the police, but I just couldn't! To tell strange men, and know they'd think I'd brought it on, and then I wouldn't even have been able to go to the grocery store without people staring because they *knew*." Still the idea was repugnant, although not so awful as it had seemed then. She took another tissue and mopped her eyes. "This won't be in the newspaper, will it?" she asked.

"No. I promise, this won't become public knowledge."

She nodded acknowledgment. "Matt left me then, and I knew where he was going. He didn't come back for a long time, it must have been an hour at least, and he had blood all over him. His hands and his shirtfront..." She swallowed convulsively. "It seemed like gallons of blood. And Matt said, 'He won't bother you ever again.' Just like that. Never another word." She lifted eyes freshly drenched with tears to Renee's. "I never asked what happened. I didn't want to know. I hated what I'd made Matt do. A peaceful man... He wanted me to talk about the rape, but I wouldn't. I said let's just forget it, and we tried. It was hard for both of us, hard on our marriage, because for a long time I didn't want—" She remembered her son's presence and stopped. "But Matt never said an angry word to me, never got impatient. And then one day we were laughing, and I felt different, and..." Through the tears she was blushing. "Well, time heals most anything. Sometimes I had nightmares, but mostly I did put it all out of my mind."

"Until you found out the bones of a murdered man had been discovered on your own land."

"And I thought it must be *him*."

"Was your husband given to using a knife? Did you find one missing from the kitchen later?"

"No." That part puzzled Shirley. "No, none of mine were missing, but there might have been a knife out in the barn. Matt did have a gun, for coyotes and such, though he didn't like using it. I suppose, if they were fighting, he might have snatched up a knife. Though you wouldn't think one would be lying around. A hoof pick, maybe, but not a knife.''

"Daniel?" The policewoman looked past Shirley.

He sounded hoarse. "Dad carried a Swiss army knife. I, um, I use it now myself. But the blade wouldn't have been long enough. Otherwise, we have a machete out in the barn—we hack open bales of hay with it—and scissors and plyers and a leather awl, but a butcher knife…'' Out of the corner of her eye, Shirley was aware of him shaking his head.

Renee's sigh was almost inaudible. "Well, our biggest trouble still is going to be identifying the bones. Without T. J. Baxter's real name or some fingerprints, I don't know how to locate dental records. Unless—'' her voice altered ''—you know of him going to a dentist while he was here?''

Shirley shook her head hopelessly.

"We don't provide dental insurance," Daniel said.

"If something of his was left around… Something he used…'' She stopped, able to tell the anwer from their faces. "But you've already told me you wouldn't have kept it.''

"So this didn't really help," Shirley said slowly.

"Of course it did! It gives me somewhere to focus. I'll have local dentists check records from back then, see if he did go to one of them. And if you think of anything…''

Shirley nodded dutifully.

Renee took her hand again. "Mrs. Barnard, I'm

grateful you were able to do what you did today. I know this wasn't easy. I hope you'll end up being glad you told someone. If it turns out your husband did kill T. J. Baxter, most likely we'll just close the file. With everyone concerned dead except for you, there won't be an arrest or trial and I see no reason to go public at all. So I don't want you worrying about that.''

Shirley nodded again.

''I have one of Anne McWhirter's cards in my glove compartment. I'll go get one right now. Will you call her, make an appointment?''

Shirley agreed that she would.

Daniel walked Renee out. Shirley wished he wouldn't come back in, not right now. Maybe tomorrow she'd be ready to talk to him, but now she wanted to be alone. She couldn't tell him that, though; he would be hurt. A good man like his father, Daniel would like to think he was needed.

Shirley sat where she was even when the living room was empty. She felt so tired, she could have gone straight to bed. Those tears had worn her out! But her exhaustion was the good kind, as if she'd worked hard all day and felt satisfied. She felt calmer than she had in weeks, more at peace. She had thought telling about such awful things would make them fresh again, tear open a wound healed but for an ache. But instead the telling had lessened the shame that had festered. She would call that counselor, Shirley decided. Talking about it all again wouldn't be so bad. Why, she might feel better each time!

Funny, she could think about T. J. Baxter now,

as she hadn't been able to ever. She tested herself by seeing it all again. Opening the door, stumbling back as he advanced. That smile... Had she ever thought him handsome?

With pride, Shirley remembered how hard she had fought. She'd raked her fingers at his face, aiming for his eyes, like she'd read you should do. That's when he'd grabbed her around the neck...

No-o, that wasn't quite right, she thought, frowning. It had hurt—oh, it had hurt!—but not his hands... She sat up straighter. A necklace, that was it! She used to wear that locket Matt had given her on a silver chain around her neck. She never took it off, until that day. In a fury, T. J. Baxter had grabbed the locket itself and yanked it sideways until the chain cut into her flesh and made her violently gag. He might have strangled her, but the thin chain broke and he flung the locket aside.

She'd found it weeks later, Shirley remembered suddenly. She was moving the couch to vacuum when she saw it, lying there like a poisonous snake ready to strike. She'd almost called to Matt, but she didn't want to bring it all up again. She didn't want to see the wrenching pity on his face. So she took a tissue and picked it up and...

Shirley gave a gasp. She hadn't thrown it away! She'd stood there with it in her hand, and thought about how it held a picture of her and one of Matt, and how her husband had given it to her with love. But she couldn't bear to see it or think about it, not then, so she'd shoved locket and chain in a box she kept in her closet that held silly things like a history award she'd won in high school and a poem written to her by her first crush, an eighth grader who'd actually noticed her, only a seventh grader! And there that locket had lain, all these years, never touched.

Why, could that mean... Even before she thought it out, Shirley hurried out to the porch. The police car was just backing up.

"Daniel!" she called. "Stop her. I just thought of something."

He didn't question her, only stepped forward to put a hand on the hood of the Bronco. The policewoman rolled down her window, they exchanged a few words, and she turned the engine right off and got out.

They came toward Shirley together.

"I do have one thing he touched," she said in a rush. "If fingerprints last fifteen years, his should still be there."

CHAPTER TWELVE

RENEE DROVE BACK to town on autopilot, completely unaware of the passing scenery or any other cars on the road.

So now she knew, she thought, frowning straight ahead.

Or did she?

Matthew Barnard had certainly had a motive for killing T. J. Baxter, no one would argue with that. If he'd been brought before a court at the time, any judge and jury would have been sympathetic to his reason for driving a knife into a man's chest, if not the cold-bloodedness of the act.

Gallons of blood, Shirley said. The heart could pump out a lot of blood. But so could the nose, if Matthew had punched the man who raped his wife before throwing him off the place. Her hysteria that night might well have exaggerated the quantity from a stained shirtfront to one soaked with a man's lifeblood.

Troubled, Renee asked herself whether she was making excuses. Did she not *want* Matthew Barnard to have killed anyone? Maybe because of Shirley? Daniel? Or maybe because the man himself sounded decent, a loving husband, a good father, a fine employer?

Well, no matter what, there wouldn't be a trial, she reminded herself. All she wanted was to *know,* once and for all. Part of her wished she could just accept Shirley's story and figure that now she did.

But she was bothered by a few things. A blade that nicked bone would have to be long, sharp and strong. Nothing dull would have made that perfect vee; not a hoof pick or leather-working awl, and not that small Swiss army knife Daniel had showed her. Was Matthew the kind of man who could have stabbed a man with one of his wife's kitchen knives, then washed it and put it back in the drawer to be used to carve the roast the next night? Renee couldn't see him that way.

Every single person she'd talked to described him as a real straight arrow, a good friend, a man with unshakable integrity.

Yes, but he'd tried, she remembered; according to Shirley, he'd wanted to call the police. His wife refused; was already hurt, terrified, wanting to pretend nothing had happened. So, did he let the man who'd raped his wife walk away? Or did he kill, though it went against his deepest beliefs, because his wife had begged for silence in which to heal?

Renee sighed heavily. She wondered what Daniel now thought, having heard his mother's story. Daniel wasn't his father, but he was a man with the same principles. What would he have done in the same spot? Could he have ruthlessly killed so that the woman he loved could retreat into pretense?

The woman he loved. The pain lancing her chest was sharp and breathtaking. Could she have been that woman? If she hadn't clung to some foolish, symbolic quest with no regard for who she hurt in her hunger to solve a mystery involving some long-dead stranger?

What was more important? she asked herself silently, and knew the answer, couldn't believe she'd ever hesitated. But she also doubted Daniel Barnard had ever loved her. Wanted her, maybe; even pursued her, sure. But the kind of love Shirley described having with her husband? The kind with mutual trust, liking and hunger that could be satisfied by no one else... The kind that meant a man wouldn't look elsewhere, even when his wife was afraid of his sexual needs, that meant angry words were quickly forgotten, laughter and joy shared...

Renee wanted that. Oh, she wanted it fiercely! But there was nothing special about her, nothing that would make a man single her out, join into an undying bond with her. She could have felt like that about Daniel, she knew she could—maybe she already did—but she could also understand why he didn't reciprocate. Maybe his pursuit hadn't been totally aimed at deflecting her from his mother, but deep down inside that's surely what he was trying to do. And then maybe getting more involved than he'd intended, maybe sympathizing with her, wanting her sexually, even feeling hurt when she chose her duty—her quest—above him. But eternal love? She never had been any good at deceiving herself.

Today she didn't cry. She felt a great echoing emptiness inside, a desert where emotion shriveled up and died like a fresh green shoot denied water. Most of her life she'd known she had that arid space inside her, and thanked God for it. Otherwise, how could she ever have quit crying? Especially once Meg left, too?

It was dangerous, not letting any emotion swell to full growth or bloom, but she'd figured she was safe. With one sister left, she knew how to love, though she wasn't sure she ever wanted to let herself again.

Now it turned out Abby had secretly despised her all this time, because she had refused to play games to get what she wanted from their father; because she had been clinging to her fears and regrets about him for so long. Abby understood, Renee had always believed, only now she knew Abby didn't, never had. Didn't feel the same way she did about the father who'd abused them.

But Daniel did understand. She didn't know how that could be, but despite everything that had happened since, she still believed he had. He'd understood even more than she had that her father's *things* had power over her.

Without his chair there to taunt her, she'd moved the television back into the living room last night. It sat on a kitchen chair, the lone piece of furniture in the room, but she had plopped down on the plywood floor with her back against the wall and watched one of her favorite programs. The best part was that she hadn't had any sense of defying him; he was just *gone*.

Now depression swamped her like sudden tiredness. Her father was gone, and she didn't care anymore. The hole wasn't one she could joyously fill. She wanted Daniel and Daniel alone to fill that lonely place in her life and her heart. She wanted to sell the damn house, to hell with her long-lost mother and sister. She loved Daniel's house, with the warm woods and the big kitchen and the windows looking out on forever. As Daniel's wife, she'd have a mother again, and Renee had a feeling Shirley would be wise, strong and loving in a way her own mother never had been.

Best of all would be waking up to Daniel in the morning, rubbing his sore muscles when he ached, being held when she hurt, talking about everything and nothing, having the right to kiss him whenever she felt like it.

She would have given anything to be the woman he would have and hold for the rest of his life.

But she guessed maybe it was time to do the best she could with her life. She would sell the house; it was time—past time. Make some new friends, find things she enjoyed doing. Follow Abby's example and live outside their father's shadow. Maybe, eventually, she would know herself to be stronger. She might even believe she *was* a woman a man might love the way Matt Barnard had loved his wife.

Voices had been crackling on her police radio, but the calls were all routine dispatches to fender benders, shoplifting, one household break-in. Now some officers were talking about the hostage situation.

Renee picked up her hand unit and called in. When Daniel had phoned earlier asking her to come out and talk to his mother, she'd left Lieutenant Pratt in charge in her stead. She wasn't needed right now, so she decided to stop by and check out the excitement.

The block of small shabby houses was cordoned

off, but a patrolman moved one of the barricades to let her past. Squad cars were parked in a semicircle in front of a white house, the best-kept on the street. The lawn had been mowed late enough in the year to look decent over the winter, and browning foliage in window boxes suggested flowers had brightened the facade. Renee parked well back and approached the knot of officers huddled behind a dark-painted van belonging to the county S.W.A.T. team.

Jack saw her coming and jerked his head indicating she ought to hurry. Her heart sped up some and she ducked behind the van.

"Is he taking potshots at you?" she asked.

"Not yet, but you never know." Jack scowled. "What are you doing here?"

"Just curious."

Inside the van, she saw Lieutenant Cunningham, the county sheriff's department's balding middle-aged negotiator, wearing headphones and making notes on a pad in front of him. He was talking, and she saw by his expression of deep concern that he'd connected with the wife-abuser inside the small frame house.

When she peeked around the van, she saw sharp-shooters positioned on rooftops and armed officers in place behind the squad cars. To all appearances, a terrorist was holed up in there.

"Any progress?" she asked.

"He's run out of beer."

"Maybe you should send him more. Let him drink until he passes out."

Jack gave her a look of dislike. "You sound like Cunningham."

Renee shrugged. "Seems pragmatic to me."

His voice hardened. "I tried to call you. They told me you'd gone back out to the Triple B. Damn it, Patton, I left you in charge and you're off chasing some kind of will-o'-the-wisp!"

She cocked a brow. "Why, Jack, how poetic."

He growled an obscenity.

"Pratt can hold down the fort as well as I can. Daniel Barnard called," Renee explained. "His mother was ready to talk."

His gaze sharpened. "And?"

"Fifteen years ago, a ranch hand raped her. She wouldn't let her husband call the police. All she knows is, Matthew went out for an hour or so and came back with blood on his shirt, saying she didn't have to worry about the man again."

"Matthew Barnard?" Jack sounded incredulous. "He's the last man I'd pick as a killer, even under those circumstances."

Renee spread her hands. "That seems to be the consensus. By the way, I promised his wife we'd keep this under our hats. She doesn't want everyone knowing what happened to her. I talked her into seeing a counselor."

Jack grunted. "After all these years? What's the point?"

"She's never dealt with it. This secret has been eating away at her all this time. She agreed."

Jack opened his mouth to say something, but was called away for a quick consultation that reminded her of a football huddle: men in a tight circle, heads together and backs out, voices barking. After a minute it broke up and he came back.

"So, are you satisfied?"

No. Her dissatisfaction was instant and emphatic. But she simply said, "We've gotten lucky. I hope. This T. J. Baxter who raped Shirley apparently grabbed a locket from around her neck. The chain broke, he tossed it away, and she found it under the couch a couple of weeks later. She didn't touch it, just wrapped it in a tissue and hid it in a shoebox in her closet. If we can lift a fingerprint..."

"You can find out who he really was."

"And whether he's still alive."

Jack's dark eyes narrowed. "You want him to be alive, don't you?"

Annoyed at herself—was she so transparent everyone could see right through her?—Renee said, "I want to know what happened. One way or the other."

"Boss!" someone called.

He turned away for another conclave, this time including Cunningham, who'd left his headphones on the table in the van. The excited buzz of voices made her guess something had happened. The negotiator and Jack were obviously arguing, although Renee couldn't hear what they were saying. Curious, she waited on the outskirts. Just as well she wasn't involved in the decision, because she knew darn well she'd be on Frank Cunningham's side. And she had a suspicion she and Jack were going to clash often enough now that she seemed to have become immune to his looks and to the knowledge that he usually made the same choices Chief Patton would have. Arguing with Jack had felt like disputing what was right and wrong with her father's ghost. She hadn't been able to question her father when he was alive, and until recently—until Daniel came into her life—she'd been just as afraid of her father dead.

Finally Jack barked some orders and the men broke off purposefully. The negotiator went back into the van and Jack came over to Renee.

"You're in luck. You may get to see the resolution." He didn't sound happy. From his gaze, pinned broodingly on the house across the street, she guessed it wasn't her presence that was bothering him.

"He's agreed to let his wife and child go?"

"He's coming out."

The policeman crouched behind the squad cars were holstering their guns and climbing into the cars, moving them farther down the street. Only the sharpshooters on the rooftops stayed put. Maybe the husband didn't know they were there. Watching the activity, Renee said, "You don't believe he means it?"

"He walks out now, the judge'll give him a slap on the wrist and suggest counseling," Jack said with disgust. "Scum like that, who'd hold a gun to his wife's head! And sure as shooting she'll welcome him back with open arms as soon as he's paroled. Hell, she'll probably bail him out!"

She shared some of his frustration, but not his obvious desire to storm the house, shoot the husband and heroically rescue woman and child. Ironic, when she thought about it, considering she'd been, in some sense, that child.

Words came out, words she'd never thought of saying to him.

"My father hit my mother. And Meg." She swallowed. "And me."

"What?" Jack swung toward her so violently, she flinched.

"You heard me." She held her chin high, jerked her head toward the scene across the street. "Your idol was as bad as that guy in there."

"I don't believe you." But he did, his eyes gave him away.

"Why do you think Meg ran away?"

"I know why—" He stopped so suddenly his teeth snapped together. After a rigid moment, Jack wiped a hand across his face and swore. "Why didn't she say anything? God damn it, why didn't *you?*"

"We were afraid of him," Renee said simply.

"Why didn't she tell me?" he said again, but not as if he were really asking Renee. Then he focused on her again, eyes and voice razor sharp. "Did he hurt her? Really hurt her?"

"He didn't torture us or hold guns to our heads. Just…lashed out when he was angry. He broke Meg's jaw once. Do you remember that? She told everyone she'd fallen down the stairs." Renee gave a brief, humorless laugh. "That's the oldest one in the book, isn't it? And you know, his hitting us wasn't the worst part. If sometimes he'd been happy with us… Proud of us… But he never was. None of us could ever measure up. You came closer than we did, maybe because you're a man. I don't think he liked women very much."

Jack groaned. "Why the hell are you telling me this right now?"

"Because of him." Like everyone else, she was riveted to the sight of the front door opening. "I'm sorry. This isn't a good time."

Jack swore again, but now he was focused on the man emerging onto the tiny porch. He bent over and set down a handgun, then straightened, arms above his head. Slowly, he started down the path. Except for him, nobody moved for what seemed the longest time. Maybe they were all paralyzed by his ordinariness; the monster was them. He was young, sandy-haired, weedy, freckled. Nice, Renee would have guessed, if she'd met him casually. Only, he stumbled, paused, swayed, and she remembered that he was drunk.

Cops closed in then, tackling him. He fell heavily and his face scraped the concrete of the narrow walk. He was yelling and cursing as the half dozen police officers cuffed him and hauled him back to his feet. Cheek and jaw raw and bloody now, he kept trying to turn back to the house.

"*Lisa!*" he bellowed, and his wife appeared in the doorway. God help them all, she was pregnant again, pregnant and holding a child who couldn't be over a year old. She was sobbing and the baby was screaming.

"I'm sorry!" he yelled. "I'm sorry. I wouldn't have hurt you. Lisa. I'm sorry." He was shoved into a police car, the door slammed, shutting him off.

Renee felt sick. "Have fun," she said tersely, and walked away.

BACK AT THE STATION, Renee left the locket, still wrapped in the tissue and enclosed in an evidence bag, with a fingerprint tech. Then she called Anne McWhirter.

The older woman had been a school counselor back when Renee's mother had walked out on her family. She'd helped all three Patton girls get through some tough weeks, and she'd continued checking on Renee every now and again since.

"Said goodbye to your father yet?" were the first words out of her mouth once Renee had identified herself.

Renee made a face. "Do you know, I think I have. Was I that obvious?"

"I worry about you," Anne said. "All of you."

"I've worked through some things lately." She took a breath. "I'm redecorating the house, and as soon as I've done the basics I'm putting it up for sale."

"Good for you," her friend said warmly. "Tell me what you're doing."

They chatted about carpet and stripping versus painting woodwork and where to buy furniture, finally agreeing that Anne would join Renee and Abby on Saturday to shop. Then Renee told her why she'd called.

"Will you let me know if Shirley Barnard *doesn't* make an appointment?" she asked. "I'd really like her to see you."

"You know I have to keep anything she says confidential."

Renee assured her she wasn't interested in what Shirley told the counselor. "But I really think she needs to see someone. I'm going to bug her until she does."

"Drumming up business for me?"

Renee smiled. "You bet. Heck, I'm trying to make up for never having stretched out on your couch myself."

"I don't do couches." Anne sounded amused. "Too Freudian for me. Besides, the last thing a rape victim or abused woman needs is to take a submissive posture or talk to some silent authority figure lurking off to the side."

"Anne...I've never thanked you."

"Don't thank me," she said crisply. "I knew your mother, you know. We were in the Garden Club together." She fell silent for a moment. "I wondered about your mother. She had bruises. I wish I'd done something. Offered to listen, if nothing else. She claimed she had such fragile skin, anything made her bruise, and I bought it, just like everyone else."

"She wouldn't have told you."

"Probably not. But her leaving the way she did, not even having the strength to take her own daughters with her... She's one of the reasons I went back to school for my master's degree and got into this kind of counseling. I thought you might like to know that."

Blinking back a sting of tears, Renee said, "It does make it seem...less pointless."

"Well." Anne's voice became brisker again. "I'll see you Saturday. Ten o'clock. Why don't we meet at McGillity's for coffee and a scone before we start?"

Renee spent the next hour catching up on paperwork. Police reports were boring to write and probably more boring to read, but a record was necessary for the long haul, and even the short. Details left an arresting officer's mind too quickly. One D.U.I. stop blended into another mighty easily, and it helped to go over notes and the official report before appearing in court. A glance at her calendar reminded her she had a court session herself tomorrow.

She heard the commotion in the hall when the troops arrived back from the day's excitement, but her office door stayed closed until Jack rapped and stuck his head in without waiting for her response.

"The wife swears she won't bail him out. Says 'sorry' isn't good enough. Do you believe that?"

"Nope."

"Me neither." He came the rest of the way in, but stayed beside the door, looking awkward. "Would you have dinner with me tonight?"

The emptiness she'd felt this morning washed over her again. "Jack, it doesn't matter. Maybe I shouldn't have told you. I don't know. But I thought maybe you should hear the truth. Anyway, there's nothing more to say."

"But I just can't believe..." He stopped, breathing raggedly. "I don't doubt you, Renee, I didn't mean that. But this is a big readjustment for me. I guess I'd like to know more. If you can bring yourself to tell me."

Who was he mourning? she wondered. His lost teenage love, or the father figure who had led him into police work?

Could she stand to cap off the day by talking about her father? Well, why not? Otherwise she'd just go home to that big lonesome house, eat a microwave dinner and watch TV. Here a man who used to make her heart beat faster was asking her out, and she was thinking of saying no?

"Fine," she said. "I can't tell you what Meg thought or felt when she left—we didn't have a chance to talk—but I can tell you anything else you want to know."

"Deal," he said. "By the way, Davies tells me he was able to lift a fingerprint from that locket. Now we just have to wait for it to be run through A.F.I.S."

Her moment of intense satisfaction was supplanted by wry awareness of that "we." *She'd* been chasing a will-o'-the-wisp, just wasting valuable man-hours. Now *we* were getting somewhere.

But she didn't care enough about who got credit for what to brood about it. Instead, once Jack was gone, closing the door behind him, Renee thought, *T. J. Baxter, now I'm going to find out who you really were.*

Or maybe not past tense. Maybe she'd find out who he now *was,* assuming those bones packaged up back in the evidence room didn't belong to him.

Knowing the FBI's backlog meant that the fingerprint ID wouldn't come back for weeks if not months had never been more frustrating.

THE PATTON HOUSE sat dark, the driveway empty.

Feeling like a damned fool, Daniel circled the block and came back to Renee's house, parking at the curb several doors down. He'd just wait for her, he figured. Maybe she was having dinner with her sister, or a friend. If it was a man...well, she wouldn't be looking for his pickup. With luck, she wouldn't spot him. He'd go home and cry into his beer.

A half hour passed. This felt all too familiar, except this time he wasn't gunning for a confrontration. He was…well, he didn't quite know what he was going to say, he knew only that he wanted to see her. Kiss her, if she'd let him. Explain his fears, and hope she understood.

He had a pretty good idea he was here with his mother's blessing, assuming he'd needed it. She'd as good as admitted that she'd told her story because she could tell her silence was getting in the way of his romance.

"It doesn't bother you that I'm seeing her?" he'd asked incredulously. "Don't you resent the way she's been riding you?"

His mother blinked in surprise. "Why would I resent her? She's just doing her job. She seems like a nice young woman. And so brave! I admire a woman who can take on a career that used to be for men only. In my day, we wouldn't have dared. Why, I just assumed I'd quit work altogether when I married your father. *He* was my work. But sometimes I'm sorry I didn't continue part-time. I enjoyed working at the library, you know."

"It's not too late," Daniel had pointed out.

"Don't be silly!" she declared, but her eyes had a thoughtful gleam.

He felt selfish not to have guessed she might be bored, having nothing to do these days but keep up a house for herself. Oh, she had friends and volunteer activities—years ago, she'd been on the library board of trustees, but they needed new blood, to use her words, and now all she did was help at the annual book sale.

Daniel glanced at his dashboard clock. 8:15. In his rearview mirror he saw approaching headlights. Two cars were coming. He saw the roof lights and E.S.P.D. emblazoned on the door as she passed and pulled into her driveway. Another police Bronco was right behind her. It slowed, she waved, and then it sped up, red taillights blinking at the stop sign down the block. Daniel watched her get out, check that the car door was locked, and let herself into the house. The porch light came on, then one in the living room.

Frowning, Daniel didn't move for a minute. He'd caught barely a glimpse under the streetlight, but he thought that had been Jack Murray following Renee home. Had they dined together? Was she turning her sights elsewhere? Or had something happened at work that had shaken her up, so Murray wanted to make sure she got home safe?

It was the last thought that decided Daniel. He started his pickup, drove the half a block and parked in Renee's driveway, right behind her 4x4.

The snow from a few days ago had melted, but the barometer was dropping again. It was damned cold. If snow fell tonight, the flakes would be tiny and dry, the powder that made skiing here in eastern Oregon world renowned.

He rang the doorbell, hearing the deep bong echoing far inside the house. Footsteps approached, hollow sounding now that there was no carpet to muffle noise. Daniel waited while she peered through the vee of glass high on the door, then unlocked.

"Daniel." Still in uniform, she looked tired and less than thrilled. "What are you doing here?"

He shifted uncomfortably. "Are you okay?"

"Oh, yeah. I'm just peachy." She didn't open the door any wider. "How about your mother? I called, but she didn't answer."

"Some friends were going to Portland and offered her a ride. She's going to stay with Mary. Mom wants to tell her what she told us."

"Good for her." Renee's expression warmed a fraction. "I imagine it'll get easier every time."

"Yeah." His breath puffed out in an icy cloud. "Uh, I was hoping we could talk."

"Talk," she echoed, as if perplexed by the idea.

"Renee, please. Can I come in? It's cold out here."

Still she hesitated discernibly, then at last, with every sign of reluctance, stepped back. He crossed the threshold and watched as she locked the door. Now that he was in, he heard tinny voices from the television.

"Did I interrupt a show?"

She shrugged and went ahead of him into the still-bare living room, where the television sat in lone splendor on a wood kitchen chair. Renee switched it off. "That's okay. It wasn't anything I cared about."

He turned his head. "You were sitting on the floor?"

"I'm shopping for furniture Saturday. New carpet is being laid Friday."

"What color?" Like he gave a damn.

"Blue. I'm doing the room in blue and white with some dashes of yellow or maybe rose, I haven't decided."

Sell the house, he thought. *Move in with me.*

They stood there, both stiff, uneasy. God, he wanted to kiss her, peel that damned uniform off, loosen her silky pale hair, find the woman beneath the cop.

He didn't dare touch her.

"I should have helped you," he said. "I shouldn't have tried to stop you."

Her eyes seemed to darken. "And I should have let it go, like you asked."

A groan tore his throat. "I've missed you."

"I've missed you, too."

They both took a step forward, meeting in the middle of that bare living room. Renee said something else, but softly, and through the roaring in his ears he couldn't hear it, but he wanted to imagine that it was, "I love you."

And then he was kissing her, and her arms were around his neck, and she was kissing him back.

CHAPTER THIRTEEN

MAKING LOVE was the easy part.

The fact that their hands were shaking didn't slow them from getting rid of clothes: a shirt draped over the banister, a bra tangled among the shoes kicked off down the hall, her gun and holster tossed on the bureau and his jeans on her bedroom floor.

The kisses, the sighs, the touches... His weight on her and her legs parting for him... The entry, long and deep and slow... Oh, that was easy. Natural and inevitable, like the sun rising in the morning or winter relinquishing its grip when bulbs burst through the soil come spring.

Afterward was the hard part.

Renee lay with her head on Daniel's shoulder and felt his chest rise and fall, the heat of his skin beneath her splayed hand, heard the heavy slow beat of his heart. He wasn't asleep, any more than she was. He just had no more idea what to say than she did, Renee guessed.

What a fool she'd been to admit she loved him! She was so afraid her impulsive words were what was stifling conversation now. She wasn't about to repeat them unless he reciprocated, and since he most likely didn't feel the same, he must be in a quandary about what to say.

What could he say? *I like you, and that was great sex, but I'm not sure about love. Maybe someday...* They'd both know that was a lie. Or, worse yet, *Sure, I love you, too,* in a false hearty tone.

"I don't know what I was afraid of," he said abruptly, his mouth against her hair.

She went completely still. Even her heart seemed to stop beating. When he didn't continue on his own, she closed her eyes. "What do you mean?"

"You made me see how much I identified with my father. Too much, apparently." Daniel fell silent again, but only for a minute. Voice strained, he went on. "It was as if...oh, hell, as if *I* was morally responsible for anything he'd done. No. Worse than that. As if I was a continuation of him. If he'd done it, I'd done it. I didn't want to believe I could commit murder, for any reason." He shifted. "Does that make sense? Am I crazy?"

Was *he* crazy? A giggle hiccuped from her. No! She had to take him seriously! Reassure him, not laugh! But she couldn't help it. Another giggle tripped over the first, and then another.

He jackknifed to a sitting position, rolling her onto her back. "What the hell?"

"Are...*you*...crazy?" Renee managed to squeak out between side-splitting laughter. "Just...go down...and look...at my living room!"

He glowered at her for another moment. Finally a crease dented one cheek and his mouth compressed. "You've got a point," he conceded, a grin growing.

"Maybe...we're both..."

Suddenly he was laughing as hard as she was.

When she didn't finish her sentence, he did. "Loco!"

"Nutty as fruitcakes." She wiped away tears and kept laughing, though her stomach muscles hurt.

"Ready for the loony bin." He swore. "I've got to pee."

"Race ya." Renee gave him a push and leaped from the bed, reaching the bathroom first.

She'd barely locked the door when Daniel whacked it with his hands.

"There's another one down the hall," she called.

"Now you tell me." She heard him retreat.

A moment later she flushed the toilet and stood in front of the mirror. Oh, Lord! Her hair was a tangled mess, her face so pale it was pasty. Maybe she should start wearing makeup to work. Just because a woman was a cop didn't mean she had to try to look like a man.

No wonder Jack Murray had never been interested! Experimentally, Renee yanked her hair back to mimic her daytime appearance. She made a horrible face at herself in the mirror. Had she been trying hard to make sure no man *ever* looked twice? Why the heck had Daniel?

An insidious voice whispered, *You know the answer. Because he was trying to influence you.*

Yes, but if that was true, why had he come tonight?

To justify his behavior? To have some good sex?

Renee had sense enough to know she was listening to fears planted by her father. No, Daniel probably didn't love her, but he might like her. Maybe something *would* come of it. She could be optimistic, couldn't she?

She ran a brush through her hair and splashed cold water on her face, toweling it dry until her cheeks glowed pink. Then she opened the bathroom door.

Darn his hide, Daniel was already sprawled on the bed again, unashamedly naked, hands clasped behind his head. The moment she appeared, he let his gaze rove over her with purely masculine appreciation. Blushing fiercely, she dashed for the bed.

"Hey, slow down!" He rolled toward her nonetheless. "I was enjoying the overall effect. You could go back and do it again."

"Not on your life." She wriggled closer. "This is only the second time I've taken off my clothes for a man, and I'm not quite ready to parade around, posing."

"Next time." His hand roved from her waist to her hip. "This is good, too."

"Mmm-hmm." She kissed the hollow at the base of his throat. She still felt terribly self-conscious, lying here buck naked in front of a man, but it was fun, too. Exhilarating. A little shyly, she asked, "Are you still upset by the idea that your dad might have killed Baxter?"

Daniel's hand stilled. "I'm not excited about it, but... Hell, I can understand why he might have. Maybe I shouldn't be saying this to a cop, but as far as I'm concerned, Baxter deserved to die. That son of a—" He stopped, his voice a deep growl of rage. "If someone raped you..."

Her thrill of pleasure took Renee aback. She was

a law enforcement officer, and she still had some kind of primitive reaction to the idea that a man would be willing to kill to protect her?

But she couldn't deny it. She *wanted* Daniel to feel that way about her.

Although there was no way on earth she could tell him that.

"I'm flattered," she said lightly. "I guess."

His throat worked. "You think I'm kidding?"

Their eyes met. "No," she whispered. "I think, just like your father, you would find it unacceptable for any woman to be treated like that. Especially one you…care about."

"Ah. So my father was just being a gentleman."

"I didn't say that."

Daniel studied her for a long time. Creases deepened between his brows. "My father would have gone to the police if the woman who'd been raped had been anyone but my mother. No matter how desperately the woman begged him to stay quiet. But Mom… He couldn't stand to see her hurt. He'd have given her anything.… His soul." He made a sound. "If he deliberately stabbed a man to death, that's exactly what he did give her."

"Now you sound as though you…oh, blame your mother. Or…or think the decision he made was terribly wrong."

Still his eyes searched her face with odd intensity. "I'd never have blamed my mother. A few weeks ago, I would have thought he should have stood by his principles and called the police no matter what. Now…" His mouth twisted. "Now I understand."

That same, atavistic thrill shot through her. Could

he possibly mean what he seemed to be implying? Or was he just flattering her?

Or, she thought ruefully, was he not talking about her at all? Maybe he'd just meant that in these weeks he'd come to understand Shirley and Matt Barnard better as people rather than as parents. Learned to see them as a man and a woman who loved each other, who were basically good folks but who still weren't perfect.

"Your father might not have done this."

"Only it all fits."

"Except for the knife," she reminded him. "And for the fact that I'm still having trouble picturing your father driving a blade into a man's chest so hard it sliced bone. It's a crime of anger, but also one a man would need to steel himself to do. Would he have taken a knife to find Baxter? Why not a gun if he were going to bring a weapon? It would be a heck of a lot easier, physically and emotionally, to kill someone by pulling a trigger. Somehow I see your father storming straight out of the house to find Baxter, not thinking about what he'd do once he found him. Do you know what I mean?"

Daniel grunted. "Yeah, and I agree. Except he might have had murder on his mind."

"And so he detoured to the kitchen and took your mother's knife?" Renee said skeptically.

Daniel lay back and stared at the ceiling. "He might have had a bowie knife. It was a long time ago. Just because I don't remember him owning something like that doesn't mean he didn't."

"That's true." She hesitated. "Well, it looks like we'll be able to find out whether T. J. Baxter died on your place. I didn't get a chance to tell you, but we were successful in lifting a couple of clear fingerprints from your mother's locket. Now we're running them. The bad news is, it can take anywhere from a week, given a miracle, to three months to get the ID back. We've got a long wait ahead of us.''

Daniel was silent for a moment. ''Well,'' he said at last, ''you were right. I'd rather know either way. I think Mom feels the same, now that it's come down to it.''

''Has she called the counselor?''

''She said she did. She hoped I didn't mind, but she thought maybe she needed to talk about what happened some more. Why the hell would I mind?'' He sounded genuinely baffled.

''She's been a wife and a mother a long time.'' Renee tried to be tactful. ''I get the feeling she's used to deferring to first your dad and now you. Maybe not on little things, but on the big ones.''

Shock showed on Daniel's face when he rolled his head to look at her again. ''Defer? Maybe to Dad, but me? On the business side, sure, but...''

''What other side is there?'' she asked softly. ''The dinner menu? You don't even eat with her most of the time.''

His brows shot together again, though he didn't sound angry. More...perturbed. ''You think I neglect her?''

''No, I think she needs to get out more than she does. It doesn't sound as if horses are her thing. What is?''

She could see him groping for an answer and being bothered because he didn't have one. ''It was always her family. The house.'' His shoulders moved, apologetically. ''She gardens some. And reads. I guess books are something she loves. I know she worked in the library back before she was married. She's still active in the Friends.''

''Well, what she does with her life isn't your choice, anyway. It's hers. I'm just guessing that, in her eyes, you've taken over your dad's role as authority figure. Unless she has her own income...''

She hadn't settled his perturbation any. ''From the ranch,'' he admitted. ''She owns half of it.''

''So you write her a check.''

''I deposit money every month in the same account she shared with Dad.''

''Which might make her feel she has to clear her spending with you.''

He swore.

Renee laid a hand on his arm and felt the muscles bunch. ''I'm not saying there's anything wrong with your arrangement. What else can you do? Really. I didn't mean to upset you.''

''I should have seen it.'' His hand caught her arm. ''Why did you? And don't tell me it's a woman thing.''

''I lived here on my father's sufferance.''

''You didn't pay your way?''

''Sure I did.'' She made a face. ''And then felt as if I had to explain where every other cent went.''

''You know that staying here even when you felt that way is illogical as hell.''

''Right.'' She smiled. ''I'm crazy, remember?''

''Yeah.'' Head braced in his hands, Daniel studied her. His mouth had a sensuous curve, and his eyes were so blue, she couldn't look away. "Are you crazy about me?" he asked, low and rough.

Was he asking her to repeat her declaration? Or... Her breath caught. Was it possible he hadn't heard her? That he didn't *know* how she felt?

Did he have some of the same doubts and fears she had? But that would mean... No. He hadn't said he loved her, and why would he hesitate if he did?

Pure cowardice had her parrying, "If I weren't crazy about you, would I be willing to discuss your mother at a time like this?"

Something flickered in his eyes; he knew she was evading the question. But he chose not to press her. "Yeah, that's an uneasy mix, isn't it?" He grinned ruefully. "I've got a beautiful woman naked in bed with me, and I'm talking about my mother. Okay, now you've got me worried about myself."

"Well..." Astonished at her daring, Renee traced his lips with one fingertip. Hoping her tone was provocative and not just silly, she suggested, "You could prove your masculine prowess and wipe this little lapse out of my mind."

His eyes darkened. "Yeah. I could do that." This smile was just plain wicked. "Maybe you could help me along. You wouldn't want my poor ego to suffer, now, would you?"

She might not be experienced, but even she could tell that Daniel wasn't going to have trouble proving anything to her. Still she arched her hips and squirmed a little, nibbled a few kisses on his neck, and trailed her fingernails down his chest.

"How am I doing?" she murmured.

A muscle along his jaw spasmed as her hand

trailed lower. He cleared his throat. "Let me put it this way. You're on the right track."

"Oh, good." Giving as well as receiving could be an exhilarating experience, Renee decided. Even…erotic.

But, running her hand over his chest and belly was one thing; actually wrapping it around his erect penis was another. She took a breath and clumsily gripped him.

Daniel winced, and then groaned, "Don't stop," when she pulled away.

"I don't know what I'm doing."

"Then practice." His fingers tangled in her hair. "I'm all yours."

His choice of words clutched at her heart, half with pleasure, half with pain because he tossed them off so lightly. How many women had he said that to without really meaning it?

But she touched him again, at first gingerly, then with more confidence when she discovered how his muscles shivered and jumped because she stroked a certain way, or squeezed him, or teased with a featherlight touch. She sneaked a look at his face, to see that his head was tilted back so that cords stood out in his neck. His cheekbones and jaw stood out in sharp relief; his eyes were closed and his lips drawn back in a grimace of sheer pleasure. Another groan rumbled in his throat.

Suddenly his hands shot out and gripped her hips, lifting her on top of him. "You lied."

"What?"

"You know what you're doing just fine," he said hoarsely. "Too well."

"Oh." She wriggled a little. "Then...then why don't I know what to do now?"

"Here's an easy lesson." He urged her hips up, positioned himself, then pressed her down.

She sank onto him, her breath whistling out of her. "Daniel," she whispered. "Yes. Oh, Daniel."

His grin was fierce. "Now it's up to you, love."

Love. Delight—or was it desire?—spasmed in her belly. She gripped him with her knees and rose, higher, higher, until she was about to lose him, and then she sank onto him until he filled her.

She did it again and again, her pace quickening, his hips thrusting upward to speed her, to bury himself more deeply inside her. She rode him like a wild woman, and loved the exultation on his face. Cries spilled from her lips, guttural sounds from his. Something inside her tightened past the point of breaking; she thought she might die if release didn't come. But she almost dreaded it, too, because nothing ever in her life had been this glorious.

When it came suddenly, the tension snapping and flooding her with exquisite rivers of heat and pleasure, she thought for a moment that she *had* died. How could something feel so good you weren't sure you could survive it?

I love you, trembled on her lips, but she held the words back. Maybe this was just sex. How would she know, when Daniel was the first man she'd ever made love with? What if she said, *I love you,* and he broke it to her that love wasn't part of it?

Now *that,* Renee didn't think she could survive.

RENEE LAY on Daniel, utterly boneless, her head on his shoulder and her hair tickling his chin. He wrapped his arms securely around her and thought about how incredible it felt, having her breasts flattened on his chest, her toes curled against his calves, one long silky-smooth leg draped between his. He'd be happy if she never moved.

He'd no sooner had the thought than she stirred. "That was fun," she said breathlessly.

Fun? Daniel lifted his head in outrage, although he couldn't see her face. Didn't she know how rare what they'd just experienced was? He'd had other women, five or six maybe, and never felt anything close to this. Renee and he together had made the earth move, set off fireworks...hell, they'd pulled off every cliché he could think of.

And she thought it was *fun?*

Of course, she *hadn't* had five or six other men. Or even one. Maybe she did think this was everyday sex.

Or maybe she hadn't felt what he had. How did he know they'd been in sync?

"Yeah." He gritted his teeth. "It was fun."

"You didn't think so?" She lifted her head then, giving him a wide-eyed look, her eyes lucid gray-green, bare of makeup and all the prettier because of it.

"I thought so," he growled.

Her smooth brow crinkled. "Then why are you grumpy?"

Grumpy? God damn it!

Get a grip! Daniel thought sharply. Don't blow it. He was thinking love and commitment and a walk down the aisle, but she was innocent, inexperienced.

For her, he was a way of dipping her toe into the water, so to speak. She was a few years younger, too. Maybe not ready to settle down.

Not in love.

The thought was profoundly depressing, but it also steadied him. If he didn't scare her away, she might come around to his way of thinking. They'd only known each other a couple of weeks, kissed four or five times. Made love a few times. *Give her time,* he thought.

"I just don't think 'fun' covers it," he said. "That's a ride on a roller coaster. This was more like rocketing to the moon."

Her forehead smoothed. "It was, wasn't it?"

"Wanna do it again?"

Her mouth formed a surprised O. "Can we?"

"Uh…not yet," he admitted. Too bad. "Maybe later. If I stay all night." He paused, waiting for an objection, for a reason why he really should leave.

All she did was lay her head back down and snuggle into the curve of his neck. "If you don't mind the bed being so narrow."

He relaxed. "It means you can't get away from me. There are worse fates."

"But your feet must be hanging over."

Yeah. They were. He felt a cool draft on them. Small price to pay. "How about if we talk?" he suggested, partly to divert her.

With her forefinger, she drew a mysterious pattern on his chest. "What do you want to talk about?"

"You."

She poked him. "Unfair."

"Okay. Tit for tat."

"Um." She apparently thought it over. "I can go for that. Is there something special you want to know?"

"What's your favorite movie?"

"Oh, that's easy. Well, no, it isn't. I love *Dave* and *Sense and Sensibility* and *Bull Durham* and *Lethal Weapon* and *Titanic*…"

"Whoa!" He held up one hand. "I get the drift. You're a closet romantic."

"*Lethal Weapon* doesn't have a romance in it." She might have sounded dignified if she wasn't naked and sprawled all over him.

"No, but it has the noble hero willing to risk everthing for a defenseless female."

"You always have to be right," Renee complained.

"Have to be? I *am* always right."

She nipped him. "So what are *your* favorite movies? Some blood-and-guts things?"

"I liked *Bull Durham,* too."

"Baseball. Figures."

"The Hunt for Red October."

She made a rude noise. "Big weapons."

"Fiddler on the Roof."

"Really?" she said in amazement.

"Hey, I'm a sensitive guy." He proved it by falling back in agony when she playfully punched him.

They talked for hours that night, sometimes serious, sometimes laughing. They made love twice more. By three in the morning, Daniel felt punchy and Renee giggled every time he looked at her.

"Time for bed," he decided, swinging his feet to the floor.

"You know, we're already *in* bed," she told him solemnly. "My bed, as a matter of fact."

He switched off the hall light and climbed back in with her. When he reached for the bedside lamp, she chopped at his arm.

"Don't! I like looking at you."

"I like looking at you, too, sweetheart." *I want to look at you for the rest of my life.* "But we need to sleep."

She pouted. "I'm having too much fun to sleep."

"We can have more fun tomorrow."

"Tomorrow I have to work." Her eyelids sank and the words began to slur. "Lots to do. If...if...what was his name? Oh, yeah. Bashter..." She frowned and enunciated more carefully, *"Baxter.* If he's not dead, who is?"

"Good question," Daniel murmured, but she didn't hear. She was sound asleep.

He kissed her gently, turned off the light and rolled onto his side facing her, pillowing Renee's head on his upper arm. Instinctively she reached for him. She fit just right, warm and slim and unexpectedly soft. He held her and she held him. The way it ought to be. Who'd want a king-size bed?

But before he slept, he couldn't help thinking about the last thing she'd said. *Lots to do.* And, *If he's not dead, who is?*

She hadn't given up, and worry stirred in him like an angina pain.

Did she care about her search more than she did anything—or anyone—else? *I have to do this,* she'd told him, letting him see that the decision hurt but making it nonetheless. Without accepting the losses in her life, was Renee capable of really loving a man?

Somewhere in there Daniel fell asleep, too, but only to dream of her. Some threads of his dream were happy: her laughter, her passion, her smile. Other threads were nightmarish: she was arresting his father—no, *him;* he was reaching for her even as she turned away, running toward an insubstantial figure he knew to be her mother. "Renee!" he cried, but she didn't hear him. She walked faster and faster, finally running, until she became as wispy and unreal as her mother.

Daniel awakened in a sweat. As if symbolically, Renee faced away from him now and he felt as though the heavy bar of his arm across her waist was imprisoning her. She made a ragged sound, a whimper, and then another, moving restlessly.

Carefully he eased back, leaving her alone in the bed. Under the hot stream of water in the shower, he washed away both sweat and the unpleasant residue of the dreams.

Why was he reading so much into her determination to solve a puzzle already begun? She was inquisitive, determined—qualities he admired and understood to be part of her. Of course she wouldn't quit! He didn't even know why he wanted her to.

No, that was a lie; he did know. He wanted her to be secure enough in herself to be able to love him wholeheartedly.

Or was it that, like a selfish child, he wanted to come first?

He looked back in at her, but she still slept. The clock radio said seven; he didn't suppose she'd set an alarm, and guessed she'd have to be getting up soon. He wanted to climb right back into bed with her, but something held him back.

Maybe it was the dreams. Or the waking uneasiness that had been their seed. Maybe just that she looked strangely peaceful, now that she was alone in the narrow, pristine twin bed.

Daniel propped one shoulder against the door frame. Before she fled into the night, had Renee's mother stood here, stealing a last memory of her middle daughter? Daniel couldn't recall how old Renee had been when her mother left. Did Renee remember at all what it felt like to have someone making her lunch, braiding her hair, singing lullabies, hiding an Easter basket? Or did she remember most the loneliness afterward?

He would have given anything to change her childhood, to make it loving as his had been, to bring back the lost mother and sister who had meant the world to her.

A private detective, Daniel thought. Maybe he could find Meg and surprise Renee.

But he knew Meg's presence now wasn't the point. Only Renee herself could either accept the loss or choose to find out the truth by hunting for her sister and mother. It was the deciding that would matter, not the finding. And that he couldn't do for her.

There must be something! he thought in frustration. If not something important, something small.

And then it came to him.

When he mounted the stairs half an hour later, he

carried a tray. He set it on the floor beside her bed and gently shook her.

"Hey, Sleeping Beauty. Upsy daisy."

Renee grumbled and buried her face in the covers.

He massaged her neck under her silky fine hair. "Come on. Time to rise and shine."

She said something, muffled by the quilt.

He bent toward her. "What?"

"My mother used to say that."

The pang he felt was sharp, bittersweet. "Mine, too."

"I smell…" She peeked from her nest of covers. "Bacon?"

"And eggs. I hope you like them scrambled. And, uh, pancakes. And I mixed up some orange juice."

Her whole face appeared. "You made breakfast?" She asked as though she couldn't believe he'd done anything so bizarre.

Again his heart cramped. Had no one ever brought her breakfast in bed?

"I…" Renee raked her hair back from her face. "I must look awful."

"You look beautiful." He smiled with sensual intent. "Your cheeks are flushed…" With his knuckles he touched them, feeling the warmth. "Your hair is tousled. And that heavy-lidded look makes a man think about sex, you know. I'd kiss you, but then breakfast would get cold, and I worked hard on it."

"Oh!" Blushing even more fiercely, she jumped out of bed. "Let me…" The sentence trailed off as she fled.

He waited patiently. She came back with astonishing speed. Some women would have showered, put on makeup, styled their hair. Renee had brushed hers and tucked it behind her ears, washed her face and donned a robe.

"I'd forgotten I bought the bacon," she said, hopping back into bed, tucking the pillow behind her and sitting cross-legged. She looked absurdly young and delighted at such a small treat.

"Milady—" he set the tray carefully in the middle of the bed "—breakfast is served."

The two plates were covered by mixing bowls to hold in the heat. Delicious smells wafted up.

"I'll never be able to eat all this," she said, even as she poured syrup onto her pancakes.

As they ate, she told him about yesterday's domestic violence case taken to an extreme. The sadness, the damage done to so many lives, the frustration for the police involved.

"You know she'll welcome him back, maybe even bail him out, and he'll hit her again, and she'll think that's the way life is. And *we'll* probably have to do this all over again, only next time he might shoot somebody, or get shot. Sometimes it seems easier to storm a hostage taker than to wait patiently until he wears down." She fell silent.

"So what's the answer?"

"There is no answer." Renee sighed. "Better education. Instant access to counseling, shelters, alcohol treatment... Would that make a difference, do you think?"

It seemed easier for a man to storm a woman's defenses than to wait patiently, too, Daniel thought. Male instincts called for action.

"I don't know," he admitted. If a woman's lot in

life was exactly what she'd expected, would she ask for help no matter how readily available it was?

"I don't, either." Renee sighed again, then smiled a little wistfully as she set down her fork. "I can't eat another bite. Oh, Daniel. This was so sweet of you."

He moved uncomfortably. "I was hungry."

"Right." She leaned forward across the tray and kissed him on the lips. Now *that* was sweet.

"Want to ditch work today?" he asked on impulse. "Stay in bed all day?"

Longing shone briefly on her fine-boned face. "I wish," she said, wrinkling her nose. "But Jack was mad at me yesterday as it was. If I take a vacation day now, he'd never forgive me. Besides…"

A chill settled over him at the change in her voice. "Besides what?"

"I've been thinking about Les Greene again. And Gabe Rosler. Something isn't right there. While we wait for the fingerprint ID, I'm going to trace them."

His gut clenched. "You're obsessed."

Her gaze, startled and defensive, flew to his. "I'm curious. Is that so bad?"

He stood up and said harshly, "What you're really curious about is what happened to your mother. Why don't you look for *her?*"

She scrambled off the bed, too, stumbling over the hem of her robe. "Because if she can't bother to contact me, I don't want to find her! That's why!"

"Maybe she can't. Maybe she's dead."

"She shouldn't have left me!" Renee cried, tears shimmering in her eyes.

"You're an adult. Wouldn't it be better to find out why she left? Why she never called or wrote?" He leaned toward her. "Wouldn't you rather *know?*"

At the echo of her own words to him, she sucked in a sharp breath. "Why are you doing this?"

"Because I want you to grow up."

He felt sick at the sight of the shock and hurt in her eyes. The cruel words weren't even true; what he wanted was for her to focus on *him,* not Les Greene or T. J. Baxter or Meg Patton.

He swore. "I didn't mean that."

"I think you did," she said quietly, her face pale. "Maybe you're right. Here I am in my father's house six months after he died. Totally inexperienced. That isn't very appealing, is it? I know you're right."

Daniel swore again and reached for her, but she shied away.

"I love you," he said, voice raw.

She shook her head hard. "Don't say that right now. Please. You don't mean it. Don't say it."

"I do! Renee..." In sheer terror, he took a step forward.

She took one back, still shaking her head. "Will you please go, Daniel? Thank you for breakfast."

Oh, God. How could he have been so stupid?

"Renee. I swear..."

"No!" she shouted, then clapped her hand over her mouth. Tears welled in her eyes. "Please... just...leave."

He closed his eyes for a moment, then backed clumsily away. "I'll call."

She said nothing.

He picked up the tray, carried it to the door. There he turned *back* for one last look at her.

"Just remember," he said, in a voice that scraped his throat. "I love you. I'm in love with you. I have every intention of marrying you."

She hadn't moved; still didn't speak. In her eyes was pain, not a leap of hope.

"Remember," he said, and left.

CHAPTER FOURTEEN

THE CLERK at the California Department of Motor Vehicle Registration was helpful and quick. On the basis of age, together she and Renee eliminated all but two of the Lester or Les Greenes who held driver's licenses in the state.

"I didn't catch that second address," Renee said. The woman repeated the information and Renee double-checked her notes.

"And not a single Gabe or Gabriel Rosler in the right age bracket."

"That's right, Lieutenant."

Renee thanked her profusely and hung up. Rubbing gritty eyes, she struggled to stay focused. If she let herself stop, she'd fall apart.

Keep busy. Don't think, was her mantra.

Okay. What had she learned?

Would Gabe have changed his name for some reason? A criminal record once he'd gone to California? Or was he lying to his parents in his annual Christmas letter about where he lived, because he didn't want them surprising him?

Heck, maybe he'd gone to Chicago, or Miami, or Enid, Oklahoma.

And maybe, with luck, Les Greene would know. She dialed information and got the two phone numbers. Chances were both men would be at work during the day, but she decided to give them a try anyway.

One lived in San Francisco, the other in Half Moon Bay, a small town half an hour south along the coast. She decided to go for the big city first.

The phone rang five times. She was about to hang up when she heard a clunk on the other end, a muffled curse, and finally the voice of someone wakened from a heavy sleep.

"Yeah?"

"May I speak to Les Greene?"

"That's me," the man said brusquely.

"I apologize if I woke you up."

"I work nights. Who are you?"

"Lieutenant Renee Patton. Elk Springs Police Department. I'm trying to locate a Les Greene who attended Elk Springs High School."

There was a long silence. The man sounded more alert when he said, "Is it my mother? Did she die?"

"Your mother's name?"

"Joanie. Joanie Greene. Unless she remarried."

"No," Renee said. "She didn't. Actually, I'm afraid your mother died three years ago. Cirrhosis of the liver."

Another silence. "Figures," Greene said. Then, "Maybe I should feel something, but I don't. She wasn't any kind of mother."

"So I understand."

"That's why you're calling?"

"No." Renee took a breath. "Actually, I'm trying to locate Gabe Rosler. I understand the two of you were good friends in high school."

"I haven't seen him since then. He took off before we graduated."

"And you left yourself a short time later."

"How did you know that?" he asked, suspicion coloring his voice.

"Gabe's mother reported you missing. I came across a police report on you."

"She reported me missing?" he repeated, sounding stunned.

"She was worried about you."

This silence was the longest yet. "I didn't think anybody would worry." Bitterly, "I knew my mother wouldn't. And with Gabe gone…"

"I was hoping you might have made contact with him after you left."

"I tried. We talked about places we'd go once we left home. S.F. sounded the coolest. I thought I might find him down here, but I didn't. I tried calling his house once, but his bastard of a father told me they didn't want to hear from me again. So—" Renee could almost hear the shrug "—I got a job and did okay. I figured maybe he'd gone home."

"I'm afraid he didn't." Renee hesitated. "May I ask you a very personal question?"

"I guess that depends," he said warily.

"Are you homosexual?"

"You want to know if Gabe was gay, too. Yeah. He was. I am. Why are you looking for Gabe, Officer? I mean, why now?"

She told him about the bones found on the neighboring ranch and her fruitless search for a name to go with them.

"I, um, actually checked your dental records, but, uh..."

"My teeth are still in my mouth."

"Exactly."

"Are you going to check Gabe's now?"

"Yes," she said slowly, "I think I am."

Another silence. "Will you call? After you've found out? I've always kinda wondered. You know?"

"Yes," she agreed. "Of course. I'll keep you informed. Um...one more question, Mr. Greene. If you don't mind. It's not important. I'm just curious."

"About what?"

"When you ran away, why did you leave your car? That's why Mrs. Rosler reported you missing, by the way. She couldn't imagine you would have left that car voluntarily."

He grunted, either with surprise or laughter. "Engine blew. The transmission wasn't so great, either. Do you know what my mother did with it?"

"Afraid not," she told him. "Doesn't sound like it was good for much but the junkyard."

"Yeah. I had some good years in that car, though." He sounded more nostalgic about it than he had about his mother. Who could blame him?

"Thank you, Mr. Greene. I'll be in touch."

Renee rose to her feet even as she hung up. *Keep busy. Don't think.* Time for another little talk with Marjorie Rosler.

As she drove, she did her best to blank from her mind the fact that this was also the route to the Triple B. To Daniel. Who had said, "I love you. I'm in love with you.'' But who had also seen through her facade to the terrified, lost little girl beneath and had no patience with her.

Don't think. Not about him.

Gabe Rosler, then.

How could those bones be his? Had his mother lied about receiving those letters all these years? Were the pride and the grief false?

Or were the letters the kind anybody could have written? The ''Dear Mom, I'm doing great, I'm an E.M.T. now'' kind.

But why would somebody bother to write them?

Now she *was* chasing a will-o'-the-wisp. But something wouldn't let her turn back. *If not T. J. Baxter, who?*

She could wait for the fingerprint ID. But she had a cop's gut feeling that the charming ex-rodeo rider, arrogant enough to think he'd still have a job after raping the boss's wife, was going to turn out to have walked away from the Triple B with no more than a black eye and bloody nose.

What could it hurt to chase down one more lead? She'd already lost everything she had to lose.

She parked in front of the Roslers' white house and went to the door. Coming in answer to the knock, Marjorie peered through the screen, just like the last time.

''Officer.'' She didn't sound very happy. ''Why, I didn't expect to see you again.''

''May I come in? I have news about Les Greene.''

''Oh. Oh!'' She unlatched the screen door and pushed it open. ''Please. That...that isn't him after all, is it?''

"No." Renee stepped inside. The house was as still as a graveyard. She'd have felt better if a soap opera had been playing in the background. "No, I actually spoke to him."

"You did?" Marjorie's tired face lit up. "He's all right?"

"Yes. He lives in the San Francisco area, although apparently he and Gabe never hooked up again. He didn't realize that Gabe was down there, too."

"But...but they were such friends. I always thought..." She fumbled her way to the rose-pink recliner and sank down, distress coming from her in waves. "Why...why, that's too bad."

Here came the hard part. "Mrs. Rosler—"

The front door slammed. Blunt-featured face flushed with anger, Dick Rosler loomed in the arched opening to the living room.

"You're back out here."

Renee faced him, thinking again what an unlikely pair he and his pretty wife must have seemed when they walked down the aisle together. "Yes. I had some news I wanted to share with Mrs. Rosler. And a few more questions."

"What the hell kind of questions do you have for us? Look at her." He brushed past Renee, went to Marjorie and placed a heavy hand on her shoulder. He glowered at Renee. "You'd better have some mighty good reason for upsetting my wife this way."

In her husband's presence, quelled by his touch, Marjorie seemed to have shrunk. She stared down as if fascinated by her hands.

Resolve hardening, Renee said, "Mr. Rosler, do you have any reason to doubt that the letters you've received from your son are genuine?"

"What?" he exploded. "What kind of crap are you talking? Of course they're from our son! Who the hell else would write?"

That was the question, wasn't it?

"Could I see them?"

"They're none of your goddamned business!"

"I'd like to check his dental records. With your permission…"

"Which you're not going to get!"

Was it fear of what she might find out that turned his face purple and glittered in his eyes? Just because he and Gabe had never gotten along didn't mean he didn't love his son. Did her suggestion confirm some deep-held suspicion that he hadn't wanted his wife to hear?

Had he wondered whether his son was dead? He wouldn't be the first to use anger to push back fear.

Only, if Gabe was dead, who wrote the letters?

"Mr. Rosler…"

"*No!*" he thundered. "I want you off our place! And don't come back. I'll be letting your superior know what kind of irresponsible accusations you're making."

Interesting, she thought, that he interpreted her request as an accusation. Did he think she was accusing him? Why would he assume that?

"Mrs. Rosler," Renee said.

Marjorie didn't move, didn't meet her eyes.

Feeling pity, Renee said gently, "I'm sorry to

have bothered you. I hope you two will discuss this. If you change your mind…''

The rancher's fingers tightened on his wife's shoulder. ''We won't,'' he said inflexibly.

Renee nodded. ''I'll see myself out.''

In her car, she sat looking up at the house for a minute. If only Dick hadn't heard her arrive! She just knew Marjorie would have given her permission, at least let her glance through her son's letters.

Now… Well, she'd done what she could without a warrant. Maybe she was wrong about the balance of power in the Rosler home. Dick Rosler wouldn't be the first man full of bluster who could be gently maneuvered by his wife. She might talk some sense into him.

Renee had to hope so, because she knew she didn't have enough justification to obtain a warrant. ''I just have a feeling,'' wouldn't cut it with the judge.

The phone messages on her desk when she got back didn't include one from Marjorie Rosler. Abby had phoned, as had the owner of a local hardware store. Renee had had dealings with him only a few weeks before, when he discovered a clerk was stealing from him. He'd fired the thief, but decided not to press charges, which she'd considered a mistake.

She called him back first.

''Thanks, Lieutenant,'' he said. ''You remember that kid I fired? Kyle Peterson? Well, shoot, this is probably nothing, but another young guy I have working for me says he's heard rumors that Peterson is talking big about killing me.''

"Killing you?" Renee repeated, startled. "You let him off easy."

"That's what I figured, but I guess he doesn't see it that way. He actually had the gall to put me down for a reference—can you believe it? I told the fellow who called that I'd fired Peterson and why. So he didn't get the job and now I hear he's worked up about it. You know nothing'll come of it, but what with all you read in the newspapers these days, I thought I should report it."

"I'll go talk to him," Renee said. "I can dig out the file, but do you happen to have his address handy?"

"Isn't that just going to make him madder?"

"Scare some sense into him, is what I have in mind. As you say, it's probably talk, but he needs to learn not to shoot his mouth off like that. And if he's at all serious...well, I'll just feel better once I've had words with him."

Nervous, the owner reluctantly gave her the address and expressed confidence in her judgment.

On her way out to the house Kyle Peterson shared with three other young men, Renee took a call to a convenience store, where the chubby clerk waved a twenty dollar bill under Renee's nose.

"Look!" she said. "It's got to be fake. Jeez, I just know it's going to come out of my pocket. God. Counterfeit money. The manager says to watch out for it, but who thinks somebody is printing up funny money in Elk Springs?"

"They're probably not," Renee said. "The customer could have picked this up anywhere."

"How was I supposed to know?" the clerk said miserably.

Renee took the bill encased in plastic. It would be sent off to federal authorities, who took counterfeiting seriously.

As she walked out of the store, a blue pickup truck pulled in beside the gas pumps. Her heart jumped and she battled a desire to scurry back inside and hide in the ladies' rest room. Was it Daniel?

No. His didn't have a rifle rack in the back window. And the man who got out had a beard.

Renee's breath left her lungs with a whoosh. She collapsed in the driver's seat of her Bronco. She was shaking, she saw with a distant part of her attention. Drained, as if she'd just been shot at. All because she saw a pickup similar to Daniel's. All because she might conceivably have run into him.

I want you to grow up.

Could she?

She knew the streets of Elk Springs well enough to drive on automatic. Not until she pulled up in front of the ramshackle house shared by four guys in their early twenties did she regain awareness of her surroundings and the neighborhood, consisting mostly of small rentals.

Climbing out, Renee tsked mentally at the lawn that should have been mowed a last time before winter, at the torn, faded flannel sheets hung in the front window in place of blinds, at the loose board on the bare, splintered porch steps.

Her father would have said that you could judge a man—he always said a man, not a woman—by how he kept up his home. Of course, he hadn't made allowances for disabilities or for a single mother's struggle to survive or a landlord's refusal to pay for repairs. Still, she often found he was right.

Much as she hated to admit any such thing.

These guys weren't much more than teenagers, though, she reminded herself. Her impression was that a couple of them were ski bums, living hand-to-mouth in wait of powder snow. The other two, including Kyle Peterson, were local boys more interested in partying than taking on adult responsibilities.

She felt a brief spurt of anger at the comparison to herself. Not far separated in years from this quartet, she felt a century removed by how she lived her life. Damn it, they needed to grow up! How dare Daniel put her in the same category?

She climbed the porch steps gingerly, noting the recyling bin overflowing with beer cans. Tinny voices from a television set were muffled by the door. Her brisk knock brought a yelled, "Come in."

Wearing nothing but sweatpants, Kyle Peterson was sprawled on a shabby sofa. A pyramid of beer cans decorated the wood crate used as a coffee table. He couldn't seem to tear his gaze from the TV screen, where Steven Seagal debonairly kicked into submission several bad guys.

"Mr. Peterson," Renee said. "I'd like to talk to you."

"Who…?" He turned bleary eyes at her. At the sight of her uniform, alarm kicked in. "You're that woman cop."

"That's right. Lieutenant Patton."

He swung his feet to the floor and stood. The gray

sweats sagged, exposing more of his groin than Renee wanted to see. "Do you have a warrant or something?"

"You invited me in."

"I didn't know—" He stopped. "Is this just some kind of follow-up?"

She planted her feet well apart. "What do you think?"

A scowl drew his brows together. "I don't know. You tell me."

"Would you please turn the television off." She didn't make it a question.

He wanted to refuse just to be a jerk, she could see it in his eyes, but abruptly he turned, grabbed a remote control and punched some buttons. The screen went dark and silence fell.

"Happy?"

"I am." Her hand rested on the butt of her gun. "I understand that you're not. I hear you're real unhappy about having lost your job."

Bitterness twisted his thin, unshaven face. "Shouldn't I be? I was good! The boss man said so himself. Next thing I know, I'm canned because some money is missing. Like he could prove it."

"He did prove it." Renee met his stare. "I urged him to file charges. He felt that firing you was enough to get the message through. Apparently he was wrong."

Wariness flickered in his eyes. "What's that supposed to mean?"

"You've been heard making threats."

"*Bull!*" he exploded, pacing a couple of agitated steps and then stopping. "I just want a job!"

"And you actually expected to get a good reference from a man you'd robbed."

"I'd have paid it back—" Belatedly, he put the brakes on. Then he swore and talked fast. "I just...I was really broke. You know? I couldn't make my share of the rent. The guys carried me one month, but they said they wouldn't another. I would've put it back as soon as I got paid. Really."

"But then where would you have come up with the next month's rent?"

"I'd have thought of something." He uttered an obscenity. "What am I telling you for?" He thrust out his hands. "Why don't you just put the handcuffs on right now?"

"That's very tempting," she said. "Let me think about it."

"Oh, God." He turned away and bumped his forehead against the wall, then stayed leaning against it, his eyes closed. "What am I going to do?"

She let no sympathy at all sound in her voice. "Lie around drinking beer and watching videos, apparently. Blame someone else."

He didn't react with renewed rage, which she figured was a good sign.

"How seriously should I take those threats against Mr. Carlton's life?" she asked.

"Oh, damn, damn, damn," Peterson muttered. "I didn't mean anything. I don't even own a gun, or... I was just... I was probably drunk. And pissed. You know? I can't believe somebody told the cops." Despair poured off him in waves, as powerful as the odor of beer.

Renee said abruptly, "I could talk to John Carlton about giving you a reference for a job where you had no access to money. He did say you were a good worker. He might consider coming through if you agree to make restitution in small monthly installments."

His head shot up. "Do you think…? Oh, damn. Why would he? I mean, I don't blame him for being really steamed. He *trusted* me."

She shrugged. "It's worth a try."

"I…" Peterson's Adam's apple bobbed. "If you mean it."

She went out to her car and leaned against the fender, dialing her cell phone. John Carlton, who had a heart as soft as spring snow, agreed immediately, as she'd guessed he would.

"Kyle's not a bad kid," he said. "Hell, who isn't impulsive at that age?"

Me, she wanted to say. *I never was.* She hadn't done an impulsive thing in her life until that night when she watched Daniel throw her father's recliner off the front porch. She'd been afraid to do anything without thinking it through ten ways to Sunday; afraid any change at all would upset the fragile balance that allowed her to cope. She almost envied Kyle Peterson, who could do something stupid and find redemption.

She went back up onto the porch to find that he'd pulled on a sweatshirt, stuck his feet in sneakers and combed his lanky hair. He cried when she told him the news, swore up and down and sideways that he'd pay Carlton back, pay *more* than he had to, mow

John Carlton's lawn, paint his house, clean his toilet. Anything.

"All he's asking is for you to learn a lesson," Renee said. She tipped her hat. "Good day, Mr. Peterson."

Back at the station, she told Jack what she'd done, half expecting him to call her a sucker.

But he nodded from where he slouched in her office doorway. "My sister used to baby-sit Kyle Peterson. He wasn't a bad kid. I think he'll come through."

Renee sat down. "We'll see."

"Update me on the bones."

"Dick Rosler called you?"

Jack's gaze sharpened. "A week or so ago. Not recently, if that's what you mean."

"I know it'll be a while before we get an ID on those fingerprints, but... Oh, shoot. I'm getting this feeling those bones might be Gabe Rosler's. Dick is determined to keep me from finding out. I don't know whether that's because he doesn't want to know if they are, or because he already knows."

"That's a pretty wild statement," Jack said.

"No kidding." Even her wry smile took an effort. In less than twenty-four hours, she'd forgotten how to smile. "I can't even defend it. It's just a hunch."

He frowned at her without speaking for an uncomfortably long moment. Then he grimaced. "Your feelings are right on more often than I want to admit." He straightened. "It's five-thirty. You're not going to accomplish anything more. Why don't you go home?"

Her stomach took a panicky leap. She couldn't!

Her house was too empty, too quiet. She wouldn't be able to help thinking. Remembering. She'd see him ripping up carpet, racing her for the bathroom, holding her close in her narrow bed.

The kitchen was about the only room where he hadn't spent much time, but she wasn't about to go back to huddling in there, hiding from life.

Grow up.

Maybe, she thought, with a flicker of hope, she was. Or maybe she already had and just didn't know it. Shoot, maybe Daniel Barnard was wrong, for once in his life.

Her phone rang. She snatched up the receiver. "Patton."

"Miss...that is, Officer Patton?" The voice was hesitant, just above a whisper.

"Yes?" Her heart took a different kind of leap. "Mrs. Rosler?"

"I didn't tell Dick I was calling." A pause. "He'd be upset, and he has that heart condition, you know. He's had a quadruple bypass."

"I didn't know that. I'm sorry," Renee said sincerely.

Marjorie begged for understanding. "He's just trying to protect me. He's always protected me."

"I'm sure he has." Renee twirled the cord around her finger. "Mrs. Rosler..."

"I mailed you one of Gabe's letters. Oh!" After a startled cry, she fell silent.

Renee sat bolt upright. "Mrs. Rosler? Is something wrong?"

Her voice came back, fainter than ever. "I thought I heard Dick coming, but I can see him

down by the barn.'' She drew an audible breath.
''He won't miss just one letter. And…and our dentist—we've all gone to him since Gabe was a little
boy… Anyway, we go to Dr. Kauffman. Philip
Kauffman.''

Renee's mind raced. ''I'll need your permission,
Mrs. Rosler.''

''I called and told them you could see Gabe's X
rays. I pray it comes to nothing, but I need to know.
I guess Dick would rather hope, but sometimes I
think the way Gabe left and never calls or anything
is worse than having him dead.''

''Yes,'' Renee said, and she wasn't thinking
about Gabe Rosler. ''I think you're right. It hurts
worse.''

''Your mama left, didn't she?''

Renee swallowed. ''Yes. When I was eleven.''

''So you know.''

''I've hoped, over and over, that she was dead.''

''Sometimes I did, too.'' Marjorie's tremulous
voice shattered, then firmed. ''Only, there were
those letters.''

''But now you wonder.''

''Who could have written them?'' The few words
expressed a world of bewildered pain. ''They would
have had to know things!''

''Les Greene?''

''Maybe.'' She sounded doubtful. ''I guess Gabe
could have told him stories. Oh! I hear the front
door.''

A click sounded in Renee's ear. Thoughtfully, she
hung up and opened her top drawer, taking out the
phone book. In the Yellow Pages, she ran her finger

down the list of dentists until she came to Kauffman, Philip, D.D.S.

A moment later, she listened incredulously to the recorded message telling her that Dr. Kauffman's office was closed for the day and he wouldn't be in until Monday. It seemed that Dr. Philip Kauffman worked only four days a week.

Renee said a word that hardly ever passed her lips and slammed down the phone. If she had to, she'd roust him out of the squash court or wherever he recreated to get in shape for ski season. The hell she'd wait until Monday!

The good dentist, however, was apparently out of town, she discovered after half a dozen more phone calls. His office manager said, no, *she* hadn't spoken to Mrs. Rosler and she couldn't possibly release those records without Dr. Kauffman's knowledge.

"He'll be in Monday morning at eight a.m.," she said crisply. "If this isn't a matter of life and death…"

Though more tempted to lie than she'd ever been in her life, Renee had to concede that it wasn't. She vented her frustration by slamming down the phone this time, too.

CHAPTER FIFTEEN

DR. KAUFFMAN'S VOICE creaked from age. Renee hoped his hands were steadier with a drill.

"Well, let me think." From the silence, he was apparently doing just that. He mused aloud, "I moved my office...oh, ten years ago. Records much earlier than that went into storage. It may take us a day or two to find the ones you want."

Renee gritted her teeth. Where had all her patience gone? "I'd appreciate anything you can do to expedite the hunt, Dr. Kauffman," she said as pleasantly as she could manage. "We're all hoping these remains don't turn out to be Gabe Rosler's, but, as you can imagine, his parents are terribly anxious. The sooner we can tell them one way or other, the better."

"Yes, yes, I can see that." He harrumphed. "Don't I remember Marjorie telling me news from Gabe's Christmas letter? I thought they heard from the boy regularly."

"There's some doubt now about those letters," Renee said.

"Ah. I see."

Plainly, he didn't, but who could blame him? The idea of a murderer writing his victim's mother for the next twenty years was a bizarre one. So bizarre,

Renee had moments of wondering whether she hadn't gone off the deep end. Did she hate the idea of failure so much, she couldn't accept that she would never identify the bones? Besides T. J. Baxter, Gabe was her last possibility. After that, she might just as well close the file.

Which was probably what she should have done in the first place, she thought with a sigh. In her quest, she seemed to have trailed unhappiness behind her like Typhoid Mary. Her job was to serve and protect. Who was she serving?

Dr. Kauffman pulled her back from some heavy-duty brooding. "I'll tell you what. I'll send Cora over to the storage center right now to find those records. She's doing billing, but it can wait. I'll call the minute we find them."

"Thank you," she told him, probably scaring the man with how heartfelt she sounded.

After hanging up, she pushed her chair back, put her feet on her desk and looked around. Usually after two days off, she walked into her office and felt as if she hadn't been gone five minutes. Today she was so damned glad to be back after the longest weekend of her life, fond feelings enveloped her at the familiar squeak from her padded chair, at the sight of her gray steel desk and brown paper blotter, the green metal bookcase filled with law enforcement manuals and the black filing cabinets. Even the corkboard with Wanted bulletins looked positively decorative. This office was home more than her house was.

Though she'd finally realized she could change that if she wanted to. The only good part of her weekend had been the Saturday shopping expedition with Abby and Anne McWhirter. She'd chosen a denim couch, throw pillows made from blue-and-white quilt blocks, and white-painted cottage-style furniture. Thrilled at the size of her purchase, the store delivered Saturday afternoon.

Her TV now reposed in a white armoire; a vase of yellow and white carnations, bought on impulse, sat on the coffee table. A painting or two, and the living room would be complete. She loved it. And she wished Daniel could see it.

Not seeing or hearing from Daniel hurt so terribly, she'd been thrown back to her childhood, remembering the disappearance of her mother, the silence after Meg left. How could this be as bad? she kept asking herself, but in a different way, it was. She had always known that someday she would grow up and leave home; her mother and sister were part of her past, not her future. Daniel *was*—could have been—her future, her forever.

She couldn't bear it if he never came back, if he didn't mean those last things he'd said. She wanted so badly to be able to show him that she was a woman, not a scared child, but she didn't know how. She didn't even know how to convince herself. Face the past, or walk away from it?

Keep busy. Don't think.

She took a call at a rental business whose manager had just discovered their chain-link fence had been cut during the night and several expensive pieces of equipment had been stolen. Unfortunately, surrounding businesses had been closed, as well. The bar behind the rental yard was just opening; the bartender hadn't seen or heard anything, but he took Renee's card and promised to ask patrons, most of them were regulars.

A broken window at the five-and-dime down the block seemed to be the work of a vandal rather than a thief. The clerk hadn't noticed anything missing and the hole punched by a rock in the glass didn't appear to be large enough to allow ingress. Renee wrote up a report without any hope of finding the kid who'd probably done it.

She stopped for lunch and sat with a couple of other women, who asked her to speak at their monthly businesswomen's luncheon. Mildly pleased, she agreed. It was always good public relations, and she'd like to see more awareness of women in law enforcement. Their invitation spurred her to call the high school and ask the principal if she couldn't come there one day and talk.

"This isn't a career girls usually consider," she said. "I'd like to see that change."

As far as she could tell, he liked the idea and agreed to discuss with various teachers the best format for having her.

"I'll get back to you," he promised.

She hung up with a feeling of satisfaction and also the dip in her stomach that reminded her she needed to find something else to do.

Keep busy.

She was saved by the bell. Renee picked up her phone. "Elk Springs P.D. Lieutenant Patton."

"This is Phil Kauffman. Cora finally located that file, Lieutenant. You're welcome to bring the X rays you have on down and we'll compare them."

Her adrenaline kicked in. "I can't thank you enough, Dr. Kauffman. I'll be right over."

She grabbed the stiff manila envelope that held the X rays the coroner had taken of the maxilla, the upper jaw still intact on the skull.

Ten minutes, and she pulled into the parking lot at the side of the small brick building that housed Dr. Kauffman's dentistry clinic. A second name in smaller letters on the sign told her he'd taken in a partner; an heir apparent, presumably, given Kauffman's age.

The starchy woman behind the counter said, "Lieutenant Patton? Dr. Kauffman is expecting you. One moment, please."

Her nameplate said *Susan Ott*. Renee asked for the Cora who'd been so quick. A matronly woman appeared through the open door to a small office and accepted Renee's thanks.

"I know the Roslers," she said. "Poor Marjorie. I'll be praying for her."

"She'd appreciate that," Renee said.

The starchy office manager sent her on back then. Waiting for her in a cubicle with a light box, the gray-haired dentist held out a hand. "Phil Kauffman."

He was stronger and younger-looking than his voice had suggested. Keen blue eyes appraised her swiftly.

"Renee Patton," she said, shaking his hand. "Thank you for putting a rush on this."

"No problem. You have the X ray here?"

She handed him the envelope; he slipped it into

one side of the light box. The other already held an X ray.

"This is Gabe Rosler's," he said absently, turning off the overhead light and peering at the two. "He had good teeth," he commented absently. "I reviewed his chart. Required very few fillings even in his baby teeth. Unusual, considering those were the days before mothers added fluoride to a baby's milk."

Renee looked from one X ray to the other. To her inexperienced eye, they were very similar. There was the filling in the back molar, and the other tiny one the coroner had spotted. The front tooth on both X rays was a little out of line—not so badly that parents would have seen the need for braces in those days, but sticking out just a little. When he smiled, it would have showed.

Renee saw in her mind's eye the photos of Gabe Rosler, the baby, the small boy, the teenager. In one picture he'd been grinning, and... Dear Lord. The small imperfection had given appeal to his too pretty face.

Phil Kauffman abruptly flipped on the light and faced Renee, his expression showing how disturbed he was.

"I'm afraid, Lieutenant, that you have a match. I couldn't believe..." He shook his head. "I still can't believe..."

"It's difficult, when you know the victim. I'm sorry to have had to ask you to do this, Dr. Kauffman."

"Oh, it isn't me! I just can't help thinking about

Marjorie Rosler. A nicer lady, you couldn't find. And Gabe was her only child!''

''You have no doubt?'' Renee felt compelled to ask.

He sighed. ''None whatever. You're welcome, of course, to have the coroner look these over. You'll probably want to do that. But... No. I regret to say that I'm quite certain.''

They shook hands. Renee took both X rays. Outside she saw how white the sky had turned. She shivered, feeling in the stillness and weight of the air the snow that would be falling soon. She hoped it held long enough for her to drive out to the Rosler ranch and make it back.

On the way, she analyzed how she felt. Now she knew, was even pretty sure who had murdered the teenager. She'd expected triumph when she found the elusive answer to the puzzle, but she'd come to know too many of the people involved. It wasn't a puzzle anymore; it was a tragedy.

Turning in the gates from the highway, Renee saw flashing lights. Cinders crunching under her tires, she drove too fast up the lane. She rolled to a stop next to the ambulance and jumped out.

The attendants were just rolling a gurney out the front door. As it passed, Renee caught a glimpse of a face covered by an oxygen mask. The E.M.T.s were moving fast, urgency in their voices and hands. Behind them came Marjorie Rosler, wringing her hands.

She turned desperate, frightened eyes on Renee.

''What happened?'' Renee asked.

''Dick.'' A sob escaped her and she looked back

at the ambulance. "He... I think he had another heart attack. I think..." Tears began to fall. "I think it was my fault. I came into the room, and he had the letters in his hand. He turned around with this terrible look on his face, and then..." She shook all over. "And then he just collapsed. He must have discovered one was gone."

"I'm so sorry." Renee tentatively put an arm around the weeping woman, who stayed stiff in her embrace. "Do you have family? Have you called someone?"

"Yes. My sister."

The E.M.T.s folded up the wheels and boosted the gurney into the back of the ambulance.

Marjorie lifted her gaze to Renee, who had the sense that the older woman had just realized who she was, what her presence meant.

"You...you've found something out, haven't you?"

"Yes." Renee hesitated. "This isn't the time..."

"Tell me." Her mouth firmed, and her expression was suddenly fierce. "Gabe is dead, isn't he?"

One E.M.T. stayed crouched inside the back of the ambulance; the other hopped out. "Ma'am, if you're going to ride along, we need to go."

Renee felt helpless to comfort, to soften the blow. "Yes," she said again. "I'm afraid so."

"Sometimes I used to think Dick hated his own son," Marjorie said.

So she knew. Renee reached out a hand; Marjorie straightened, rejecting her touch.

"Ma'am," the ambulance attendant repeated more urgently.

"Your husband loves you," Renee said. "He went to a lot of trouble to send those letters."

"Oh, love." Grief, rage, bitterness, all tangled in her voice. "Is that love?"

She turned away then, and accepted the E.M.T.'s hand to help her into the ambulance. Just before the doors closed, she looked back. "Why? That's all I want to know. Why would he have killed his own boy?"

Renee could guess. What she couldn't decide was whether she should tell a grieving mother that her husband had probably found out his son was homosexual and murdered him out of rage and pride that wouldn't accept his neighbors knowing what his son was.

Renee watched the ambulance go, a lump in her throat.

Marjorie had said she'd rather know. Now she did, but this knowledge was grievous.

Staring after the ambulance until it disappeared toward town on the highway, Renee wondered again: who had she served?

SHE'D GO TO THE HOSPITAL. And hope, for the first time in her life, that a man died. If he survived, could she come up with enough evidence to convict him? She'd have to focus on the letters. Who had mailed them for him?

What would be gained from sending a sixty-year-old man to jail for a murder committed so long ago? He wasn't a danger to society.

And yet, how could she let him go back to his life, a free man?

What kind of life would that be, now that his wife knew what he'd done?

Perhaps, Renee thought, Dick Rosler had chosen the time of his going.

Before she went to the hospital, she'd drive out to the Triple B. Although no one could be certain what had happened to T. J. Baxter until the finger-print ID came back, they now knew the most important thing: the remains found on Barnard land were not his. Renee felt, after all she'd put her through, that she owed it to Shirley to tell her as soon as possible.

Renee swung the Bronco in a circle and headed for the R & R gates. This was something she needed to do.

Never mind that she might see Daniel.

She'd be just as glad if she didn't, she tried to convince herself. Seeing him would hurt. She'd hope he wasn't there, or didn't notice her arrival. The news would come better from his mother.

Which didn't explain why her heart was pounding so hard when she drove under the Triple B name burned into the gate arch.

But her luck was out. As she drove by the barns, Daniel stood talking with another man beside a strange pickup. A chill and then a flush washed over her face. Despite her dark mood, he looked so good to her in boots, dusty jeans and a denim jacket; a Stetson was pushed onto the back of his head.

She saw him, as if in a pantomime, turn to stare at her. The other guy, who appeared to have been talking, mimicked him exactly. Scarcely able to breathe, her heart was so constricted, Renee lifted a hand in greeting, and continued on to the white farmhouse. Without looking over her shoulder although she knew he would come, she went up the steps to the front door and rang.

"Just a minute!" Shirley called from inside. A moment later, she opened the door. She took a sharp breath when she saw Renee. "You…you have news."

"Yes." Better this time; easier to give.

"Come in." But Shirley didn't move. "No. Tell me now. Please. Was it Baxter who died?"

"We still don't know anything about T. J. Baxter," Renee said straight-out. "But I do know those bones aren't his."

Shirley sagged. Renee took a quick step forward across the threshold and grabbed her elbows.

"Do you need to sit down?"

"I'm just…" Her voice was a wisp and she trembled all over. "Dear Lord, I'm so relieved." She lifted a face already damp with tears. "That means…"

"Yes." For some absurd reason, Renee felt close to tears herself. "It's pretty unlikely a second body is lying out there somewhere. I think you can go back to believing your husband would never have done something so against his principles."

"I'm ashamed even to have been afraid…"

Neither woman had noticed Daniel's arrival until he said urgently, "Mom. What is it? Are you all right?"

It somehow felt natural to slip her arm around his mother's waist as Renee turned to face him.

His eyes, always bluer than she remembered,

bored into hers even as his mother was the one to speak. Had to be the one to speak. Renee wasn't sure she could.

"The bones aren't that Baxter man's. Your father didn't kill him."

The intensity of his gaze didn't waver. "Then whose…" He stopped, his tone changed. "Not Gabe?"

Renee nodded dumbly, her tongue still paralyzed.

"Gabe?" his mother exclaimed. "The neighbor boy? Not Gabe Rosler!"

"Yes." At last she could talk. "I'm afraid it was. Is. I just told Mrs. Rosler. I would have rather put it off. Her husband has had a heart attack. I'm on my way to the hospital, but I wanted to let you know first."

"Oh, no! Poor Marjorie! Is there anything I can do, do you think? Does she have someone with her?"

"She'd called her sister, she said."

Shirley shook her head. "Dick had a heart attack…oh, three or four years ago, you know. He had bypass surgery, one of those triple or quadruple ones that makes it sound like his heart must be a maze now. And—oh!—another attack so soon."

"He didn't look good," Renee said.

"Oh, no! Well, you be sure to tell her to call on me for anything at all."

"I will." Renee could tell she meant it, which was a good thing. Marjorie was going to need all the help she could find to get through these next months, whether her husband lived or not.

Shirley looked at her son, then Renee, then back

again. "Well," she said. "I'll let Daniel walk you out to your car. Bless you for coming today. I feel like I did after losing all that weight! Remember how plump I got?" she asked her son.

He didn't appear to have heard her. Gaze never leaving Renee, he stood between her and the porch steps, just waiting, big and solid.

Shirley gently slipped away from Renee and gave her a slight push so that she had to step over the threshold onto the porch. Behind her, the door quietly closed, leaving her alone with Daniel.

"Renee," he said, voice low and gritty. "I was going to come by your place tonight. I figured this was long enough. That you'd know how you felt by now, one way or another."

Her heart was pounding so hard she could hardly hear herself. "I'm going to find my mother," she said, as if that were the most important thing she could offer.

"I don't care." He took a step closer. "Find her or not. Suit yourself. You're all that matters to me."

"But…" She searched his face. "No. Don't say it doesn't matter. It does! If only because I've been so self-righteous! Remember how I said you had to know about your father? Your mother had to face up to what had happened so that she'd *know*. And then Marjorie Rosler. Oh!" Renee said in shame. "*I* was so certain that everyone else should face reality. And all the time I couldn't face my own! How did you stand me?"

"But you were right." His mouth twisted, and for the first time he looked away. "What you were pushing us to do was have the guts to find the answers to questions that needed asking. That's not the same thing as you not wanting to know for sure why your mother walked out. Whether she's dead or still alive and just didn't give a damn. It'll hurt either way. What's the good of finding out?''

"Maybe…" Renee groped for an answer to this question. "Maybe if I did know why and what became of her after she left us, if I could understand, then maybe it *wouldn't* hurt as much. Do you see? Because I wouldn't be just a little kid who's lost her mommy anymore. I'd be a woman who could empathize. Maybe she had no choice. Maybe she did try to contact us. Maybe she even tried to take us, or fight for custody, or…" Renee's hands balled into fists as she shared her childhood dreams. "My father would have been careful not to let us find out. He never mentioned her." Her voice felt thick; her mouth worked. "Oh, damn. Now I'm going to cry."

"I love you." Daniel reached for her.

Renee backed away, holding her hands up, palms out. "No. Please. Let me finish. What I'm trying to say is, if the woman I am now could understand why my mother did what she did, then maybe the part of me that's still a scared little girl could be shown, too."

He made an inarticulate sound. Letting her finish wasn't easy on him; tension and frustration and anguish poured off him in waves. His blue eyes were almost black as he listened. But he did listen, which was the most loving thing anyone had ever done for her.

"What I'm trying to say is, you were right. I guess my development was kind of…arrested." She struggled to explain, knew she had to articulate how she'd felt. "It was like, if I stayed where I was, if I didn't grow up, I thought she'd come home and we could go on where we'd left off." She shook her head. "Oh, that sounds crazy!"

"But then, we're agreed that both of us are nuts." His voice was hoarse. "Remember?"

"Loco," she whispered.

He broke then. Swore, and hauled her into his arms. Not to kiss her, although she hoped he'd do that sooner or later. He just squeezed her into an embrace that probably hurt, although she didn't care, because she was holding him just as tightly.

"I love you." His voice broke. "I wish I'd ripped my tongue out before I said what I did. All I really wanted was to be sure I mattered to you more than your mom and sister do."

"Well, of course you do!" She pulled back in astonishment, seeing for the first time how haggard he looked. The grooves in his cheeks had deepened; more lines feathered out from the corners of his eyes, which were puffy and tired. He had suffered, she saw. She liked the idea she wasn't alone in that, or in any other way.

Her future.

"If Mom and Meg were still at home," she told him, voice shaking with her need to convince him, "I wouldn't be planning to live with them forever, for Pete's sake! I mean, when a man… That is…" Her face flushed as she tried to take back a mighty big assumption. What if he still wasn't talking marriage? She'd given him plenty of reason to be cautious!

"But they're not still home," he said, with odd grimness. "Maybe them leaving hurt you in a way I can't heal. I guess that's what scares me."

"No," she said. "I mean, yes. Of course you can. You have! I'm going to sell the house and…and…"

"Marry me." Daniel framed her face with his big hands. "Come home with me."

"Yes. If you want me."

He gave a laugh that brought a lump to her throat, it held so much emotion. "You know the answer to that."

"Is it this simple?" she asked wistfully.

"Yup. This simple. If you love me." He swallowed. "You never have said you did, you know."

For one moment as he waited, Renee saw him again as others might, a plain, simple man who questioned whether he was worth loving, just as she questioned whether she was.

"Oh, yes," she said in a rush. "I love you. Oh, Daniel, I do love you!"

Heartfelt emotion made his eyes blue again, brought a slow smile to his face. It started out sweet, joyous, stealing her breath, slowly becoming a wicked, sensual grin.

"Then," he said, "let's go to my house."

"Yes." She tumbled back into his arms for a kiss that accelerated from gentle to hungry so fast, it buckled her knees.

Still kissing her, he scooped her up and started down from the porch, one fumbling step at a time. Her feet whammed into the newel post; she tugged at his hair and tangled her tongue with his.

"Oh, hell," he muttered suddenly. "You'll have to drive."

"Drive?" Her brain wasn't interested in anything so mundane, not when she could string kisses down his rough cheek, feel the pulse jump when she pressed her lips to his throat.

"If you don't want to have sex on my mother's front lawn," he groaned, "you need to drive."

Put that way... "Oh, all right," Renee conceded.

He let her slide down his body until her feet touched the ground. Feeling his thigh muscles and his erection with every nerve ending, she closed her eyes on a spasm of need only partly sexual.

Trying to make light of it, she said, "Oh, that really helped," but her whisper was husky and unnatural.

He opened the driver's side door to her Bronco and bundled her in without much finesse. Voices on the radio crackled, tugging her back from never-never land.

"Oh, no!" she said, as he jumped in the other side. "I can't come home with you. I have to go to the hospital."

"Why?"

"Because I told Marjorie Rosler..." Well, no, she hadn't, Renee remembered. She took a breath. "I think Dick killed Gabe. He's the only one who could have written those letters."

Shock and then understanding crossed Daniel's face. "Does Marjorie know?"

Renee bit her lip and nodded.

"Will he live?"

Recalling that glimpse of his face, blue and still, she said quietly, "No. I don't think so. I hope not."

"You being there might make it all worse for Marjorie."

Renee went still, thinking. "Maybe," she admitted. "But..."

"You can't let it go." His tone was carefully nonjudgmental; he wasn't expressing anger or disappointment or hurt, although Renee guessed he was feeling all of those.

She turned to look at him. Would he be waiting an hour or three hours from now, if she *didn't* let it go?

But all she had to do was look deep into his eyes to know that he would be. He would never issue her an ultimatum.

He wouldn't leave her.

Tears clogged her throat and burned her eyes. "I'll call the hospital," she said with a sniff. "You're right. Nobody there needs me."

"Somebody here does."

"I need to be here." She had one of those moments of profound understanding that came to her like a lightning bolt but, she suspected, would have seemed obvious to anyone not as dense about love and family. "I need that," Renee said steadily, "more than I've ever needed anything in my life."

Daniel's eyes closed; a muscle ticked in his cheek. Then he looked at her with stark vulnerability. "I will make up for everything you've ever missed," he vowed.

"I believe you will," she whispered. "But it won't be one-sided."

"No." He reached out a shaking hand, touched her damp cheek. "Let's go home," he said roughly. "I want to make love to my wife-to-be."

EPILOGUE

RENEE DID CALL the hospital that afternoon. Dick Rosler had died en route.

She attended his funeral, as she did his son's, a simple ceremony held two weeks after the father's. Besides Marjorie, Daniel was the only one Renee ever told about her suspicion that Gabe's father had killed him. She closed the file, noting that after so many intervening years the murder was unsolvable, and sent a copy to Marjorie Rosler.

Theon Josiah Harris, aka T. J. Baxter, turned out to be alive if not content, ensconced as he was in the Washington State Penitentiary in Walla Walla. He was serving a twelve-year sentence for rape as well as violation of parole for a previous conviction.

Shirley went through agonies of guilt, thinking she might have prevented at least one of the other rapes if she'd gone to the police, but with Anne McWhirter's help, she came to terms with the pain and helplessness of that night.

Renee's house was sold within weeks of the sign going up in the front yard. Abby was maid of honor at her wedding.

She did plan to institute a search for their

mother, but after all these years, what was the hurry?

And then one day, Meg came home.

Watch for Meg Patton's story—
THE BABY AND THE BADGE—
coming next month from
Superromance.

HARLEQUIN®
SUPERROMANCE®

by
Janice Kay Johnson

The people of Elk Springs, Oregon, thought
Ed Patton was a good man, a good cop,
a good father. But his daughters know the truth....

Renee, Meg, Abby
Sisters, Cops...Women

They're not like their father. And that's all right with them. But
they still feel they have something to prove to the
townspeople—and to themselves.

Daniel, Scott, Ben—three men who can see past the
uniforms to the women inside. They're willing to
take on—and ready to love—Patton's Daughters.

Look for Janice Kay Johnson's newest miniseries:

August 1999—*The Woman in Blue* (#854)
September 1999—*The Baby and the Badge* (#860)
October 1999—*A Message for Abby* (#866)

Available at your favorite retail outlet.

HARLEQUIN®
Makes any time special ™

If you enjoyed what you just read,
then we've got an offer you can't resist!

Take 2 bestselling love stories FREE!

Plus get a FREE surprise gift!

"Fascinating—you'll want to take this home!"
—**Marie Ferrarella**

"Each page is filled with a brand-new surprise."
—**Suzanne Brockmann**

"Makes reading a new and joyous experience all over again."
—**Tara Taylor Quinn**

See what all your favorite authors are talking about.

Coming October 1999 to a retail store near you.

#858 TALK TO ME • Jan Freed
By the Year 2000: Celebrate!

When Kara Taylor left her husband on their disastrous first anniversary, she figured she'd just call her marriage a bad experience and move on. Sure, Travis was handsome and charming and wonderful, but they were mismatched from the start. He was a true outdoorsman, and she was the ultimate city girl. Success mattered more to her than it did to him, so who would've thought that nine years later he'd be the only person who could save her business?

#859 FAMILY FORTUNE • Roz Denny Fox
The Lyon Legacy

Crystal Jardin is connected to the prestigious Lyon family by blood—and by affection. And she's especially close to Margaret Lyon, the family matriarch. Margaret, who's disappeared. Whose money is disappearing, too. At such a critical time, the last thing Crystal needs is to fall for a difficult man like Caleb Tanner—or a vulnerable young boy.

Follow the Lyon family fortunes. New secrets are revealed, new betrayals are thwarted—but the bonds of family remain stronger than ever!

#860 THE BABY AND THE BADGE • Janice Kay Johnson
Patton's Daughters

Meg Patton, single mother and brand-new sheriff's deputy, has finally come home to Elk Springs. It's time to reconcile with her sisters—and past time to introduce them to her son. And now her first case has her searching for the parents of an abandoned infant. But Meg can't afford to fall for this baby—or for the man who found her. No matter how much she wants to do both....

#861 FALLING FOR THE ENEMY • Dawn Stewardson

When crime lord Billy Fitzgerald, locked away in solitary confinement, arranges to have prison psychologist Hayley Morgan's son abducted as a bargaining tool, Hayley's life falls apart. To ensure her son's safety, Hayley has to rely on Billy's lawyer, Sloan Reeves, to act as a go-between. Trouble is, he's the enemy and Hayley is smitten.

#862 BORN IN TEXAS • Ginger Chambers
The West Texans

Tate Connelly is recuperating from near-fatal gunshot wounds. Jodie Connelly would do anything to help her husband get well—except the one thing he's asking: divorce him. Maybe the Parker clan—and Jodie's pregnancy—can shake Tate up and get him thinking straight again.

#863 DADDY'S HOME • Pamela Bauer
Family Man

A plane crash. An injured woman. A courageous rescue. All Tyler Brant wants is to put the whole thing behind him. But the media's calling him a hero. And so are the women in his life: his mother, his six-year-old daughter and Kristin Kellar—the woman he saved. If only they knew the truth....